On My Knees

Meredith Wild

Copyright © 2014 Meredith Wild.

Cover Design by Meredith Wild.

Cover photographs: Dreamstime.

Paperback ISBN: 978-0-9897684-7-4

PRINTED IN THE UNITED STATES OF AMERICA

For all the survivors.

PROLOGUE

My survival hinged on his love in a way I couldn't appreciate until he'd left. The days were only days. Time served. Tolerable only because, once past, they would bring us closer to being together again.

I glanced at the clock, the only object of interest in the otherwise lifeless room that I shared with an absent roommate. Late afternoon light came in through the bay windows. They were an exceptional feature for the room, but the old campus was filled with houses like mine and rooms like this one that had hosted the youth of New England's elite for decades—centuries actually.

Being here nearly by myself the past couple days had been strange. An unusual calm fell over places that were otherwise filled with the hustle and bustle of students and faculty. The rare quiet, combined with the void of coursework, had made missing Cameron almost unbearable. Of all the days of missing him, today—with no purpose and no distractions—had been the worst.

I wanted him back with a gnawing hunger and was silently counting down the minutes until he would be. A persistent fear fed by my own insecurities and the break in our recent communications kept interrupting the fantasy of having him in my arms again. Would he still feel the same way for me after all this time? From the stories I'd heard, few people came out of basic training the way they went in. I had nothing but a handful of letters and a few abrupt phone calls to reassure me that he would return to me as the same Cameron I remembered.

Over the past couple weeks, I'd spent less time missing him and more time worrying. But when all was said and done, I was the first and only person he wanted to see when the Army granted him leave. Since then, I'd held tightly to our shared memories when the apprehension of losing what we'd had together took hold. I quietly prayed enough would be left between us, enough time together, to keep us solid through the commitments that would keep us apart for weeks more.

I startled at a sudden knock. Only one person could be at my door. I checked the clock again. He was early. I hadn't expected that. I got up from the bed, tossing my book to the side. My heartbeat sped, and I straightened my white sundress, my one decent looking dress. I tugged out my ponytail and let my hair fall loose down my back. I fussed a minute longer until he knocked again. Energy and excitement coursed through me, and I took a deep breath before opening the door.

There he stood, almost too gorgeous to be real. I released the doorknob and found my other hand, twisting my fingers in tremulous anticipation. He looked different. His familiar blue eyes bore into me, but the Texas sun had darkened his olive skin. He appeared at least twenty pounds lighter. The strong lines of his jaw and cheekbones were sharper. Between that and his nearly black hair trimmed into a short crew cut, he looked older. I should have expected changes in his physical appearance, but an irrational worry tempered the flood of emotion that rushed over me at the sight of him.

Did he still feel the same way? Could he have changed this much on the inside too?

Struggling for the right words, I opened my mouth to speak. His lips quirked into a small smile, setting off a relieved one of my own. He stepped in and caught my fidgeting hands in his, rubbing his thumbs over the white of my knuckles until I relaxed. The warmth in his eyes melted away any lingering doubts. I exhaled a shaky breath.

"Come here," I whispered, still afraid to break the silence and unable to do justice to how overwhelming being in his presence again was.

I stepped back, pulling him after me. He followed and once inside curved his arm around my waist, tightening his hold until we were firmly chest-to-chest. My body molded to the hard lines of his. My breaths came fast, my entire body responding to his closeness. His gaze locked me in. He traced my lips with the pad of his thumb, his smile fading as he did.

"I missed you so much, Maya. Every day…"

Out of habit, I hooked my hand around his nape. I mourned the overgrown locks that would have tangled between my fingers, but none of that mattered now. Changed or not, he was here. His heart, the heat of his body pressed against me. This was all I'd wanted. My love in the flesh. It all felt like a dream. Maybe I'd wished for him so hard and for so long that somehow he'd come true. The separation had been almost unbearable. I couldn't—wouldn't—consider how we'd face it again.

"I can't believe you're really here." My voice wavered.

He feathered his fingertips over my cheek, calming me. I released a tentative breath. I went to kiss him, but before I could meet his lips, he stilled me, gently cupping my cheek.

"I love you," he whispered, his soft breath dancing on my lips.

My heart twisted, a bittersweet ache pulsing through my chest with each beat. We'd written it, said it so many times, worn it out. The profoundness of those words from his lips, now, nearly knocked me down. My entire being warmed from the inside out. Possessed with a fervency to prove how much I felt it too, I lifted to my toes and kissed him. Our lips met, then our tongues, tangling, teasing, and tasting.

"Maya," he breathed, breaking our contact with the words.

"What?" I got lost in his eyes, never wanting any of this to end. I'd never loved him more. My soul was brimming for everything I felt for this man.

He hesitated, seeming to search for words as I had before. Before I could press him, he pulled me into another wild kiss, deep and passionate. I moaned, losing my ability to think clearly as our bodies shifted over each other. A hand slid down my thigh and back up, cupping my butt over the thin cotton of my panties. He toyed with the hem before pushing them down my hips. They fell to my knees, and I kicked them off the rest of the way.

He pushed the thin straps over my shoulders, and my

dress fell to the floor. His heated gaze roved over my nakedness. Until now, his eyes hadn't left mine. My skin burned under his touch as he caressed down my arm, over the jut of my hip, over my ass to press me to him firmly again.

I roamed my hands over the hardened planes of his stomach. Eager to see and feel all of him, I shoved his shirt up and he tugged it off. God, he was gorgeous. Every muscle was more pronounced, taut and lean. I ran my fingers over the curves of his abdomen, over his pectorals, and down the corded muscles of his arms. I bit my lip, unable to hide my smile.

"You approve?"

"You're like a different person." Physically anyway, he was a new man. He'd been gorgeous before, but this was icing on the cake...with a cherry on top.

"I'm not all different," he muttered.

"I hope not." I wanted nothing more than to find out for myself. I wanted all of him, now, at once, and for as long as possible. I kissed his chest, dragging my tongue over the hard muscles straining under his tightened skin. Slowly I lowered to my knees. I looked up at him, emboldened by the heated lust in his eyes. Unfastening his pants, I tugged them low enough to access the hard length of his erection loosely reined in through his boxer briefs.

He flinched under the cotton. I breathed hot air through them and traced the outline of the head with my tongue. I hooked my fingers over the band, ready to release every delicious inch of him.

"Wait." His voice strained.

"I want you."

He caught me by the hair. "It's been too long. I won't last with your mouth on me. Come here."

He lowered next to me. Sitting on the floor with his back to the bed, he guided me to straddle him. A fleeting shyness warmed me as I spread my legs wide astride him, my nakedness on display.

His lips parted. His gaze journeyed over my curves, his hands following its path. "Jesus, Maya. You're so beautiful."

My cheeks heated. "You're just saying that because you've been starved and tortured for months."

"No, I'm saying that because you're the most gorgeous creature I've ever laid eyes on." He leaned in and kissed me, wrapping his arms tightly around me. "Mmm, missed these sweet lips."

He grazed over my ribs and over my breasts, squeezing them and teasing the tender tips. "And these."

His eyes darkened. His touch blazed a path between my thighs. Tantalizing me with light touches, he sifted through my curls to tease the wet folds of my arousal.

"I missed this too," he whispered, licking his lower lip.

I gasped and leaned eagerly into his touch, wanting more. I brought us chest-to-chest, rabid for the feel of his skin against mine. I wrapped my arms around him and kissed him frantically.

"I want you inside me." I jerked my hips against his touch, a silent plea for more. Heat rushed over me, my lips tingling from the urgency of our kissing.

His fingers answered, dipping into me. I clenched around him and moaned at the penetration, rocking into his hand.

"More." I wanted so much more.

He slipped another finger inside and massaged the tender flesh, fucking me gently until I grew slick around him. He rubbed the rush of moisture over my clit and back inside. Flames of desire licked over my skin. My hips pumped against his deliberately slow movements.

"Cam, please. I'm going crazy."

"I want you ready for me."

"I've been ready for weeks."

He lifted me slightly and pushed down his pants and boxers, revealing the thick virile cock I'd fantasized about more times than I could remember. If sex with Cameron were a drug, I was fully prepared to overdose. I'd never wanted anything so damn bad.

I shivered in anticipation, circling his hot flesh with both hands, milking him. A bead of moisture glistened at the tip. My mouth watered. I wanted to taste him. We'd have time for that. Right now I needed him inside me before I lost my ever-loving mind.

He sucked in a sharp breath. I took the cue, satisfied that he was as eager as I was. I hovered over him, notching the blunt tip to my opening, and guided him inside.

He caught my hip, stilling my movement. His eyes were serious, the cool blues dilated. "Go slow. I don't want to hurt you."

I complied, resisting the urge to drop down and have all of him inside me at once. Inch by inch he filled me, his gaze never leaving mine. I shifted from desire to relief to pain, back to frenzied need, every transition on display as he watched me work his body into mine.

He kissed my lips gently, breathing in my tiny moans and gasps. I'd taken him to the root, and my body stretched to accommodate him. I tensed against the simultaneous bite of his depth and urge to allay it by riding him hard and fast until I forgot my own name.

His hands traveled up my ribs and down to where my ass met his thighs and squeezed gently.

"Perfect," he murmured. "You have no idea how amazing you feel."

"We fit," I whispered, tracing the curve of his ear with my tongue. I kissed his neck, sucking the salt from his skin. I filled my lungs with him, intoxicated on the scent, all musk and man.

He lifted and lowered me again slowly, relieving me of the effort to decide how and when to move. I whimpered, overwhelmed with sensation. Unable to escape the searing pleasure of being filled after such an absence, I clung to him. I gripped his shoulders, hoping they could anchor me through the impending storm.

Our bodies fell into a steady rhythm. The flutter of desire that started low in my belly grew with every stroke. Bold and demanding, I kissed him like the starved creature I'd become with distance.

He shifted his hips so I could take him deeper. I threw my head back and cried out as pleasure took its hold. My breasts became heavy and tender as he sucked my nipples to hard hypersensitive points. I gasped and tightened around his penetration, increasing the friction of every thrust.

He worked me over his cock until my grip on reality began to slip. I wanted to make this last for both of us, but he was launching my body into overload. Sweat misted over my skin.

I groaned. I needed an orgasm like I needed my next

breath. I matched his thrusts, leveraging them with my weight to drive him deeper. My body was slick around him. He pumped quickly and easily. *Faster, harder.* My mind was lost in a flurry of silent wants and demands. Anything to bring us closer.

"Maya, look at me." He wove his fingers through my hair, bringing my focus back to him.

Our gazes locked on each other, our breathing ragged and uneven. Something in his half-lidded eyes and the firm set of his jaw as he thrust inside me broke through my single-minded need to come. The fierceness in his next thrust robbed me of air. My jaw dropped in a soundless cry. I thought my heart might explode if he held me this way much longer, but I couldn't escape... Didn't want to.

"Cam." The quiet plea signaled a certain surrender. I was giving him everything now. My body, my heart, my trust.

"I've got you." The rasp of his promise sent a tingle over my skin.

Cameron wasn't only fucking me. He was loving me with every touch. Caressing my lips with his, guiding my motions with a firm grasp at my hip. Churning inside me with a fierce pressure that had me on the brink of rapture, he satisfied every raw need, inside and out.

He licked the pad of his thumb and rubbed tiny expert circles over my clit. I shifted over him, thrashing and grabbing as the tension mounted within.

"Oh my God," I cried.

"That's it. Stay with me." He held me tight, holding my focus and forcing me to pinpoint all my energy on his eyes, now dark and intense.

"I'm going to come... Oh, fuck." I squeezed my eyes closed, unable to focus on anything. I could only feel.

And I felt everything.

Everywhere we met clashed and clenched, as if something precious might slip away if we didn't hold on for dear life. His cock lengthened, throbbing and rigid, as he drove his pelvis deep into my sensitive tissues. I dug my nails into his skin, raking down his chest as mindless release took over.

"Fuck," he growled.

My eyes flew open. The sight of him losing that last thread of control did me in. The orgasm, the weight of our separation and our love, and the acute need to be fucked like I'd never been fucked before, crashed down onto me like a tidal wave. Pleasure and relief racked my body with a string of violent shudders. I screamed. I grabbed feebly at the bed behind him, fisting the fabric in an attempt to ground myself to earth when my body was soaring with delirious pleasure.

"I love you. Love you so much." I suppressed a sob as the words left me. Tears prickled the corners of my eyes as I came back down.

His hips arched off the floor, extending the moment as he chased his own release, setting me off again. He swallowed my last cry with a desperate kiss. Uttering a feral moan into my mouth, he froze and then came, the warm rush filling me.

Weakened, I leaned back on his raised knees, letting all the tension go. His arms wrapped around my waist, and his damp forehead rested between my heaving breasts as I struggled for air.

I held him to me, so grateful for everything. For

x

Cameron, for this moment, for whatever miracle brought him into my life. I swallowed over the painful knot in my throat. I felt stripped. I wanted to cry and rid myself of all the fears and doubts and worry that I'd carried before today. I wanted to be rid of all of it, until only our love remained.

He lifted his head, reflecting a look of complete and utter emotional wreckage.

"Jesus, Maya. That was…"

"Amazing." I finished the thought. "Amazing" was a weak description of what had just happened between us. Epic and earth-shattering also fit the bill. Rug burn-inducing even, I thought, vaguely aware of the sting on my knees where they met the area rug protecting us from the wood floors. I didn't care.

I feathered my fingers over his skin, still drunk on our passion but, like a true addict, still wanting more. He reached up to kiss me. Our soft lazy kisses quickly became urgent, stoking the warm embers of my desire anew. He thickened inside me.

"Let's do that again," he rasped.

★ ★ ★

We had the week to ourselves, to simply be together, which was all we really needed or wanted.

While my dorm mates frolicked on Southern beaches for spring break, we spent our days in bed. At night we'd walk downtown, have dinner, and get tipsy. We'd rush home so we could make love again or fuck wildly and loudly, our uninhibited sex sounds echoing through the mercifully empty halls of the house.

We soaked up every precious minute and talked endlessly about the future we wanted together. Marriage and babies and happily ever after. With so much of the future unknown, we let ourselves dream and imagine the life we could have. I had no idea when or how our future would take shape, but I prayed that when the time came, I could give him everything he wanted.

As the days passed, our touches lingered. Our kisses were deeper and the wild fucking gave way to tender, unhurried lovemaking. I let the tears come, finally, and he kissed them away, never asking why. He held me, loved me, and helped me forget, if only for a moment, that we were running out of time.

As hard as we tried, loving slowly couldn't delay the passing of time. We walked along the edge of the campus, and I tried not to think about the dwindling days. Soon he'd fly back, and I'd return to my monotonous and work-filled life as a student. I leaned against his shoulder, wishing I could freeze time or kidnap him. Surely my roommate wouldn't mind a third.

The pond sparkled with moonlight as it fed into the river. Cameron slowed, turning to me. Held my hands in his. I looked up at him, mesmerized by how his eyes glittered in the semi-darkness. He was beautiful. Perfect. And at least for now, all mine.

"You okay?"

"I'm fine," I lied. I didn't want to waste time talking about the inevitable.

"I don't want to go either," he said, echoing my thoughts.

I stared at the ground between us. "I can't even think about it."

"We'll get through it. After I get through tech school, everything will be easier, I promise."

My heart ached at the thought of enduring another long separation. "Summer will be here soon," I said, offering a ray of hope, but I swallowed the tears that threatened. I had to save the rest of them until he left. I couldn't taint our last couple days with sadness over the unavoidable.

"About that…"

I looked up, questioning the sudden tension in his pose. His jaw was tight, and he looked down to our intertwined hands. He took a deep breath.

"What? What's wrong?" My stomach knotted. Had he waited to drop more bad news on me?

"I know you said that you were going to try to work up here over the summer."

I nodded. "The housing is cheaper with my tuition. It makes the most sense."

"I know, but maybe instead of visiting me wherever I get stationed, you could come live with me for the summer."

I frowned. "But you said you couldn't live off base. I couldn't afford it, Cameron." I hated admitting my financial woes. Such limitations had never existed for him.

"I can't live off base right now, but I could…"

I tried to finish his thought in my mind, but I knew nothing about the intricacies of the military. Already the institution had more rules than I could fully comprehend.

"How?"

"We could get married."

I widened my eyes and dropped my jaw slightly as I

sucked in a sharp breath of the cool night air. "Married?" I barely recognized my voice as I said the word. The sound, strained and high, betrayed my panic and ran in stark contrast to how we'd spoken of it hours ago, a far off dream we'd both shared.

"If we got married, I could live off base. We could be together. I'd make plenty of money to support us both until you came back to school. And after, of course."

The intensity that once hummed between us now hung frozen in the air as I absorbed his words. I struggled to reply, my lips moving wordlessly. Panic seized my lungs. I couldn't breathe.

This wasn't how it had happened in my fantasies. We were older, my life was far more stable than it currently was, and I was smiling and crying and jumping to kiss him with one yes after the other pouring from my lips. Yet now I fought a wave of nausea. My vision blurred. The subtle sounds around us muffled behind a jumble of broken thoughts flooding my brain.

"I don't understand what you're saying," I finally said. True enough, I had no idea where this proposal had come from.

He gripped my hands tightly. I was vaguely aware of the dampness of my palms, but my thoughts were too scattered to care.

"Maya, I want to marry you."

The earlier softness in his voice gave way to determination. He looked at me intently. He was serious. I was scared to death that he was.

"There are logistics with the military, yes, but none of that matters as much as wanting to be married to you. Everything we've had this week... I want that forever, to know that nothing can take that away from us."

"But—" I stumbled over my words, hoping I didn't look as scared as I felt. "Are you... Do you mean, like, now?"

He paused. "We could do it this weekend, before I leave. Just you and me. We don't need anyone else."

I took a small step back and out of his grasp, hoping it would allow me to breathe easier. My chest heaved with labored breaths. My mind had spun straight out of the love coma that we'd been living in for days. For all my loving him, I could not have been more shocked by this.

"I don't have a ring..." His shoulders sagged.

My uneasiness only grew with the asking in his eyes.

"I don't care about a ring, Cameron, but this is so sudden. Do you realize what you're asking me?"

"I know exactly what I'm asking you. Trust me, I've thought about little else for weeks. I wanted to ask you the minute I saw you."

My gaze darted between the ground and buildings in the distance. I needed something to hold my focus, because my thoughts were running rampant.

The future we spoke of seemed a lot closer for him than I'd realized. The dreams we shared were within reach now, but I couldn't feel anything but crushed emotionally. The warm blanket of the past few days had been ripped away, and I was left with the shock of his request.

"Why now?"

"Why wait?"

"I can't just run away. I have things I need to take care of. Things here."

A confused frown marked his brow. "Like what?"

"I don't know. Work, I guess." I offered the weak half-truth, not wanting to get into the real reasons why I couldn't skip town with my would-be husband come May.

"You can find work wherever I am, or don't worry about it at all. Take the summer off. I'll be making more and can take care of you, of us."

As if anything could be that simple.

Frozen, I tried to think of how I could convince him this was rash. Too soon. "I don't know, Cameron," I murmured. "I need time to think about this, I guess."

I chanced a look in his eyes. His jaw was tightly clenched, his whole posture on edge.

"Do you want to marry me or not?" His voice was a mere whisper.

I'd asked for time to think, but this wasn't a negotiation of terms. This was a moment—one that demanded an answer, not an excuse.

Fine mist swept over my skin, and I fought a new wave of sickness. I couldn't. It was too much. Too fast. As head over heels as I was, as we both were, I couldn't go through with it. One day, yes. But I couldn't say when that would be. He wanted to take care of me, but he'd never really understand the weight I carried.

"I do want to marry you, Cameron. I really honestly do, one day, but not...*today*. We shouldn't rush into this."

"Rush? I've spent two months away from you and it's killing me. I thought you felt the same way."

I fought the tremble in my hands, wringing my fingers together. With each word, I felt him slip further from me. I stared past him to the pond. The campus had darkened under the night sky. This was my life, and I hadn't really thought seriously about what it might look like outside of our idle dreaming. He was calling me out on all the promises we'd made, and here I was reneging.

I loved Cameron, but being with him was like being in a dream, a fantasy where I could believe that everything was possible, that everything was going to be okay. But he didn't know everything. He'd never understand the forces that weighed me down, the battles I fought away from the eyes of my friends here. He'd only known a life of privilege. Security, normalcy, a family that by most standards would be considered perfect. Certainly compared to mine.

I'd hinted about the situation with my mother, but I'd never shared the embarrassing details of how I'd grown up, or how her life had fallen into woeful disrepair since I left for school. What chance would I have with him if he knew who I really was?

"I want to be with you, Cam." I prayed that could be enough.

"Then marry me. There's never going to be anyone else for me. This is it." The look of love in his eyes, the look I'd seen so many times before, left no doubt.

"Marriage?" I shook my head, pleading with him to relent on this dream that I couldn't give him.

He winced. "You say the word like it makes you sick, Maya."

"It is making me sick." I half turned away, wrapping my arms around myself to chase away the chill of the night. He was pushing me so hard. Everything I was saying was disappointing him, hurting him. I hated it. I hated everything about this conversation. I wanted to go home and fall asleep in his arms and wake up as if we'd never had it.

The hurt in his eyes lanced through me. My heart fell.

"You're telling me no, then."

I shook my head, my heart breaking. I had no other choice, and I'd never be able to make him understand my reasons. "I can't."

"What was this week about?" His voice strained, laced with hurt frustration.

I shrugged, wishing we could forget all this, turn back time, and go back to the place where we were both happy simply being with each other, without this looming expectation that I'd never be able to live up to. "Us, being together, like it's always been."

"This is so much more than it's ever been. You know that. What do I really mean to you? What does any of this mean if, when it comes right down to it, you don't want to be with me?"

"You're everything to me, Cameron."

His hard laugh tore through me. "Apparently not."

"Stop it." My voice was watery. My guilt was giving way to despair, and I felt weak and powerless over where this was all going.

"What am I, then?"

"You're my lover, my friend. I don't know how I would have gotten through this year without you." Being with Cameron had given me hope, something to look forward to every weekend before he left. Our all-consuming love held so much promise.

"So I'm a crutch? Someone you can rely on emotionally but don't really want to commit to?"

I exhaled sharply at his words, my eyes burning with

unshed tears. "No."

"Then what? Explain it to me."

"This is crazy. You're being crazy, asking this of me. People don't do this anymore."

"I don't give a shit what people do." He rubbed his forehead, breathing audibly through clenched teeth. "So this is it?"

My heart thudded against my chest. "What do you mean?"

"This is it, Maya. I can't..." He shook his head, avoiding my gaze. "You have no idea what I've been through. All I've thought of is you and this moment. But if this is how you feel, we should stop wasting our time."

I gasped, panic flooding me. "No."

I reached for him but he stepped back, raising his hands as if in surrender.

"Let's talk about this." He was slipping away. I couldn't lose him over this.

I could no sooner find the words to make him stay as I could stop the tears from falling free down my face.

"Cameron, wait. Please."

I suppressed a sob as he turned and walked away without another word.

CHAPTER ONE

Five years later

MAYA. Over the hum of a room full of machines, papers shuffling and dozens of people typing away, I swore something in the air changed every afternoon around this time. The anticipation of freedom, of sixty minutes to call our own away from this place. It was 11:55 again, and I fidgeted anxiously with my purse, checking that I had everything for my sprint. Noon struck, and I made for the elevators. I used my oversized handbag to maneuver my way to the front of the pack. Every fucking day was like this. They let us all out at the same time, like cattle.

I ignored the bitchy stares shot my way. I was still too hung over from celebrating Vanessa's birthday last night to care. I wasn't wasting another five minutes of my break trying to be polite. Not today. Not most days actually, if I really thought about it.

I hadn't always been this way.

I pushed the thought away as I stepped out of the revolving doors and into the street. I stopped for a second when the icy chill of winter hit me. Someone slammed into me a second later, lurching me forward. I caught myself and went into motion, not caring to look back at the asshole who'd nearly knocked me down. I'd been that asshole a few minutes ago, anyway.

I stuffed my bare hands into my jacket pockets, cursing the cold. Delaney's was a bit of a walk, but after a few blocks, the sea of black pea coats had already thinned significantly. Several minutes later I slipped into the dark musty air of the bar. I pulled myself up onto a stool and sat frozen for a few seconds, willing the chill away. I took a breath and unwrapped myself, dropping my coat onto the empty seat next to me. As I did, Jerry appeared from somewhere. He nodded in my direction and called my usual order into the back.

"What's new today, Maya?" He grabbed a rag and wiped the already clean bar.

"Same shit, different day." I ran my fingers through my hair to get the static to die down.

"The usual?"

"Yup."

He nodded and returned with a tall glass of diet Coke and a shot of Jameson.

I swore my body relaxed at the mere sight of them. My two best friends. Caffeine and booze. I couldn't remember exactly when I'd started drinking during work hours. I hadn't been caught yet, and no one from my office would ever be seen lunching here, so I honestly didn't think much of it.

I'd turned twenty-five over the summer, marking

almost four years working in a cubicle crunching numbers. After the bailout and the economy going to hell, working in finance wasn't as glamorous as it used to be anymore. Except the money, of course. The promise that greed would somehow keep our financial system upright and that the people who managed to do it could still get rich with the effort. Money wasn't something I'd ever had much of, so the lack of it was all the reason I needed to go in that direction.

Still, landing a job making as much as I did straight out of college felt impressive. Like I'd finally made it and all my hard work had paid off. But the glitz of a Wall Street job had worn off a lot faster than I'd expected when I realized that getting ahead was going to take a hell of a lot more than being good at my job. Nothing was ever easy. At least for me. Something always seemed to lurk around the corners, threatening to knock me down. But I'd come this far and was still standing.

I took the shot of Jameson and let the liquid burn on its way down to my empty stomach. My insides twisted a bit in protest but relaxed again when the alcohol absorbed. Hair of the dog.

Stella was sitting at the other end of the bar. She was a regular. Her hair was long like mine, but straggly and gray down to the blond tips from the last time she'd dyed it. That could have been years ago, and so much could change in the span of a few years. Even in the darkness of the bar, her pallid features seemed stark. The faint light from the windows of the tavern hit the side of her face, drawing lines of age and experience across her skin.

"How's it going, Stella?" I called down to her. A few of the familiar faces looked over to me before going back to whatever they were doing—reading the paper, watching TV, staring into their beers looking for answers.

"Going real good, honey. Real good."

She'd had an early start from what I could tell. Her eyes were glossed over and she shot me a slanted smile. If I looked hard enough, I could believe she used to be young and beautiful, but her face was so worn and sunken now from too many long days and cold nights. Or maybe it was cold days and long nights. I didn't know her history, but somehow I knew there wasn't a trace of who she used to be in the person I saw before me now. People passed her over. Hell, half the people in this seedy bar, who didn't look too much better, passed her over.

I didn't want to, though. I wanted to ask if she had a family, but I didn't, knowing a question like that could hurt more than it could help.

Jerry returned with my food. Chicken fingers and fries, my favorite. I still ate the same food as I had when I was a kid. We'd order off the dollar menu or make a batch of Ramen when Mom was short on funds, but as a kid I never argued since that had been—and still was—the good stuff. Between my poor culinary cravings and my cubicle-dwelling lifestyle, I'd kept my college fifteen, plus a few. I regretted it, but not enough to do much about it.

"Thanks, Jerry."

"No problem. Let me know if you need anything."

"Actually, you want to get something for Stella? Just put it on my bill." I dropped my debit card on the bar so we could settle up well before I had to jet out again.

"You sure?" He raised his eyebrows, as if an extra ten bucks wasn't worth spending on someone as hopeless as

Stella.

"I'm sure." My voice was harder than it had been before.

He walked over and tossed her a paper menu.

"Pick something out here, sweetheart. Your little friend over there's buying you lunch again. What'll it be?"

"Oh, honey. You don't have to do that. You save your money." She waved her hand at me, almost knocking it into her half-empty beer.

"I don't mind."

She gave me a sad smile. The kind that told me she wished she could refuse, or turn the tables and buy my lunch instead. But who knew when she'd last had a full, decent meal? She drank away any money she had. I could tell because she was rail-thin. The old clothes she wore barely stayed on her. She chose booze over food, every time. That's why people like Jerry shook his head.

He took her order and hollered into the back again.

I'd eaten all my chicken already and was taking my time with my fries now. I was at the point in my moderate hangover where food was the cure. I needed something in my stomach to ward off the rest of the day's nausea. I checked my watch. Plenty of time still. I wasn't like the rest of the cattle who stood in line for a half hour only to have cafeteria-style lunch stuffed next to a complete stranger. The long walk to Delaney's was always worth it.

I reached into my bag for my notebook. The bag was one of those enormously impractical designer bags, filled with God knew what shit I definitely didn't need to be hauling around with me every day. I finally found it and opened to an empty sheet. I clicked my pen a few times and set the tip to the page.

I wrote about Stella, about all the things I thought about her. Things I imagined, having never really known her beyond this vantage at the other end of the bar. In a way, I was afraid I already knew her. I wrote a page and then turned it, flipping back and forth between the two, grabbing words until a poem formed. Then I rewrote it again, whittling it down further.

Stella

gray
a damp, leafless tree
arms branch across her face

cold
a barren, lifeless mother
her soul prays for spring

Something about the jagged sparsity of a poem settled me. *Wabi-sabi* or the minimalist imperfection of it, or maybe the simple knowledge that no one would understand it but me. I was fine with that, preferred it actually. I'd come to terms with the fact that most people I met would never really know me.

I checked my watch again. Time to go. I paid Jerry and bundled up. I waved goodbye to Stella on my way out, but she didn't see me.

I lit a cigarette before stepping back into the cold. Menthols. My stomach protested again when I took a drag. Too many cigarettes last night. I really should quit.

Despite that, I was warm now, a little loose, and ready to face the last half of the day. Hump day. Two more days. Two more days and then what? Maybe I'd finally get my shit together and go the gym or something. *We'll see how it goes*, I thought.

Lost in my fitness fantasy and the promise of a slightly smaller ass, I barely noticed the sound of my name. Seemed like I wasn't in range of being recognized yet. I had a little way to go.

"Maya?"

I stopped short and looked up. A pretty girl with chocolate brown hair falling loose around her face stood before me. Her piercing blue eyes met mine.

"Olivia. Hey. How are you?"

"Good." Her smile tensed with the short reply.

We didn't do the hugging thing, which is weird to do with people you haven't seen in forever, but it was weirder now that we weren't doing it. Like we had a good reason to not do that. I was certain she had her reasons.

"I didn't realize you lived here," she said, breaking the awkward silence.

"Yeah, I've been here since graduation. Working on Wall Street as an analyst." I stamped out my cigarette, suddenly embarrassed by it. I wasn't sure why. Not like I needed to impress her, but a part of me wanted her to know how together my life was now. Beyond that and the whiskey that likely lingered on my breath, I looked good. Expensive suit, expensive coat, stupidly expensive shoes. I tucked my hair—stylishly cut in meticulously straightened layers that fell down my back—behind my ear.

"How about you?"

"Just moved here actually. Still finding my way around. Thought I'd take a spin through Manhattan. I have a couple friends who live nearby."

"Picked quite the day for it."

"No kidding. It's freezing." She shifted her weight back and forth a couple times, staring down at the ground.

Something told me she still hadn't forgiven me for Cameron.

"I should let you go, I guess. I have to get back to work."

She glanced up. "Right. Well, it was good seeing you, Maya. I'm glad to hear you're doing well."

"Thanks, you too," I replied awkwardly, realizing I hadn't bothered to ask what she was doing. God, I was such a self-involved jerk now. I'm sure she could tell.

"Okay, I guess I'll see ya." She gave a terse nod and slipped by me, heading in the direction I'd come from.

I couldn't think straight by the time I got back to work. I tossed about ten mints in my mouth and set to work.

A couple people were out sick at the office so I picked up the slack. A few hours passed and I was caught up. Alone with my thoughts again until the markets closed.

CAMERON. "You'll never guess who I ran into."

Olivia peered over me as I pressed the weights rhythmically above me. I'd had a long day and it'd been an even longer night with little sleep. While I welcomed

31

the distraction if it kept me awake, I was not remotely interested in gossip hour with her.

"Who?" I grunted between silent counts.

"Maya."

My grip slipped slightly but I recovered, pushing the bar back up onto its cradle. I sat up, letting her name echo in my mind until it conjured a vision I'd spent the past several years hoping to forget. *My Maya?*

"Maya Jacobs?"

She leaned on the mirrored wall across from me and answered with a quick nod that confirmed my suspicions.

In the reflection, I saw the rest of the gym filling with members who hurried here after work, vying for prime real estate at the treadmills and ellipticals. The leisurely daytime mom crowd was being replaced by the nine-to-fivers. I usually tried to sneak in my work out between the two so I didn't get caught in the fray. People in this city were intense, and after a year I was still getting used to it.

"Where did you see her?" I tried to sound casual, but curiosity was already burning through me.

She raised her eyebrows. "A few blocks off Wall Street. That's where she works now, I guess."

"She works on Wall Street? You're kidding me."

Her narrowed eyes were fixed on me, as if she were studying my reaction. "Please tell me you're not still hung up on her after what she put you through."

I pushed off the bench and grabbed a towel, wiping the sweat from my face and draping it around my neck. "Just curious. I haven't seen her in a long time. How'd she seem?"

Olivia looked past me, seemingly distracted by a guy

positioned at the bench press. I followed her gaze. One of the regulars. I frowned, making a mental note to keep an eye on him.

She sighed quietly. "She seems different."

"That's descriptive."

"Maybe you'll run into her one of these days and you can see for yourself."

"There's eight million people in the city. Doesn't seem likely."

"I'm sure she's the last person you want to see anyway. I mean, you haven't seen her since—"

"No, I haven't." The last thing I wanted to do was relive the day I left Maya, least of all under Olivia's scrutinizing stare. She harbored a grudge that rivaled my own. "Listen, I've got to shower and take care of some paperwork. I'll meet you back at the house for dinner, all right?"

"Sure. I still need to straighten things up."

I eyed her warily. "Don't color code my shirts or anything."

She laughed. "Not today. I will get you organized though, if it's the last thing I do."

"I have my own system. Stop moving shit around."

"Right, good luck finding a woman when she gets a load of your organizational skills."

I waved her off and headed to the back of the building where my office was hidden behind another wall of mirrors. I sat behind my desk, staring at the piles of papers in front of me, not remotely interested in any of it.

Olivia might have been right. Revamping the three story partially renovated condo I'd taken over as my bachelor pad was one thing, but I was getting in over my head with running the gym. When Olivia offered to help me out, I'd taken her up on the offer, figuring she was just as eager as I'd been to get away from our parents. I cringed at the thought of working for my father and letting them run any part of my life, as they were inclined to do with her. Thankfully they'd already given up on Darren and me.

I was glad to give Olivia a stepping-stone to start the next chapter in her life, but she'd only been in town a couple weeks and already she was driving me half mad. Between that and the recent string of sleepless nights, I could hardly see straight.

The door swung open and Darren walked in. "What's up, man?"

"Not much. Paperwork, I guess."

"Need any help?"

I contemplated his offer, but my thoughts were too scattered right now. "Nah, I'm going to hit the shower and take care of some of this in the morning. I'll see you tomorrow."

"Sure thing. Everything okay?"

"Yeah, why?"

He shrugged. "You seem a little off. You hormonal again?"

"Fuck you," I muttered.

He laughed and shoved his jacket in a locker, replacing the fire department shirt he wore in favor of one with the gym logo on it. I'd asked him to come onto the team to help with training shifts so I could have some downtime. I paid the price with tolerating his daily dose of crude sarcasm. I often wondered how we shared a bloodline.

"Hey, do you want to grab some beers this weekend? You haven't been out in a while."

I hesitated, my thoughts drifting to Maya. Her name was like an old song, and I was struggling to remember the lyrics. Why was I doing that to myself? Like I needed another memory to haunt me.

"Come on, man, you haven't been out in forever. You act like you're the old man. Have a few, meet some women, kick back a little."

Darren was the oldest. He was pushing thirty with a social life that easily surpassed Olivia's or mine. Women flocked to the gym for a chance to train with him. We both knew what else they wanted, but so far he'd done a good job of not creating drama at work.

"I'll think about it, all right?"

He gave me a twisted smile. "Just say yes, man."

"Yeah, fine. We'll grab a beer."

"Cool."

I relaxed a little, glad he'd finished prying. I hesitated, contemplating what I was about to ask. "Hey, can you cover me for a few hours tomorrow? I might have to run some errands."

"Sure, I'm off all day."

"Thanks."

I took a long shower, ready for the day to end. My wet hair froze in a few seconds after I stepped outside. It was still snowing, but I walked anyway. You never knew what might happen on the streets of New York, who or what you'd see. Every day was an opportunity, and today was certainly living up to that.

After an extended layover in the city on the way back

from a tour overseas, I'd decided this is where I'd come when I got out. Turned out, four years and three tours were enough. Olivia was worried. Our parents were freaking out. I'd made a solid effort to crush out the memory of Maya in the desert, and when the time came to move on, I took it.

Maya. I did a double take at every long-haired blonde I saw. Olivia said she seemed different. *How?* Would I even recognize her if I saw her? Maybe we'd already crossed paths in some random place, and I'd been too lost in my own world to even see her.

No. I couldn't miss her face.

I still couldn't believe Olivia had run into her after all this time. Proof that not only did she still exist somewhere out there in the world, but she was close.

Close enough to find.

CHAPTER TWO

MAYA. I nearly slipped on the wood floors as I stepped into the apartment. A light snow had started not long before I came back to the office and my Manolos did not agree with the accumulation on my brief walk home from the metro.

I steadied myself and kicked them off, grateful to be home and warm at last.

"Home sweet home!" Eli sang from the living room, which was only two feet away, separated from the entryway by a partial wall. "You want some wine, hon?"

"Sure."

I stepped farther inside as he rose from his perch on the couch. He was wearing his usual uniform, faded black skinny jeans and a T-shirt from one of the many concerts he'd attended in his illustrious and excruciatingly low-paying career as a freelance music journalist. He disappeared into the small closet that our landlord claimed was a kitchen.

I carried on to my bedroom—entirely mine and,

unlike the rest of the apartment, a decent size. We lived modestly, but I refused to sleep like a sardine. I had a queen-sized bed, and I could walk all the way around it. I stripped off my suit and found my oldest pair of blue jeans. They were faded and ripped in several spots. They felt like home. I pulled on a hoodie and padded out to the living room where Eli had just returned with two generously filled glasses of our favorite red.

"Here you are, my sweet." He handed one to me.

"You're amazing. Thank you."

"I know, and you're welcome." He smirked and settled back into the couch. "So tell me about your day. Did you see Vanessa?"

"No, we were going to grab lunch, but her boss had her running around doing something."

"I'm surprised either of you made it to work based on how you looked last night. You two are pros."

I sighed. The discomfort of my earlier hangover was not nearly a distant memory. "Yeah, I barely survived. Don't know about her, but I'm guessing she made it."

Along with Eli, Vanessa had become one of my best friends since I'd moved to the city. She was also one of the only people who could make a Tuesday night feel like a Friday night and didn't judge me for it. Most people went hard in college. I blossomed a little late in that department, and Vanessa hated her job equally if not more than I did, so we commiserated often.

I stared past Eli to our bookshelf filled with random books and framed candids from our various inebriated adventures.

"You seem distracted. What's up?"

I met his gaze again, hesitating whether to tell him.

Seeing Olivia was nothing, a blip in my day. But I hadn't been able to shake it.

"I saw an old friend today."

"Who?"

"Olivia Bridge. We were friends in college." I picked at the frayed fabric of my jeans, still in disbelief that I'd seen her. I'd run into plenty of people here. Tons of people, really. New York was like a Mecca for rich Ivy League kids, and that's who I'd been rubbing shoulders with for years now. But I hadn't seen Olivia since graduation. She hadn't changed much, if at all. Physically she was the same beautiful, put-together girl who I'd shared a house with in college.

Eli's eyes went wide. "Wait... She's not the one who's brother—"

"Yeah, she's Cameron's sister." I said.

"Oh, wow. I didn't realize they were from around here."

"They're not. I guess she just moved here, so it was pretty random."

"Was it awkward?"

I shrugged. "I don't know. She was nice enough." She'd been guarded but friendlier than I remembered. She had spoken to me after all, but I suspected that the passing of time hadn't eased the resentment she'd held toward me. As much as I didn't want to care, I did.

"Let me guess. You've been thinking about Cameron all day, and this is why you are in a super funk."

He cocked his head, his dyed black hair feathering over his forehead. We both knew he was right. I'd told Eli about Cameron before, so admitting he'd slipped back into my thoughts after a merciful absence wasn't a big deal.

I blew out a breath, still feeling thoroughly mixed up. Seeing Olivia threatened to resurrect an entire volume of unwanted memories. Cameron's chapter in my life was ancient history, yet a familiar ache penetrated the fatigue and the dulling anesthetic of the wine when I thought of it.

"I swear, I should be like one of those nine hundred number psychics or something." Eli pulled a blanket down from the top of the couch and covered both of us with it. "Do you ever think about trying to reach out to him? You know, clear the air or something."

I shook my head. The memories felt ages old, but our breakup had been a painful one. Losing him had nearly broken me. I couldn't relive any part of that.

"You don't think that maybe he might want some closure?" Eli's voice was soft.

"He's the one who left. If anyone deserves closure, it's me, but I don't need it. I'm over it."

Silence fell between us, and I poured a second glass.

"Do you ever regret telling him no?"

I rolled my eyes, hating where this was going. "People don't just run off and get married like that anymore."

Eli shrugged.

"I don't know anyone who could have said yes under those circumstances," I continued.

"Okay, but that's not really an answer. Do you ever think about what would have happened if you'd said yes?"

I had lived that day over and over in my mind, playing out any number of scenarios that didn't end with me watching Cameron walk out of my life forever.

"You know why I couldn't," I mumbled before a surge of anger rushed over me.

While Cameron shunned his privilege, I'd had to claw my way past everything that threatened to hold me back, with more than my own survival to think of. Nothing was as simple as everyone seemed to think it was. I'd explained this all to Eli, but he was still poking me about it, stirring up my guilt all over again.

"Whose side are you on, anyway? You're a shitty therapist."

"I said I was psychic, not a licensed shrink. And you know I'm on your side. I get it, but things are different now. All I'm saying is that obviously you two really cared about each other. Maybe enough time has gone by that you could reconnect and at least be friends." He reached over and patted my leg over the blanket. "Everyone can use closure, trust me. Emotions were running high, but he's had time to calm down. You both have."

I shook my head. I went back to that day. I'd been so overwhelmed by seeing him again, only to have his love ripped from me. I'd never forget it. I cried myself to sleep for weeks thinking about it, filled with regret but knowing I'd had no other choice. I'd beaten myself up for months, years, that I couldn't hand over my heart and run away from my life, as much as I may have wanted to.

Marry me. Those two little words had ruined everything. No proposal ever wanted to go the way ours had gone.

After he'd left so suddenly, I'd called Olivia in a panic. She'd gone back home for break, so I assumed that's where he'd go next. No. He flew back to base, voluntarily skipping the rest of the leave that he'd been granted. He'd relinquished the time we would have spent getting used to calling each other husband and wife to be farther away from me.

Weeks went by with no word. He'd never given me the address to his new base and Olivia claimed not to have it, telling me that he'd deployed as soon as he got out of tech school. We didn't speak much after that. She could barely look at me.

"You loved him once, Maya." Eli's soft words broke through my thoughts. "I know you still care about him. You could keep carrying the weight of that day with you, or you could try to create a new memory."

I swallowed over the burning sensation in my throat. I'd cried too many tears over him already. What we shared then had been more than a fleeting infatuation. Cameron had been everything to me, and I'd believed it was the same for him. He was my escape, every hope and dream wrapped up into one beautiful package. True enough, he'd been my crutch when I'd desperately needed one.

I cringed at the word and how he'd wielded it against me in the heat of the moment. In the end, that's what he thought he was to me, an emotional crutch, because I couldn't commit to more. Maybe that had been true and he was better off without me.

"Can we drop it?" I downed a big gulp of wine, convinced that everything would make more sense once I hit the bottom of this glass, possibly the bottle. I could forget Cameron, my soul-crushing job, my fucked up family, and boil everything down to the blissful numbness that crept over me.

Eli sighed, seeming to relent. He grabbed the remote

from the table and turned on the news. An international story started to put things into perspective, but my mind kept returning to Cameron. The way he'd looked at me that day was burned into my mind, so in love and then so defeated, as hurt as I'd ever seen him.

I hadn't forgotten any of it. I was afraid if I ever saw him again, I never would.

★ ★ ★

"Hey, you."

Alex interrupted my laser focus on the spreadsheet I was working on. I looked up at him for a second. He was holding what was likely his third cup of coffee and smiling at me with bulgy eyes, like he had something juicy to share.

"What do you want?" I trained my eyes back on the screen. I was in my mode.

"Nice to see you too."

I sighed and waited for him to start. Considering Alex was male, straight, and engaged, he was a terrible gossip at work. I suspected it was a result of absolute boredom, which I couldn't exactly blame him for. Our office sorely lacked culture and energy. When I wasn't working, I usually welcomed the distraction—and the information— since I wasn't in the habit of making friends at work for intel.

He leaned into the side of the cubicle, bringing his head lower to mine. "Have you met the new assistant VP?"

"The chick?"

I'd seen her walking between her office and the

senior VP offices. She was olive-skinned, gorgeous, and had a throaty laugh that made me wonder how many guys had propositioned her since she'd started last week.

"Her name is Jia. She's our age. I'd like to know how she landed that gig. They didn't even pretend to hire internally for the position."

"Is she nice?" I asked, assuming she wasn't. No one climbed the ladder that fast being nice. Not that I would necessarily know. More women worked in the field now than a decade ago for sure, but our small contingent didn't exactly share a strong female camaraderie. Every woman for herself, and you never really knew who would sell you down the river if given the chance. I'd seen it happen a few times and accepted this as yet another facet of office politics that I'd never fully buy into as long as I was here.

"I don't know. I haven't met her yet, but Jason said his cousin used to work with her before she came here. Said she was a real bitch. That might have been because she wouldn't sleep with him though."

"Great. Can't wait to meet her." I looked back at my screen, trying to figure out which cell I was on.

"Shit, boss is coming. I'll see you later."

I nodded without a word, and he disappeared with lightening speed.

I finished what Alex had interrupted, and then headed downstairs for lunch well after the herd had cleared the office. I waited patiently by the elevator when someone joined me.

"You're Maya, right?"

"Yes." My reply came out as a question.

"I'm Jia."

Up close, she looked impeccable in a blue silk blouse, a fitted black skirt, and heels that I envied. Her jet-black hair was pulled into a tight twist, her features accented with enormous diamond stud earrings and a simple platinum chain that sparkled against her skin. She was pretty. Too pretty.

"Congrats on the new position." I acknowledged her with a quick smile and shook her hand before turning back. I stared up to the elevator numbers, hoping they'd hurry. I was running out of time to make it to Delaney's.

"Thanks. I noticed your name on the roster. Not many women around here."

"You noticed?"

She laughed, revealing a set of perfectly white teeth. Not only was she gorgeous, she was dazzling. Her naturally dark red lips sealed it. The elevator arrived empty and we stepped inside. I punched the button for the lobby, and she leaned back against the elevator wall as we descended.

"How long have you been with the company?"

"Four years," I replied.

She nodded, no doubt unimpressed at my inability to climb the corporate ladder with the breakneck speed that she had. I wasn't sure I wanted to know how she'd done it, but maybe I could use some tips, because doing the work of two or more people wasn't enough apparently.

"We should get lunch sometime."

"Sure," I agreed. I could feel her eyes on me, and a quick glance to the side confirmed it. I tried to shake the mild discomfort of being assessed in such close proximity by this beautiful stranger.

"I have meetings this week, but we should plan

something for next week."

"Yeah, that sounds great. You know where to find me."

Despite my general pessimism about excelling professionally, I was interested in getting to know her better. Maybe this was what I'd heard about in my women's college pep rallies, women helping women. She might surprise me.

We stepped out of the building and went our separate ways. I hadn't taken two steps toward Delaney's before I saw him.

My heart stopped, and a rapid heat washed over me. His lips parted and his breath clouded in the cold air when our eyes met. I forgot everything. Where I was, where I was going, who I was. In that split second all I could think about was who I was the last time we saw each other. Vulnerable, heartbroken, so in love with him I was sick over it.

I'd packed the photos of us away long ago, but every memory came rushing back. He was everything I'd remembered and more. Literally, he was more. The coat couldn't hide the broadness of his chest and shoulders. I marveled anew at the definition of his cheekbones and strong jaw line covered with fine stubble. His hair had grown out again, but not long enough to obscure the blue eyes that he and his sister shared. They cut through me now, filled with an intensity I couldn't name.

He stalked closer, his expression unreadable. I couldn't breathe. Actually I couldn't stop breathing. I was heaving like a maniac and the fog in the air left no doubt.

"Hey," he said softly.

"Cameron." His name fell off my lips and my body

weakened, a remembered feeling he'd given me so many times before. I fought the urge to touch him, curl up against his body, knowing he'd hold me up. Eli had been all wrong. This was a terrible idea.

I swallowed hard and lost myself in his eyes. "What are·you doing here?"

"Olivia said you worked down here. I thought maybe we could catch up."

"Catch up?" Why did I sound so desperate? Where was corporate Maya? In a matter of seconds his presence had reduced me to a blithering idiot.

For a split second, he looked how I felt. Overwhelmed, a little lost, paralyzing me with those amazing, penetrating blue eyes. "Do you want to get lunch?"

"Lunch?" I repeated the last word because I still wasn't completely in control of my brain. He might have been speaking another language for all the sense this made to me.

A slow smile came across his lips. Fucking hell, those lips. They looked good, and it'd been far too long since I'd had anyone's lips on me.

CHAPTER THREE

CAMERON. Olivia was right. Maya was different. I recognized her, but after a few minutes, I knew that she'd changed more than her hair and the way she dressed.

We sat in a little bistro a few blocks away from where she worked. Everyone in the place was wearing a suit. She didn't seem to care that I wasn't, which was reassuring because I didn't care either. I'd watched my father put on a suit every day, and that had been enough for me. Of course Maya was probably more concerned with me showing up out of nowhere than with the dress code for lower Manhattan bistros. She hadn't interrogated me yet on why I'd sought her out.

After Olivia told me about their run in, I'd stayed up half the night, trying with little success to push her from my thoughts. By morning I realized I couldn't wait weeks, years, or maybe forever to run into her by chance. Something about knowing we were in the same city at the same time felt karmic. I needed to act on it—open the door, walk through it, and see what was on the other side, even if it was only friendship, or nothing at all.

"So what did you want to talk about?" She tucked her pale blond hair behind her ear. She wore it long like she used to, but the soft waves that once framed her face were sleek and straight now.

"I don't know." I hadn't thought this through too well. I should have known what I wanted to achieve before ambushing her. I had no idea what to expect from her after all this time though, so I'd have to make it up as I went.

The server brought our meals, and I distracted myself with mine, grateful for an excuse to regroup. We had to have some common ground still, but as the seconds passed, the gulf between us created by years of not speaking grew wider.

We hadn't stayed in touch. Some breakups have no place to go afterwards. I'd had no interest in watching her life take a turn away from mine, with other people who weren't me. We cut ties, and I'd let her memory fade as much as it would. I had no idea what her life was like now.

"How long have you been in New York?" Her smile was tight and polite.

"About a year. I started a gym in Brooklyn."

She lifted her eyebrows. "That's great. What's it called?"

"Bridge Fitness."

She nearly choked. "Wow."

"What?"

"That's a few blocks away from my apartment. I can't believe we never ran into each other before."

"You work out there?"

She laughed. "No."

"Why is that funny?"

She shrugged and looked out the window. "It's not. I don't really have time for stuff like that."

"That's what everyone says. It's the most popular cop out."

"Right."

"What about you? You like your work?"

Her gaze lingered on the busy street outside for a moment before focusing on her food. "It's okay. Pays well."

I could sense the gulf getting bigger. Lecturing her about working out probably wasn't the way to go. I was totally fucking this up. We hadn't exactly parted on good terms, and here we were, trying to talk like none of that had happened. Like we were old friends reunited. We were anything but.

"Listen, I'm sorry for just showing up out of nowhere."

"It's okay. I mean, it's nice to see you."

"I know we never really stayed in touch. I just wanted to see you. It's been so long."

"It has." She closed her eyes and took a breath, as if her thoughts might be taking her someplace else for a second. "Seems like we've both moved on, and you're doing well, so that's great."

I tensed at the words. "You're seeing someone?"

Her eyes widened. "What do you mean?"

"You said we've both moved on. I assume that means you're with someone."

"No, not really."

She studied her food again. I released a breath I didn't realize I'd been holding. Why the hell couldn't she look me in the eye?

Her hand trembled slightly as she reached for her glass of water. A faint blush colored her cheeks, her chest rising softly under the soft fabric of her button down that hugged her breasts. I wasn't blind to the effect I had on women. Since Maya, there'd been others, but somehow I couldn't remember noticing how their bodies reacted in all the subtle ways that Maya's was right now. She mesmerized me.

I tore myself away from studying her and straightened in my seat. "I guess I don't know where to start here."

She was silent for a moment, tracing tiny circles into the tablecloth. "If this is about closure, I get it. Things obviously didn't end well between us. If you want to talk about it, I understand."

Closure? The way she said the word felt like a punch in the gut.

I laughed quietly. "Closure, huh?"

She leaned back in her chair, tossing her napkin over her picked-over salad. For all the attention she'd given it, she'd barely eaten. "I don't know. I could live without rehashing everything." Her tone was matter-of-fact, cold, as if talking about what happened between us really was the last thing she wanted to do. Ancient history.

"You don't ever think about us?"

She took a deep breath. "Sure. Sometimes."

"And it doesn't bother you, the way things ended?"

"Does it matter? It ended. That's what happened. That's what we decided, one way or the other." She cleared her throat. "What you decided, anyway."

I bristled at the last words. Of course she blamed me for being the one to leave. In the heat of the moment, walking away had seemed like the best thing—the only thing—I could do.

"I wanted to spend the rest of my life with you. The feeling wasn't mutual. What did you expect?"

She finally looked up, a painful grimace taking over her beautiful mouth. "People don't get married in college, Cam."

"We talked about marriage. All the time. Don't pretend like we didn't." I kept my voice low, not wanting to show her how much her rejection still hurt. Fuck, I'd spent years trying to get her out of my system, and here we were. Our last night together could have been yesterday for how in control I felt.

"Can you seriously imagine us married right now, Cam? I mean look at us."

My lips tightened into a thin line, as I tried to make sense of the woman sitting across from me. How much of the person I'd loved might possibly still be there?

"No. I can't imagine it at all actually," I finally said. At the moment I couldn't.

A flash of pain passed behind her eyes, and I immediately regretted it. Maybe the Maya I loved was hiding somewhere under this new life and look after all. She blinked, her brown eyes glistening before she glanced down at her watch. Big and covered in sparkling crystals, it engulfed her tiny wrist.

"I'd better go. I only get an hour and I left late," she mumbled, reaching for her purse.

"Let me get the check," I said quickly.

"No, I'll get it."

"I insist." When the server came, I gave her a smile that guaranteed the check came to me.

"Cameron. Please, you don't have to buy me lunch." She started digging almost frantically in her purse.

"I'll let you pick it up next time." I dropped some bills onto the table and stood, reaching for her hand.

She pretended not to see the gesture and slung her purse over her shoulder, leading the way to the exit.

We stepped out and she paused.

"You don't have to walk me back."

I frowned. "I don't mind."

She relented without a word and set a brisk pace back to the office. We wove past pedestrians, and with every step I hated the awkwardness between us more and more. *Fuck*. The way she'd looked at me moments ago—I knew that hurt look. I'd put it there the last time I'd seen her, and though she'd quickly masked it, she'd revealed it all the same.

A knot formed in my stomach as regret filled me. This wasn't the reunion I'd hoped for, and it was going to be over all too soon. I couldn't leave her like this again, believing that I'd hated her. Not knowing if she hated me too.

We were steps away from the revolving doors of the building entrance when she slowed and turned. Before she could say goodbye, I caught her arm and tugged her to the side, out of the way of the foot traffic.

"What are you doing?" A panicked look passed over her features.

I struggled for words. "Maya... I'm sorry."

"Why?"

"I wasn't expecting things to go this way. Can't say it's

the first time that's happened with you though."

"Sorry I'm not what you expected." She tightened her jaw, and it was there again—that look that made me want to cringe and apologize and make everything right that had been wrong between us for so long.

She turned to walk away and I pulled her back, close to my chest. She sucked in a sharp breath before her body softened in my arms. I brushed her cheek, remembering her skin. Soft, warming under my touch. "I want to kiss you."

"What?" Her eyes went wide, her body suddenly stiff in my arms.

"I can't explain it. I need to know if I'll feel anything, kissing you." I traced the bow of her mouth, the tremble in her lip mimicking the pounding rhythm of my heart. "Call it closure," I whispered, lowering my mouth to hers.

"Stop," she said a second before our lips met.

I opened my eyes when she pushed me back. Doubt clouded her expression but the motion was firm. I let her step away, creating more distance between us, too much distance.

Her normally porcelain complexion colored, a flush working its way up her cheeks. Was she embarrassed? Pissed? I couldn't really tell. All I knew was that I wanted her as badly as I ever did—possibly more. I wanted to remember more, her smell, her taste. Harnessing my need took more than a little restraint. I wanted to touch her the way I used to, but I didn't have that right. Not yet.

MAYA. I waited impatiently for the elevator. I briefly

considered the stairs if they might burn off the surge of desire and epic confusion rocketing through me right now.

Sometimes I'd wondered if, after all this time, there could still be magic between us. Now I had little doubt. I was on fire, and he hadn't even kissed me. I couldn't bring myself to let him. I'd wanted him to, of course, but sitting through lunch pretending like he was just a blip in my history was nerve-racking enough. I couldn't go down that road with him, not knowing if I could realistically survive the emotional aftermath of a failed fling with an ex. I was already a frazzled fucking mess.

"Hey, girl."

Vanessa wedged beside me. "I called you about lunch."

"Oh, you did?" I padded my pockets for my phone. "Sorry. I probably shut it off at work and then I got sidetracked."

"Whatever. What's up?"

"Not much," I lied. I'd fill her in later, once I'd figured out what the hell had just happened between Cameron and me. "How's work?"

"Oh, you know." She kept her voice quiet as we piled into the elevators with a dozen others. "Yesterday was hell. I swear he knows when I'm worn out and runs me harder just to watch me suffer. I honestly think he gets off on it."

He was David Reilly, Vanessa's boss. He was one of the big bosses, superior to Jia and any of the others on my floor. He took unique pleasure in making her life a living hell. She'd landed the job with little experience through a connection and refused to quit and have it reflect poorly on the person who'd gotten her the gig. If I didn't care so much about keeping my own job, I would have given him a piece of my mind. But then who would I commiserate with?

"We still on for this weekend?" she asked.

"I'm pretty sure there'd have to be a zombie apocalypse to keep me from having drinks with you on a Saturday night. Consider it a running open invitation."

She laughed and nudged me with her elbow. As we ascended, she caught a few errant tendrils of her auburn hair that had escaped from her clip and tucked them back away. The doors opened at my floor and I prepared to push through.

"Wish me luck," she said.

"I would if I thought it'd do any good."

"Touché." She rolled her eyes.

I exited the elevator toward my own personal hell.

I made several unsuccessful attempts to focus on work, grateful that I'd had a productive morning. Thoughts of Cameron invaded every moment. I'd gotten off easy yesterday, having only his memory turning my world upside now. Now he was, in the flesh, which was far more disturbing. Whatever gorgeousness I'd remembered and imagined on lonely nights had been swiftly replaced by the vision of the man he'd become. I'd entertained half a dozen fantasies of rediscovering his body over lunch, and now my body was screaming for it.

Unfortunately nothing was simple about this craving. Cameron was more than a pretty face and what I imagined was an incredible body under his clothes. Cameron was a beacon of my past and so many emotions that I'd long buried. I wasn't sure how I felt about revisiting all of that again.

Cameron... I swear, he looked at me like he still loved me, hypnotizing me with his cool blue eyes. And he touched me like he used to, tender, possessive.

No. That was impossible. He'd hurt me. He'd broken me in a way that no one ever had. I couldn't reward him with a kiss, or a second chance.

CHAPTER FOUR

MAYA. "Wake up."

Eli nudged my shoulder, exacerbating the dull headache that surged upon waking. Vanessa and I had gone out for drinks after work to ring in the weekend. Too much champagne. Cheap champagne too, second only to boxed wine in the guaranteed terrible hangover department.

"Go to hell. It's too early," I groaned into my pillow, feebly shielding myself with another layer of blanket.

"It's almost noon, Maya."

I groaned again, a long sad moan that I hoped would inspire Eli to take pity on me.

"Come on. Get up. You've been bitching about going to the gym for weeks. I can't take it anymore. *We are going*."

I threw off the covers and glared at him. If he poked me one more time, I was going for blood. He reared back, hesitant, but determination glared in his eyes.

"Fine. Coffee first."

"You want to put coffee on top of all that champagne you drank last night? How about some water?"

"I don't care what the hell it is, as long as it buys me an extra fifteen minutes to wake up. Please go away."

After a shower, I emerged from my bedroom. Eli shoved a warm cup of chamomile in front of me before I could start berating him again. I sulked into the couch. The warm tea was simultaneously easing my stomach and putting me back to sleep. Eli sat with me, and I debated telling him about my run-in with Cameron.

His eyes narrowed as if he were reading my mind. "You're not telling me something."

"How do you do that?"

"I told you." He tapped his temple and grinned. "What's up?"

"Cameron Bridge. That's what's up."

"Shut up. You saw him? Last night?"

"No, at work the other day."

He frowned. "Explain."

"You could say we created a new memory."

"Okay, that could be really bad or really, really good."

I shook my head, unsure how to categorize our very unexpected and heated encounter. It couldn't be only good or bad. Seeing him yesterday was in a confused category all its own. I ignored Eli's question. He could decide after I told him about it.

"He found out where I worked from Olivia. When I left the office for lunch, he was downstairs waiting for me. Totally blindsided me but we had lunch, and... we talked."

"What did you talk about?"

"Small talk mostly, but I mentioned something about closure that I think pissed him off, and somehow we ended up right where we left off. He basically implied that he couldn't possibly imagine being married to me now."

"Ouch."

"Yeah. I didn't really need to hear that." The mere thought made me want to run back to bed and sleep until it didn't hurt anymore. I would have if I'd had any faith that I would ever be rid of the pain that surrounded my relationship with Cameron. After yesterday, I was more convinced than ever that our breakup was a wound that simply wouldn't heal, no matter how much time or distance we put between us.

"So he was a jerk, and then what? Did you just leave it like that?"

I finished my tea and set it on the table, not wanting to talk about what happened next.

"Spill it, Maya. For Christ's sake. You're killing me here."

"He tried to kiss me."

"Whoa. Okay, *tried* to kiss you?"

"I told him to stop, and he did. Then I left."

"What?"

"I wasn't going to let him kiss me out of nowhere. He walked out on me without a word five years ago, and I'm supposed to melt in his arms like a wilting fucking violet?"

"I don't know." Eli crossed his arms. "You might be right. Actually, yeah, fuck him. He doesn't deserve you."

"Or *don't* fuck him," I corrected.

He shrugged. "He may be a jerk, but he sounds like a

hot jerk, and it's never too late for breakup sex. One for the road, you know. Could be therapeutic."

"I highly doubt it." I rolled my eyes and hauled my ass off the sofa. Working out suddenly seemed better than spending another minute talking about Cameron. "Let's do this."

We headed out, and I was instantly freezing. Thankfully we weren't trudging through snow, otherwise I would have definitely vetoed this excursion, again. After several blocks we were nearing the entrance of Cameron's gym. I stopped short.

"Wait, I didn't realize we were coming here."

Eli frowned. "I've heard good things about it. It's fairly new."

"This is Cameron's place."

"What do you mean?"

"He owns this gym. Bridge Fitness... Cameron Bridge... Get it? I can't go in there. What if he sees me?"

I was talking fast, the sudden prospect of seeing Cameron again so soon sending me into a mini meltdown. Eli rolled his eyes and hooked his arm in mine.

"Let's go."

I didn't budge. "No," I said through clenched teeth, in disbelief that he wasn't sympathizing with me. "I told you, I'm not going in there."

Eli pulled away and put his hands on his hips. "Maya Jacobs, grow up. We've braved five city blocks in the freezing cold. *Let's go.*"

I shook my head again, and he left me in a huff, disappearing through the entrance.

My jaw dropped. I couldn't believe he would ditch

me like this when I was clearly freaking out. I yanked the braided strings of my winter hat down farther, hoping it would disguise me if I ran into Cameron. I took a deep breath and entered.

The gym was surprisingly inviting, with muted cool tones. Gyms freaked me out. Or maybe just the people who frequented them did. I always felt out of place, like everyone knew I had no idea what I was doing there. Today was no exception, but something about the place had an unusually calming effect. I scanned the reception area and the rooms I could see into. I released a sigh of relief that Cameron was nowhere in sight.

Eli was at the counter, getting details for the yoga class, when I joined him. He glanced back at me and took my hand in his. I followed him down the hall. We entered a spacious room with mirrored walls, light wood floors, and some new age soundscapes drifting over us from the surround sound. We grabbed mats and found two spaces. Eli strategically positioned himself next to another young guy, a blond slice of heaven who was chatting with him in no time. The only other spots open were in the very front. My anxiety immediately kicked in, but I couldn't bail now.

I got situated and lay back on my mat, waiting for the class to start. Between being horizontal again and the music, I was nearly asleep again when the instructor spoke up, asking us to take a seated position. I rolled up, wishing I'd had an extra five minutes for a power nap.

The instructor introduced herself. Raina was a petite girl about my age, thin and toned with pixie cut brown hair. She pretzeled her legs into a comfortable lotus. I looked down at my crossed legs. *No. That won't be happening.*

The rest of the class went better than expected. Raina had realistic expectations and gave us enough options so no one felt left out. I left the class both exhausted and rejuvenated. I waited for Eli to finish chatting with his new friend, and we walked out together. Still no sign of Cameron, but I pulled on my hat just in case.

"So that was good," I said, my voice markedly peppier than it had been an hour ago.

Eli cocked his head. "See, aren't you glad you came? You were being such a baby about seeing Cameron, I thought I was going to have drag you in there."

"Maya?"

I jumped back at the sound. Cameron emerged through an adjacent doorway. In front of us now, in a gym T-shirt and mesh shorts, he was impossible to ignore. I gave him an involuntary once over, swallowing hard.

"Hi," I mumbled.

A broad smile crept over Eli's face as he held out his hand. "I'm Eli, Maya's roommate."

"It's a pleasure." Cameron shook Eli's hand. "You guys come to work out, or...?"

"Yoga," I replied.

He cocked an eyebrow. "You always wear a hat to yoga?"

I frowned and pulled it off, my hair instantly going in every direction from the static. I nervously tried to tame it when Cameron continued.

"Let me give you guys a tour. I could even do a quick training session if you're interested. I don't have an appointment for another thirty minutes."

"Awesome. I'll leave you two to it. I think I see

someone I know at the treadmills." Eli winked at me and waved goodbye.

I followed his retreat with a glare, my zen waning at a rapid rate.

"So what'll it be?" Cameron crossed his arms and leaned against the wall, his powerful legs on display. I thought he'd come back changed after boot camp, but this was a whole new level. I tore my gaze away and forced myself to meet his eyes.

"I don't know. I'm not really up for a work out. I'm kind of wiped out."

"From yoga?"

I rolled my eyes, not wanting to explain that I also happened to be epically hung over. "Listen, I did a lot of planks in there. She's intense."

"Oh, Raina?" He laughed a little and he shifted his gaze past me. "Speak of the devil."

Raina bounded beside us, her eyes locked on Cameron. "Hey, Cam." She lifted up on the toes of her sneakers and gave him a quick kiss on the cheek.

A pang of jealousy hit me, and then I remembered that he hadn't exactly made it clear that he wasn't seeing anyone. Even if he weren't, someone as good-looking as Cameron wouldn't stay on the market for long, as evidenced by Raina casually rubbing her sports-bra harnessed tit on his arm.

"Hey," he said. "Raina, this is Maya."

Her gaze shifted to me. "New member?"

"Actually, Maya's an old friend. I was about to give her a tour."

She gave me a tight smile and extended her hand. "Nice to meet you, Maya. Enjoy the class?"

"I did actually," I admitted.

"I hope you'll be back?"

I nodded wordlessly, not wanting to commit verbally.

"Cool. Well I'll see you two later then. I have another class in a few."

She took off, leaving Cameron and me alone again. Before I could come up with another excuse to get out of performing any kind of exercise in front of him, he took my hand and led me into the main area. The gesture seemed bold, but I appreciated the extra sense of security the connection gave me in light of my gym anxiety. I assessed the rows of fit, clearly habitual gym people, their presence somehow reinforcing how I was not supposed to be here.

We stopped in front of the free weights. "You okay with doing arms? After the planks and what not?"

He did a poor job of hiding his smirk, which stirred me enough to take the challenge.

"Bring it."

He hit me with a mega-watt smile and picked out two dumbbells. They looked puny in his strong hands as he faced the mirror and started demonstrating the motions he wanted to me to make. He seemed to know what he was talking about, but I was too entranced with his body to really listen. I still couldn't handle how changed he was. He'd always had a great body, tall and lean, but now with the massive amount of muscle tone that he'd gained, he was downright imposing. The front of his T-shirt lifted slightly every time his arms pulled up to touch the dumbbells together above his head. I caught a glimpse of his abs. I licked my lips, daring myself to look lower.

"Got it?"

My eyes shot up. "Yeah, sure."

I took the dumbbells and tensed against the strain of lifting their weight as he'd so easily done.

"Keep your shoulders straight."

His voice was low and even. He placed his hands on my shoulders, coaxing them back slightly with his fingertips. The simple contact shocked through me. In our reflection, I could see his eyes trained on my form. His hand slid down my back as he circled to the side.

"Hold it."

I froze, my arms holding the weights above me.

"Step your legs apart a little."

I sucked in a sharp breath at the quiet command.

"Good. If your posture is right, you're going to feel it here too." His hand brushed over my lower abdomen. The dull ache created from my earlier planks and holding these damn weights in the air transformed into a red hot energy pulsing through my core and between my legs from the contact that felt far too intimate.

Fuck, I didn't sign on for this. I took a shaky breath and lowered the weights to my side and up again, slowly repeating the motion. I was pretty sure a few members would pay extra for this level of attention. Or maybe they didn't need to. Maybe Cameron was hands-on like this with everyone. But I couldn't drag my filthy mind out of the gutter long enough to believe he wasn't touching me for the sheer, animal fun of it.

CAMERON. I'd never had to work so goddamn hard to focus on training someone. No shortage of attractive women had come through the gym, all too eager for the chance to train with Darren or me. But Maya was in a class of her own. Her body had changed since we'd known each other. Her clothes couldn't hide the fullness of her breasts or how her hips curved out from her waist in a way I didn't remember. At least blatant staring was justified under the circumstances.

She finished her set, breaking my steady survey of the intricacies of her body. We moved away from the free weights, and I set her up on the cables.

"I'm not sure I'm cut out for this," she said.

"You're doing really well."

She blushed, reinforcing how uncomfortable I suspected she was. Half of my job was making people feel more comfortable in the gym. Though I had a few clients who basically paid me to watch them work out in one-hour increments. Business was business, so I didn't argue. When they realized they weren't getting anything more out of it, they typically moved on. Sometimes to Darren.

Maya had always been headstrong though. I knew she'd take the challenge, even if it meant spending time with me that she might not have wanted. After I'd nearly kissed her and she left me in front of her office, I'd had mixed feelings about the whole thing. We hadn't exchanged contact information, and I sure as hell wasn't going to keep stalking her at her office.

"I didn't think I'd be seeing you again so soon," I said, hoping to get her to open up.

"Me neither."

"Why is that?"

She winced, straining against a motion, her biceps flexing with the effort. "Eli dragged me out for the yoga class. I had no idea we were coming here."

She stepped back and took a breath between sets. Her face was flushed from exertion. Time was ticking down. I couldn't push her hard just to spend more time with her.

"I didn't know you had a roommate."

"Yeah, well there are a lot of things you don't know about me." She shook out her arms.

"Maybe we can change that."

Her calm expression didn't change. "Oh?"

"I don't know." I shrugged, trying to sound casual. "I'd like to be friends, I guess, if you think we can."

She looked down at her feet, toeing the floor beneath her, a chink in her otherwise cool demeanor. "I don't know."

"What don't you know?"

She huffed. "How are we supposed to be friends when you're... You know, you kind of blindsided me yesterday."

"I know. I didn't plan that. I'm sorry."

"We have too much history, Cam."

"Mostly good history, don't you think?" I leaned against the machine, crossing my arms.

Her eyes went soft for a moment. Her throat worked on a swallow before her features hardened, an impassive blanket washing away any emotion I might have recognized moments ago.

"What's next?" she asked, her voice clipped.

I frowned. "What do you mean?"

"Are we almost done or what? I'm dying here."

"One more," I muttered, straightening again.

I switched out the hardware and demonstrated the motion for her. I adjusted the weight again when I finished. When I stepped away, she'd launched right into the first set of curls with fevered determination. With every motion her cleavage pushed up out of her tank top. I blew out a slow breath and tried to look anywhere else. I caught her reflection in the mirror and studied her ass in her skin-tight yoga pants. *Christ.* I'd have no chance of hiding a hard on in my gym shorts.

"Take a break after this. Then do two more sets. I'll be right back," I said brusquely.

I left her there without making eye contact. I needed water. What I really needed was a cold shower, because I was losing my damn mind reliving the memory of her body. I grabbed a couple waters from behind the front desk. I chugged the first one, stopping to take a few more steadying breaths. I needed to get her out of my head. She didn't want this trip down memory lane either. What the hell was I doing?

"Everything okay?"

Darren strolled up to the counter, his eyes narrowed. Fuck, he could read me like a book. Unlike Maya. Her thoughts were still a mystery. I'd been able to read her so well, once upon a time.

"Yeah, just grabbing a water for a client."

Maya walked up with Eli at her side, her eyes as cool and calm as they had been earlier. "Okay, I think you've tortured me enough. I'm heading out."

Darren swiveled to face her, his face lighting up when he sized her up. I tensed.

"Hi, I'm Darren," he said, holding out his hand.

She shook his hand and her eyes brightened. "You must be Cam's brother? I'm Maya."

Darren's smile slipped for a second. They'd never met, but they sure as hell knew of each other. He flashed me a look before returning to her. "Yeah. You're *the* Maya?"

"I guess," she muttered, almost too quietly to hear, as she put on her coat and tugged her hat back on. She looked to Eli and turned to leave.

"So, Maya. You interested in coming out with us for drinks later? Old man Cam is going to tie one on. You wouldn't want to miss that, would you?"

"Darren—"

He lifted his hand to silence me. "No, no. I'd love to get to know the infamous Maya who I've heard so much about."

"Maya never misses a happy hour," Eli chimed in, lifting his shoulders to his ears.

She glared at him and he recoiled slightly, giving her a frozen smile. "That's not true."

"Judgment free zone, hon," Darren said. "Let's hit the bar down the street around seven. What do you think?"

She stared hard at him. Between Eli's comment and Darren's impossible grin, I wasn't sure how she'd be able to shoot him down. I almost felt bad for her.

"Fine." She grabbed the second water from my hand, turned, and hooked arms with Eli.

He smiled back at us as she pulled him out the door. Through the glass, I could see her mouth moving at a rapid rate the second the doors closed. She was pissed.

I suppressed a smile.

CHAPTER FIVE

MAYA. "Do you want to explain to me what the hell that was all about?" I started as soon as we cleared the exit from the gym.

Eli sighed dramatically. "Here we go."

"You completely sabotaged me in there!" I had to keep myself from screaming at him as we made our way back to the apartment.

"You ran into your ex. It's not world news, okay? Get a grip."

Rage pulsed through me. "And you basically pushed me into a private work out with him, and somehow I'm supposed to be totally fine with getting drinks with him and his brother tonight?"

"So what, Maya? You've been moping around all week since you found out Cameron was in New York. You obviously still have feelings for him. Why don't you give it a chance?"

"Give what a chance? What we had is over. I'm

71

attracted to him, but that doesn't mean I'm going to go running into another relationship with him. And who knows if that's even something he wants?"

He rolled his eyes. "Right."

"Right…what? What does that mean?"

He turned toward me. "Outside of my own personal experiences, I've never actually felt chemistry between two other people. Until today. The freaking air crackled when you two saw each other. Whatever is going on between you is so obviously more than you're making it out to be. I just gave you a little shove in the right direction." He swept his hair away from his eyes. "Maybe you'll thank me one day."

I stopped in front of the apartment, too irritated to take the next steps up to the entrance of the brownstone we shared with a handful of other tenants. "This is not a game for me. You're supposed to be on *my* side, Eli." My tone was low, my voice thick with emotion. This situation with Cameron was taking me on an emotional roller coaster, and somehow Eli was driving the ride.

"*You're* not even on your side. Do you know how difficult it is to live with you and your self defeating attitude sometimes?"

"Well no one's forcing you to stay here. It's not like I'll miss the rent that you never pay me," I snapped.

His jaw dropped. The silence that fell between us was almost painful.

"Wow."

I was about to speak, somehow soften what I'd just said, when he beat me to it.

"I'm going to grab some groceries for dinner and try to forget you just said that. I'll see you back here later."

"Eli…" My shoulders slumped as he walked past me.

I cursed and made my way upstairs and out of the cold.

Despite feeling energized by my workout, I sulked most of the day. Eli and I barely spoke, though he made his movements around our small apartment known. I tried to ignore him every time he slammed a door a little too hard, made a clatter putting the dishes away, or sighed a little too loudly. If I was self-defeating, he was classically passive aggressive.

I tossed aside a book that wasn't grabbing me and looked out the window. The streets were empty, the trees that lined them now barren. The dead of winter had come early this year, with the kind of cold that borders on painful the second you step outside, the kind of cold that made me wonder why I came here, of all places, after school. Though I had no way of knowing, I wanted to believe I was close enough for my mother to find me if she needed to.

I opened my laptop and a new tab in my browser. I typed *Lynne Jacobs* into the search bar and scanned the results. I checked all the usual places where I thought I might find her—police reports, regional news, and finally the obituaries. I had no way of knowing where she could be, if she were even alive.

No less than six months after things ended terribly with Cameron, I'd lost touch with my mom. We rarely saw each other after I'd left for college, but we always kept in touch somehow. Then the phone number I'd had for her was disconnected. At the time, I panicked, angry and scared that I'd never bothered getting contact info from her newest boyfriend, or even the address where she'd stayed last. She moved around so often, I'd stopped keeping track, figuring she'd always circle back and find me wherever she landed. I closed my eyes, seeing her face. I'd never forgive myself.

"Find anything?" Eli's voice was soft when he settled beside me, glancing over my shoulder to the screen.

I shook my head.

"Truce?" he said.

I shut the laptop and shifted closer, pulling him into a tight hug. True enough, I'd taken on the brunt of our shared expenses, but my friendship with Eli had been my lifeline in so many ways—ways I could never put a price on. I'd lashed out at him in a moment of weakness, and he didn't deserve it.

Having Cameron in my life again was sending me into an emotional tailspin that I had no control over. I could almost visualize the past and future colliding. I simply wasn't the person I used to be, sentimental and lovesick and profoundly in love with this man. I'd given up on love after a few unsuccessful rebounds. Nothing held a candle to the love I'd shared with Cameron, and in the end, I decided to stop wasting my time. I didn't date, and I didn't fall in love.

Yet I couldn't shake the sinking feeling that bringing Cameron back into my life could challenge me on both fronts.

CAMERON. The minutes ticked by as I waited for her to meet us at the bar. Every time we met seemed like a gamble, a chance that could be easily missed. And I didn't want to miss any more chances. The attraction to her was fierce enough, but the void I'd lived with for so long wanted to be filled, more than ever now that I'd seen her again. Self-preservation told me to run hard in the opposite direction, but deep down, I knew I wanted her back somehow.

The problem was I had no idea if that was something she might want too. I could have been reading all the signals wrong, but surely she couldn't deny that outside of the breakup and its aftermath, we had something worth salvaging. Not just the sex, though that had been remarkable, but simply being together had always been great. I'd never been so at ease, so fundamentally happy with another person. We were comfortable with silence, comfortable with ourselves. Not like now. She was a beautiful mystery to me now, and I was putting myself out there in a way that had every alarm going off, and not in a good way. With every word, I was waiting for her to say no again—no to friendship, to seeing me ever again, or to something more that I still wasn't sure if I wanted.

I strummed my fingers on the bar, twisting around to scan the room in anticipation of her arrival.

"Relax, man. You're stressing me out."

"She's my ex. If anyone's stressing out here, it's me."

Darren broke his concentration on the televisions above the bar. "You think you'll hook up?"

I shot him an annoyed look. "Are you fucking serious?"

Darren went wide-eyed. "Uh, yeah?"

"You really need to try out an actual relationship sometime. I can barely hold a conversation with you."

He laughed. "A couple weeks living with Liv and you sound exactly like her now."

I sighed and leaned back into the bar stool. He might have been right, but he was also being an idiot, as usual.

"Maya isn't some random girl you pick up and take home."

"What kind of girl is she then?"

"She's someone I have history with. I was ready to marry her. Obviously that complicates things."

"Why? You haven't seen her in years. She's smoking hot, and if she's into you, why not? You really need to loosen up, man. How long has it been since you've been laid?"

I took another sip of my beer, refusing to get sucked into another inane conversation.

"That long, eh? How about this? I'll give you one week to get Maya into bed, and if you can't bite the bullet, then you're letting me hook you up with some people I know. This celibacy thing isn't working for you."

"I'm not celibate, and if you're talking about hiring a professional, you can fuck off right now."

He laughed loudly. "You worried you can't seal the deal in a week?"

A subtle charge went through me at the challenge. Maya wasn't a conquest, at least not a purely sexual one, but Darren had a way of capitalizing on our non-stop competitive natures. "I'm not worried about that, no."

"You probably want to romance her and shit though. See if she'll go steady with you first?"

I rolled my eyes.

"Maybe I'll give you a week and then I'll give it a go," he prodded.

I fisted my hand in my lap, anger simmering through

me. "Maybe you should mind your own fucking business. I'll sleep with her when I'm good and goddamn ready. You even think about touching her and I'll kill you. Understand?"

A glint of mischief passed over Darren's eyes. His gaze shifted past me and his smile widened. "Hey, Maya."

I swiveled in the chair to find her standing by my side, her light brown eyes glimmering under dark lashes. I had no idea how much she'd heard, but if she'd heard any of it, I couldn't imagine what she'd be thinking now.

"Hey." She stood frozen in place. "Am I interrupting something?"

"No." I pulled out the stool for her to join us. "I was about to haul Darren into the street and beat the hell out of him, so you arrived just in time. Saved by the bell, I guess."

"Or by the lovely ex, in this case," Darren quipped, his eyes lighting on Maya.

I was kicking myself in the ass for letting Darren coordinate this meeting. Now I'd have to contend with him being an asshole all night. As if all of this wasn't difficult enough.

The comment earned a small smile from Maya, and she lifted herself onto the stool. She ordered a drink. I took advantage of her distraction to look her over. She looked good, dressed casually, but nice. A dark blue sweater dress, the hem of which rested mid-thigh, showing just enough of her sheer stocking-sheathed leg to make me want to see more.

"You look great, Maya." Darren's voice mimicked my thoughts.

"Thanks." Maya flashed him, and then me, a smile.

Everything seemed to go out of focus except her when she looked up at me then. That moment of levity was swiftly interrupted.

"Cam, how come you never told me Maya was drop-dead gorgeous?" Darren said.

I released a breath that hissed between my teeth, resisting the urge to rip him off his seat and set him straight right now. "Darren, you want to go harass someone else for a while so we can catch up?"

He grabbed his beer and slid off the stool. "Sure thing, bro. You can take it from here." He slapped me on the back and winked at Maya before making his way toward two women positioned at the far end of the bar.

I seriously pitied them.

"What was that about?" Maya took a slow sip of her freshly poured martini.

"Darren was just being ignorant, as usual. Don't mind him."

"For complimenting me?"

"No, of course not."

I wasn't about to give her the full history on what an irritating ass he could be, or the fact that his only goal was to expedite his little brother getting laid.

"You did well this morning," I said, hoping to change the subject.

"Thanks. Working out isn't really my thing."

"You should come in more. I could get you into a pretty good routine."

She shrugged. "I don't know. I work a long day, and frankly I just need to unwind with a drink after."

"Exercise works just as well as a nightcap, trust me. "

She laughed a little. "Somehow I doubt that."

"Try me."

Her eyebrow went up at the challenge.

"Give me a week. I'll show you how to use your body to work off stress, blow off some steam, and I guarantee you'll sleep like a baby and have more energy the next day."

A slow flush worked up her cheeks, and I realized that my trainer spiel sounded a little different in the context of speaking with someone I'd once slept with. Despite Darren's taunts, I wouldn't mind using her body to blow off some steam either. I sat back in the stool, forcing my thoughts in a different direction. God knew, after overhearing the tail end of my conversation with Darren, she probably already thought I was only out to fuck her. I silently wished for an easier way to go about this. There probably was and I was too out of practice to figure it out.

"I'm not sure if that's a good idea," she finally said.

"What do you mean?"

The last of the martini slid into her mouth. She moved the glass away and swiveled in her seat to face me. She straightened her shoulders. "You said you wanted to be friends."

"Yeah."

"Is that really true? I hate to kill the mood here, but I just need to know what I'm getting into. I mean, I run into Olivia one day, you track me down at work the next, and now here we are. We could keep dancing around this for the next few weeks if you want, or we can lay it out right now. If this is about sex and you're just interested in a hook up, you can tell me that. I'm a big girl."

I blew out a breath. Shit, she'd never been this direct before. "Are you saying you'd be open to having a sexual relationship with me if that's what I said I wanted?"

She didn't flinch. "Not necessarily, but at least I'd know what your intentions were. I heard the tail end of whatever you and Darren were talking about. Something about sleeping with me when you're good and ready?"

I winced, cursing Darren and his big stupid mouth. "I'm sorry, Maya. I really wish you hadn't heard that. He was egging me on and..." I cursed, shoving my hands through my hair. There was no way to regurgitate that conversation in a way that didn't make us both sound like grade A pricks. "I don't have a hidden agenda, if that's what you're worried about."

She shut her eyes and shook her head slightly, her expression softening. I relaxed a little, hoping she was going to let me off the hook for that slip up. I really, really hoped that's what was happening. Otherwise Darren was going to get a beating of a lifetime.

"Honestly, I don't know if I can even be friends with you, Cameron. Nothing was simple after you left, and maybe some of that is still unresolved for me. Being around you is mixing it all up again, things I put away a long time ago. I'm not sure I want that in my life right now."

I couldn't speak for a long time. She'd dropped a lot on me, and as usual, I wasn't prepared for any of it. These impromptu reunion meetings were not my forte. How could I blame her though? I'd left suddenly and severed contact. We didn't even have a chance to fight it out. So much had gone unspoken between us. I turned to face her, trying to rapidly collect my scattered thoughts.

"If we're being honest adults, then I'll admit that being around you now makes me feel like I want more than friendship. But you're not the only one who's worried that even considering it is a terrible idea."

She nodded, her gaze cast to the ground. Her body language was so subtle, a slight hunch in her shoulders, a sad kind of aura settling over her features. My heart twisted at the thought of her hurting, especially because of me. I reached out, grazing the curve of her cheek.

"I still care about you, Maya. That's never going to change."

Her gaze flew up to mine, her eyes like warm caramels. She could always captivate me with a look. Her lips parted. The fear in my gut dissipated, replaced with the urge to hold her, to make her believe it again. That pull was returning with greater force each time we met. An inexplicable energy drew me to her, to her lips and her body. I wanted us so close that neither of us could think straight. But I couldn't rush us into that.

"Why don't we just try to get to know each other for a while? It sounds strange to say, but it's been a long time and I don't know you that well anymore."

"I'll save you the suspense, Cam. I'm not the girl you used to know. My life is...different." She waved her hand, returning it to rub her forehead anxiously. "Just a hunch, but I have a feeling we have very different lifestyles that even friendship may not be able to accommodate."

I nodded. The fear that we'd already grown too far apart rooted in my gut, but I pushed past it. I couldn't give up before we'd even started. That was worse than disappearing from her life years ago, a mistake I intended to rectify if given the chance. "We've both changed.

That's obvious."

"Maybe it's not a good idea to go down this road right now." She tucked her hair behind her ear. "I mean, we can stay in touch. Facebook or whatever."

"Fuck Facebook."

She laughed. "Okay."

"Start by seeing me at the gym next week."

She looked away for a minute as if she were restoring her resolve. "You really think you're going to get me to work out every day?"

"Give me a week."

"No cocktails?"

I hesitated a second. "No cocktails."

She canted her head to the side. "Says the guy holding an empty pint glass."

"This is an exception. Darren coerced me here. The bar isn't really my scene."

"Now I know why he calls you old man Cam." She gave me a crooked smile. The gesture saved me from bristling at Darren's insulting moniker for me.

"I don't find mingling with random inebriated strangers especially fulfilling, no. I guess that makes me old."

"I'm not a stranger."

"No, you're not," I said quietly. Her long bangs fell across her forehead, resting on her eyelashes. I wanted to reach out to her again, to remind us both that we weren't strangers. Even if it felt that way sometimes.

"Okay, I'll do the workouts, but I'm reserving the right to a nightcap," she said, lifting up her finger to make her point.

"You breaking the rules already?"

She quirked her lips. "Are you going to be a stickler?"

"Old man Cam. I have a reputation to live up to. Plus I'll have a better chance of converting you to a paid gym member if you experience a full week of healthy living."

"And what if I decide that your workout regimen isn't cutting it?"

"It will."

"Your confidence is noted, but shouldn't there be some sort of counter effort after I bust my ass and deprive myself for a week?"

I shrugged, unconvinced that she'd possibly feel that way by the time we were through.

"How about I take you up on this proposed week of fitness hell—because I can already see that it will be—and then we can celebrate my way. I can show you how I blow off steam and you can tell me how they compare."

I was intrigued. "How do you blow off steam?"

"I dance."

"Uh, okay. Where?"

"There are a few clubs I go to with friends. We toss back a few and dance all night. It's a great workout. But I guess that's not your 'scene' either."

"No, not really, but I'd like to be fair. And I wouldn't mind spending some more time with you, so let's do this."

She raised her refilled glass to my empty one, which seemed fitting.

"Are we toasting?" I laughed.

"I think it's only appropriate that we do. Having little faith in your ability to convert me into a gym rat, I'd feel better if I bookended this experience with some vodka."

I raised my glass and clinked it with hers. "Cheers, then."

"To new memories." She tipped the glass to her lips.

MAYA. The waiter sat us by the window and the steady rush of traffic outside held my attention until Jia spoke.

"So who's the guy?"

I gave her a blank stare. "Who?"

"I mean the one who had you pressed against the building the other day." Her lips curved into a secretive grin. "I was having lunch across the street when you came back."

I couldn't see myself but I knew I'd turned beet red. Mortifying just wasn't the right word. "Oh, God. I'm sorry. That was—"

She laughed. "I don't care. Looked pretty intense, actually. Is he your boyfriend?"

"No. An ex."

"That's always interesting. You getting back together?"

I bit my lip and glanced across the restaurant, wishing the server would return so I didn't have to divulge any of my confused thoughts surrounding Cameron's reemergence into my life.

Rejecting his advances that day had been easier than it was to push away from his attempts to simply spend time with me. Letting him get close was too natural a reaction. I could almost fool myself into thinking we were young and in love again, that nothing or no one else mattered. Only I had no interest in falling in love with anyone. The mere thought of it scared the hell out of me. So did simply eliminating Cameron from my life again, even though that seemed like the only way to keep myself safe from any potentially painful fallout.

Maybe taking him up on his offer was an emotionally reckless thing to do, but I wasn't ready to see him walk away again. Plus this could be the shove I needed to get my ass into shape, and staring at his beautiful body wasn't a bad way to do it.

I looked back to find Jia waiting for my answer. "We're catching up, I guess."

She smiled. "I see."

"Not like that. I mean, we haven't seen each other in years, and we realized that we live in the same neighborhood. I guess I'm seeing how it goes, getting to know him again. I'm not really looking for a relationship though."

"I can see that. Not like work isn't consuming enough. I don't really have time for dating either. Serious dating anyway."

"Seems like you're doing really well at the company."

She nodded, but I wanted to know more.

"You're young to have come as far as you have, Jia. I hope you don't mind me saying that." I hesitated as the words left me, briefly regretting them. She was being blunt asking me personal questions though. Plus she'd invited me here, not the other way around, so I might as well see what she was made of. The server came to take our orders, delaying her response, which made me even more nervous.

As soon as he left she spoke. "Not at all. You're saying what everyone is thinking, and I realize that. It's not easy being a young woman in this field. Plus if you're attractive, everyone assumes you're fucking your way to the top."

I bit my lip, not wanting to let on that everyone I'd talked to about Jia had had something to say about her rumored history at the other firm. People were so shallow. Was that what I wanted if I ever managed to crawl out of my cubicle and get promoted? People speculating on the cause for any success I earned?

"I know I'm younger than most of my male colleagues, but I'm not here to make friends," she said. "This is my career, and I intend to keep it moving forward, no matter what."

"Me too. I just want to get the job done. But that never seems to be enough."

"It isn't. You have to play the game. There's no way around it."

My heart sank. She'd confirmed what I'd believed to be true and had refused to engage in for years now. "Don't you find the politics tedious?"

She shrugged and lifted the water glass to her lips "Not really. I consider it part of the job. You have to know what you want, and more importantly, you have to know what other people want. That's the key."

"How do you mean?"

"Look around yourself, Maya. Look beyond the numbers. Look at the landscape of the company and the people who make it up. Have you gotten to know anyone who you work with? Any of your superiors?"

"Not really. I do my job. That's what they want, isn't it? I thought you said people shouldn't be here to make friends."

"You listen. Good." She smiled. "But no, they don't only want you to do your job. Different people want different things. If you venture outside of your comfort zone a little, eventually you'll find the connections that will open doors."

"Right." My thoughts went to people like Dermott, my boss, or Reilly—hard and focused men who barely noticed people like Vanessa and me unless they happened to step on us. I wasn't sure I wanted to open a door that they were on the other side of.

"Consider me one of those doors."

I raised my eyebrows.

"I like you, Maya, and I'd like to help you, if you're open to it."

"Help me?"

"This is your career too. I'm assuming you'd be open to having a mentor, a friend?"

"Well...yeah. I mean..." I didn't quite know how to accept or acknowledge such a blatant offer of support. Jia seemed shrewd and charismatic. Being able to call her a friend was an intriguing opportunity all its own.

"Good." She smiled and reached out, feathering her fingertips over the back of my hand before returning to her meal. "I'm glad we did this."

CHAPTER SIX

CAMERON. I'd cleared my schedule for the week's evening training sessions. Maya had only committed to an hour each night, but I planned on taking her out after if she'd let me.

Darren grumbled about picking up the slack, but I didn't care. He owed me. I'd let him off the hook a few times so he could take off early to continue his training sessions with one of his new recruits, the flavor of the week. That routine was going to catch up with him eventually. As far as he spread his affections, his no-drama track record wouldn't last forever.

I leaned against the reception desk, making small talk with the young kid running it, when Maya arrived.

"Hey." I smiled, all too aware of how her mere presence lit up the room. But maybe that was just me. That I'd been waiting all day to see her became painfully obvious. She was still dressed for work, and her tired look tempered my excitement. "You okay?"

She smiled too quickly. "Yeah. I'm good. Long day, you know."

"Right. We'll make this quick then."

"Whatever. Don't feel like you have to go easy on me."

I grinned. "I wouldn't dream of it. Lockers are that way. I'll meet you out here when you're ready."

Before she could take a step away, Olivia walked in behind her. The smile she greeted me with quickly faded when she recognized Maya.

"Hey, Maya."

Maya gave her a weak hello.

Olivia flashed a subtle glare in my direction. "I'm guessing this isn't another coincidence."

"Actually it kind of was. Maya dropped into the gym last week. She lives nearby."

Olivia nodded, her expression emotionless. "Uncanny."

Maya straightened. "I'm going to go change. I'll be out in a bit."

As soon as she'd disappeared into the women's locker rooms, Olivia started in on me, her voice hushed.

"Do you want to explain to me what's going on?"

I crossed my arms and leaned against the front desk. "I don't need to explain myself to you, Olivia."

"Like hell you don't."

Christ, here we go.

"You went to see her didn't you?"

I looked past her, refusing to answer. I wasn't about to let my baby sister berate me. "Go home, Liv."

She shook her head. "I shouldn't have told you. I knew it. I had a feeling something like this would happen. I don't know what I was thinking. God, the stupid things you've done for her, and here we are—"

"It's fine. I wanted to see her, and it was friendly. She came to the gym today and we're just catching up."

"No, it is not fine. She basically destroyed your life, Cameron."

"I think it's safe to say that you're being a little dramatic."

"You could have died on those deployments. Do you not think of that?" Her voice was strained, laced with the concern I knew she carried with her during those hard times.

"You can't blame her for a war that I drafted myself into."

"I sure as hell can. Don't bullshit me and tell me she had nothing to do with you staying out there. She was the *only* reason you were out there as long as you were."

I clenched my jaw, forcing the words back down. "This conversation is over. If you came here to help, then help. If not, you can leave. I don't need you hanging around here making her uncomfortable."

"What are you saying?"

I straightened, no longer casually shrugging off her comments. "I'm saying that if you continue to give me shit about this, or if you say *anything* to upset her, you can leave right now. This is my gym, and you're living in my house. You may be my sister, but those are my rules. Get used to it."

Her jaw dropped, her small hands fisted tightly by her sides. More people came and went, which was the only reason she wasn't cursing me out right now, I suspected.

"Wow. I guess I know how I rank. So much for family."

Before I could say anything more, she stormed out.

MAYA. I sat on the bench along the wall leaning my head back. I let my eyes fall shut, fighting the fatigue. I briefly contemplated grabbing my bag and sneaking out. With my luck, Cameron was probably still standing guard by the door, with Olivia, no less.

Any semblance of politeness I'd enjoyed before must have worn off after our brief chance meeting, based on the narrow-eyed look she'd cast my way. The way she glared at Cameron had me unsettled too, like we were both in trouble.

I'd had another soul-draining day at work, but somehow I'd gotten my ass to the gym for a workout that was sure to strip the last of my energy. Now I was going to be subjected to Olivia's cattiness after a five-year reprieve?

Determined to carry on, I rose and checked myself in the mirror. I'd pulled my hair into a tight ponytail and changed into a snug black sports tank and matching yoga pants. I sighed. Now or never.

I emerged a few minutes later. I wrinkled my nose when the smell of sweat and metal met it. Across the room, Cameron was lifting what appeared to be an incredible amount of weight by a bar that rested across his shoulders. Where did he find the energy to do this all day long? I wanted to find a soft mat in the corner to take a nap on.

I joined him as he returned the weighted bar to its cradle and shot me a bright smile. "Hey, you ready?"

"You're at a ten, Cam. I'm at about a two. Any chance we can meet in the middle?"

He laughed. "I'll see what I can do. How do you feel about legs?"

I cocked an eyebrow. "I like them. I have them?"

"I mean doing legs. Have you ever done squats?"

I made no effort to disguise a grimace. He rested his hand on the long metal bar.

"We'll start with three sets of fifteen on this."

I went wide-eyed when he started toying with weights. "Whoa."

He paused, straightening again. "What?"

"This is freaking me out. Can't I just run on the treadmill for like a half hour and we can do those arm things from the other day?"

He gave me a serious look. "You told me not to go easy on you, and I don't plan to. Cardio is fine, but I want to focus on weight training, and you need to learn how to work all areas of your body."

"It may be worth noting that I'm not interested in having He-man legs."

"You won't. Legs help you burn calories everywhere though. Gets your whole body to pay attention."

I cursed inwardly and huffed. "Whatever. Show me what I'm supposed to do, and let's get this over with."

He walked me through the motions. We negotiated about the weights, agreeing that I could start with only the bar. He insisted I could do more, but I had no idea what I was doing. I had no interest in pushing the boundaries of my strength today. This was day one, after all.

I did exactly as he asked, determined to stay focused. I didn't want to look like a fool since I was venturing so far beyond my comfort zone in the work out department.

"Perfect, Maya. You're good at this."

I ignored his encouragements and the burn in my thighs as I pushed through the last set. Shit, this was hard. I powered through the last lift and returned the bar.

"How do you feel?"

I took a swig of my water and caught my breath. "I feel like this was a rotten idea. My thighs are on fire, and I want to die. How long are we doing this?"

"I started you with the most intense set first. Should go easier from here. We've got another forty-five minutes. Don't give up on me yet."

I groaned. He led me to some of the machines, instructing me as we went. He was right. The rest of the workout was less intense, but I was going to definitely feel it in the morning.

He stood in front of me, arms crossed and legs wide, staring me down as I struggled through my last set of leg lifts.

"Enjoying the show?"

"You always this wiped out after work?"

"Pretty much." I counted silently in my head. Almost done.

"So what is it? Stress, or just the work itself?"

The thought of work weakened my already taxed muscles. "Can we talk about something else?"

"I thought we were going to get to know each other better."

"Suffice it to say I'm not nearly as passionate about my work as you are about yours. It's inconceivable to me that you are this peppy after my work day has long ended."

"Peppy?"

"You're like aglow with energy. Makes me sick." I relaxed back into the seat of the machine, grateful for the break and praying that we were nearly finished.

He smiled. "Maybe you have that effect on me. I'm not usually this energized on the second shift."

"I think you enjoy torturing me."

A ghost of a smile curved his lips. "Come on, next one." He jerked his head in the direction of another machine.

I glared at him.

"What? You maxed out?"

"If you burn me out tonight, I might not be back tomorrow. My couch and a glass of wine are looking really nice about now." The prospect of forgetting the whole day with a drink tugged at me, a familiar craving I wasn't used to denying.

He twisted his lips and narrowed his eyes.

"I'm not bluffing. There's a reason I don't work out," I said. "I have zero will power."

"Fine. One more set, and we'll call it done. But we're doing abs tomorrow, and we're going to go hard on those."

I rolled my eyes. I was never going to survive this. "I'll be sure to run right over here after work then," I said with no small amount of sarcasm.

I finished up and escaped to the locker rooms before he changed his mind about sneaking anything else in. I took my time in the shower, letting all the tension leave my body. I was utterly spent. My head started swimming from the heat. I finished up and dressed, emerging makeup-less and ready for my bed, too drained to care about appearances.

Cameron was waiting for me. He'd changed too, into blue jeans and a crisp white T-shirt. Somehow, the simple ensemble made a mouthwatering combination. I hadn't forgotten how good he looked in and out of clothes.

"I guess I'll see you tomorrow for day two of hell," I said.

"Are you hungry? We could grab dinner."

"I'm good. I ate on the way here."

"How about tomorrow?"

"I would, but Eli is having his new boy over so I can meet him before they go to a concert."

He chewed his lip for a second. "I'm afraid to ask about Wednesday."

I scuffed the toe of my tennis shoe on the floor. "I think I could do Wednesday. As long as you promise to go easy on me. I'll be lucky if I can walk home tonight."

"I'll escort you, just to make sure you get there safely."

I canted my head slightly. Cameron's eyes glittered, beckoning me. A subtle surge of energy flowed through me. I wasn't up for much, but spending a few more minutes staring at his gorgeous face could probably be penciled in.

"You know, you're kind of a stalker," I teased.

He grinned and caught my hand in his. My heart leapt at the contact. "Yeah, but at least you know what you're getting into with me."

Did I? I pondered that as we started the short walk toward the apartment. "I'm sorry about Olivia," he said.

I didn't say anything right away. I wasn't sure I wanted to get into how *not* surprised I was by the tone of my second run-in with Olivia. Maybe he could assume that she'd spent our last year at school giving me the cold silent treatment, which was more than he'd given me.

"It's fine. But if you'd rather I didn't come by anymore, I understand. I don't want to make things awkward between you two. I realize she's not my biggest fan."

"It won't be awkward. I talked to her."

I raised my eyebrows. "Great." I couldn't imagine that conversation and how awkward my next meeting with Olivia would be as a result. As a former friend, I remembered how ruthless she used to be when it came to her friendships. People were either in or out in her book, and I was most definitely "out" with no prayer of getting back "in." I wasn't petitioning anyone to get into her good graces either. She could glare all she wanted. I had my own life and my own friends.

"She doesn't usually come by in the evenings, but even so, it's not something to worry about. You're welcome at the gym anytime."

We stopped in front of the apartment. I stared at the ground, battling with my renewed doubts. Was this going to be worth it?

"Hey." He tipped my chip up so our eyes met. "I'm not letting her scare you off, okay?"

His thumb grazed my lower lip, leaving a tingle in its wake. I exhaled slowly. Every time he'd casually or accidentally touched me tonight, my concentration scattered. Maybe he'd always have that effect on me. That scared me far more than Olivia's scathing looks.

"I'll see you tomorrow, okay?"

He nodded, releasing me slowly. Eager to be out of his grasp so I could think clearly again, I hurried up the stairs and disappeared into the apartment.

I gave Eli a small wave on the way to my bedroom before collapsing onto my bed, letting exhaustion win.

CAMERON. Having to hold back with Maya was beyond frustrating. I hated that I needed to. She was hesitant, and rightly so. We had to take things slow and get to know each other better. I could almost hear Darren's snarky remarks about going steady in my head. In truth, I wanted nothing more than to drag her into my bed. I had a feeling that's what we both ultimately wanted, but rushing into a physical relationship would be reckless. We'd both been through too much.

I entered my apartment quietly, hoping by some miracle that Olivia wasn't home. I wasn't in the mood to have it out with her again tonight. When I didn't see her, I went to the kitchen and pulled out some leftovers.

"Back so soon?"

I jumped back and shut the refrigerator door. Olivia was leaning against the counter, her arms crossed tightly.

"Don't fucking sneak up on me like that. What do you want?" I tried to ignore her persistent stare.

"Are you kicking me out?"

I paused. "Do you plan on giving me a reason to?"

She looked away, her lips pursed.

"Is making Maya uncomfortable important enough to you to go back to Mom and Dad's?"

"Obviously not. And I'm not trying to make her uncomfortable. I just don't want to see you get hurt again. You really should rethink what you're doing, inviting her back into your life."

"I'm a big boy, Liv. I appreciate the concern, but I can look out for myself."

"Have you thought this through, or are you going to rush back into something with her? That didn't work out so great last time, you know."

"We're not rushing into anything. We're trying to get to know each other better, to be friends, before we decide if we want anything more."

She sighed. "God."

"What?"

She shook her head. "Nothing."

"Liv, is this going to be a problem? I can't really see myself kicking you out, but don't make me consider it, okay? She's important to me."

"You barely know her, and you're putting her above me? Your own family?"

"I'm not ranking anyone here. I know her better than you ever will, and this is the last time we're going to discuss whether I decide to have her in my life. Understand? This is it."

She glared at me from under her lashes. I walked past her and went upstairs.

MAYA. It was past midnight on Tuesday night when Eli walked in. He had raccoon eyes and a stupid smile on his face. I sat cross-legged in front of our small coffee table, sheets of paper scattered around me as I scribbled. I stopped when he walked in.

"What are you still doing up?" His voice was high and slurred slightly.

"Can't sleep. I've replaced wine with caffeine," I

joked. If I was telling the truth, I would admit that Cameron was right. His regimen seemed to be giving me more energy while simultaneously wiping me out at regular intervals.

"How was your workout with Cameron?"

"Good actually." Except my abs were fucking killing me.

He raised an eyebrow. "You're being super positive about this."

I shrugged. "I don't mind it as much as I thought it would."

Somehow I'd resisted the urge to cheat on our bargain. Without a nightcap to look forward to, I had to fill my nights with something other than the slippery descent into inebriated bliss. My thoughts were sharper and my feelings more acute. That meant facing my emotional demons—many of them inspired by Cameron's reemergence in my life—was more of a challenge lately. When I couldn't shut them up with a glass of wine, I simply gave them a voice. I'd written more in the past week than I had over the past few months.

"How was the show?"

"Fantastic." His smile was impossibly wide and giddiness rolled off of him. He'd had his fair share of wild concert nights, but this seemed exceptional.

"Aaaand how did things go with blond boy?"

"Show stopping."

"Do tell."

He dropped onto the couch behind me and sighed loudly. "I think he's a keeper."

"Really?"

"Could be new boy excitement, but it seems like we have a lot in common. We love all the same bands. And he's a great kisser. And so fucking hot, my God."

I smiled, genuinely happy for him. "That's great, Eli. I can't wait to meet him sometime."

"I know." His shoulders sagged. "I was bummed he couldn't do dinner tonight. Did you go out with Cameron instead?"

"No, we made plans for tomorrow. I'm sure he's probably sick of me by now anyway."

"I doubt it."

"All he does is torture me, and all I do is complain." True enough, but we seemed to be feeling each other out with humor. The banter helped me find some boundaries with him, and a little part of me enjoyed hurling fresh and clever insults his way.

"You don't talk about other things?"

"Yeah, we do. Nothing too deep though, which is fine by me."

He leaned in, taking a peek at my notebook. I shut it quickly.

"You're writing?"

"Yeah."

He narrowed his eyes at me. "Have you showed him any of it?"

"Cameron?"

He rolled his eyes and gave me a *duh* look.

"No way. It's way too personal for that."

"He probably doesn't even know you write, does he?"

"He used to."

"Do you write about him?"

I took a long drink of the now lukewarm breakfast tea I'd been ignoring. "Sometimes. I mean, I used to all the time."

"And now."

I shrugged. His return to my daily life was conjuring thoughts that I'd never admit to out loud. I'd written them down for the sole purpose of putting them and the emotions they represented away. That's how I'd gotten over him the first time, and that's how I'd keep my head this time.

"Read me something."

"No, Eli. This is like...therapy. It's not really for sharing."

"Come on, I'm three sheets to the wind. I won't even remember it in the morning."

I didn't flinch.

"Maya Jacobs, if you do not read me something, and soon, I will steal your notebook, photocopy it, and distribute it to every man you bring home for as long as you let me stay here and freeload."

I gasped. "You wouldn't dare!"

He grinned mischievously. "No. But you need to stop keeping all that shit to yourself. It's awesome that you write it down, but that's just the first step." He blinked a few times. "Please?"

I rolled my eyes, and reached for my notebook, and flipped through for something that was close to finished. I never wrote anything down with the intention of having it read. Skimming over the words, I imagined how any number of people would receive them. The exercise was nothing short of petrifying.

"I don't know, Eli. This is all really rough. I'll work

on something and read it to you tomorrow, okay?"

He snatched up a loose sheet that was on the floor beside me. "This will do."

I reached to take it back but he twisted out of reach.

"Relax!" He cleared his throat and his gaze darted down the page.

I bit my lip, replacing it with my fingernail after a couple minutes passed. This was nerve-racking.

"Eli, enough. Give it back. You've read it, right?"

"I'm re-reading. Chill out, woman."

I took a breath and waited for him to lower the page. When he did, his eyes were more focused than they'd been before. "Maya, honey. Promise me that you will try to make this work with him. For your sake, for his sake. For my sake even."

I ripped my nail off and stacked the rest of the papers that were strewn about, tucking them safely inside the now worn notebook.

The relief and satisfaction I'd relished moments ago at having poured my soul onto the page was quickly replaced with a frightening vulnerability. My heart and stomach seemed to be inextricably connected now, constricted over what I'd shared and Eli's drunkenly honest assumptions about it.

"Maya."

"What?" I rose.

"Promise me."

"Goodnight, Eli. I'll see you in the a.m., okay?" I leaned over to kiss him on the forehead and disappeared into my room.

CHAPTER SEVEN

CAMERON. We sat at a table in the quiet corner of the restaurant. The place was casual enough that we could swing by after the gym, but Maya had still spent extra time getting ready before we left. I'm not sure how she managed it, but her makeup was fresh, and her jewelry sparkled in the dim light of the restaurant. She was sexy as hell in an all-black ensemble, a scoop neck sweater that showed her cleavage and snug jeans that were driving me crazy the whole walk here. I wanted to think she'd dressed up for my sake, but I couldn't be sure.

I tried to reprogram my thoughts every time they wandered. I had to keep my head straight. We were still a long way from where I wanted to be in terms of getting to know each other. That's what this week was about.

"Tell me how you ended up working on Wall Street." I still had a hard time imagining her crunching numbers for corporate America.

"The company recruits right from the college, so it

seemed like a good opportunity to make some money, pay off loans and what not."

"What's your day like?"

She shrugged, a wordless answer. "What made you decide to start the gym?" she asked.

"You know, I wasn't really interested in taking over the family business." In all our dreaming about the future, no one had known better than Maya my desire to break away from my parents' expectations. Degrees and suits and plans for the future that always involved some kind of bullshit ladder. She'd been hurt most by my joining the military, yet she'd supported it because it meant taking control of my future.

She nodded. "I remember. Did they help you?"

"No, I got the funds from investors. Somehow I managed to do it all on my own, which frustrates the hell out of them."

"I'm proud of you." Her eyes softened with a warm smile.

"Thanks."

"Why a gym?"

"There's not a lot to do in the desert, so I got pretty good at working out. Not exactly a page-turner as far as stories go."

That earned a small smile. "How long were you over there?"

I did a quick tally in my head. "The better part of three years over a handful of deployments."

The sparkle of interest in her eyes dulled with a new emotion. "That's terrible."

"It's fine. I volunteered for them. Swapped with a few guys with babies on the way, otherwise I probably could have gotten away with one or two."

"I don't understand. Why would you volunteer to go over there?"

I thought back to that life—a life that could not be more different from the one I was currently living. Peace, sometimes quiet, and safety were simple luxuries that I often took for granted now. At the time it all made sense, but lately I wondered how I'd managed it. Now that I was on the other side, the only answer I could come up with was that I was a glutton for pain, that I needed to experience something as intense and disturbing as war to put the war in my heart into perspective.

"I don't know," I lied.

"Were you scared?"

"It was stressful. I mean, I definitely saw things that I'll never forget. But after awhile, you get used to it. There aren't any bills or...I don't know...superficial bullshit, like which store in the mall to shop for Christmas gifts. It's simpler in a lot of ways. I think that was what kept me there, kept me going back. Every day being the same, like some sort of self-imposed purgatory."

I ran my thumb along the clothed edge of the table. Did she know that I'd served my time in the outskirts of hell because of her? That sometimes I'd wished for danger with a blind courage, trying to cure the dying place in my heart where she'd once been.

"There were times when I'd been there for so long, I could convince myself that time was actually standing still. Every day looked the same as the last, with so many days still ahead of me."

"Yet you kept going back."

I nodded. "That's what I thought I needed."

She worried her lip gently. "And then you left."

"When the time was right, I did. I finished up the last tour and came back ready to start over."

We were quiet for a long time. The stab of a few particularly heinous memories flashed through my mind—visions that my brain wouldn't forget. I pushed them away, focusing instead on the beautiful woman in front of me.

"So what made you change your mind and get out?" she asked quietly.

"My family was understandably worried. They'd email me every other day asking if I was close to what was happening on the news. They just wanted to make sure I was still alive. I could have stayed in longer, but I didn't want to put them through that anymore."

"And you like it here?"

"I love it. Completely different, of course, but the business has been a great challenge. And I like the energy of the city. The possibilities, I guess."

"You never know who you might run into."

"You're proof of that."

She smiled and my heart twisted. Thank God for chance meetings.

"Are Olivia and Darren partners with the business then?"

"No, Darren's invested in his own way, but he can't commit to a woman, let alone a business. He's a great help though. Gives me a break and does well with the training."

"You two seem close."

I shook my head, guessing she gathered that from me cussing him out at the bar. "Yeah, at the end of the day, he's my brother. What are you gonna do? He's a pain in the ass, but somewhere under that thick skull he cares, I guess."

"You're lucky."

I nodded. Olivia, Darren, and I were all independent in our own way, but knowing that we had each other meant the world sometimes.

"And Liv needed a change," I continued. "She'd been working for our father's private equity company upstate. Not surprisingly she started to feel kind of smothered. Dad was trying to set her up with guys at work. He means well, but Mom was making wedding plans before she could blink, trying to track out her whole life."

"Sound stressful."

"Of all of us, she's been the one they wouldn't really let go of. After a while they gave up on Darren and me, but she's their little girl. You know how she is. She didn't want to let them down. But the whole situation started eating at her, so I told her to come stay with me for a while, help me get things organized with the business until she was ready to make her next move."

"How about you? Anything new with your family?"

She sliced off a hunk of steak and popped it into her mouth, shaking her head. I guessed she didn't want to talk about that either. She'd always been vague about her family. Her father was out of the picture early on, and her mother seemed to be a bit of a rolling stone. I had a hard time believing that Eli and Vanessa were the only significant people in her life since I'd left though.

"So how does a beautiful, successful woman like you not have a boyfriend in this city?"

Her eyes met mine. "You're intent on figuring me out, aren't you?"

"Hell bent. Might as well start filling me in now."

She spun her water glass by its base. Light flickered off the liquid like a prism. "You might not like what you hear."

My body tensed in anticipation. "Let's get it over with then. Spill it."

"I don't really date." Her voice was clipped. Her pink lips pursed slightly.

"Ever?" I cocked an eyebrow.

"I'm not joining a convent, if that's what you're thinking."

I tightened my jaw, not enjoying the fleeting thought of her with anyone who wasn't me. I would have preferred the convent. "I didn't think so, but what's the alternative? Friends with benefits?"

"Benefits. Relationships all come down to sex, anyway. It's just simpler that way. No games, no drama." She sighed quietly. "No one gets hurt."

Hell, who was this woman, and where was my Maya? I rubbed my jaw, no less tense, and tried to wrap my head around what she'd just told me.

"Isn't that a bit pessimistic?"

"I like to think of it as realistic."

"Assuming that every serious relationship you have will hurt you?"

"I've tested the theory enough to be convinced of it," she said simply.

The remark shut me up for a while. I got the strong sense that her theories were now overlapping with our history. Had the outcome of our relationship inspired this cold and emotionless perspective? We finished eating in silence, and I tossed my napkin on the table.

"If you don't date, I suppose technically this isn't a date either. Am I interviewing to be the next notch in your bed post?"

I laughed, but I wasn't entirely sure I wanted to know the answer. An imperceptible frown marked her brow.

"This is us getting to know each other." She gestured between us. Our eyes clashed across the table.

"Sounds like that could get complicated."

She rolled her eyes. "I thought you wanted to be friends."

"I do. I also said I might want more. Call me crazy, but I thought that was something you were considering too."

"I've managed to avoid being in a relationship for years. I don't plan on making an exception now."

I regarded her intently, searching for an indicator that she didn't really buy into all of this. I couldn't believe this is who she'd become, that deep down she didn't harbor some of the same feelings that I did, the same desires I had started to want for us too.

"So you think I'm just like everyone else then?"

She closed her eyes, holding them shut a second too long.

"I know you're not."

MAYA. We walked through the park. Manhattan was lit up over the river, a thousand city lights danced across the water. I didn't mind the cold when Cameron had me at his side, his arm draped over my shoulder, warming me and keeping me close. Tonight had all the earmarks of a date. I didn't want to admit it, but Cameron was already an exception. He wasn't like everyone else. Far from it, in fact.

Cameron, had been my first and only love, but holding it against him was difficult when, despite our painful past, I still wanted to be near him. Being together had always been easy, a natural state that neither of us had to work too hard at. Even with all the time we'd spent apart, that hadn't seemed to change at all.

When he reached for my hand I took it now, out of habit maybe. When he pulled me to him, I leaned in, reveling in the small touches, uncertain where each might lead. All my instincts responded to Cameron. Even my heart did—the battered soul of me that would have been safer at a distance.

"I'm glad we did this." The low hum of his voice vibrated through me.

"Me too. Dinner was amazing. Thank you."

I'd eaten my fill, perhaps in defiance to this new health kick, but mainly because after working out all week I was perpetually starving. My stomach almost ached now from all the amazing steak I'd stuffed in it, followed by dessert.

My fingers touched on the pack of cigarettes tucked deep in my coat pocket. The urge to partake in my post-food ritual tugged at me. I pulled out the pack and tapped one out.

"What are you doing?"

"I need a smoke. Do you mind?"

He stopped us abruptly. "Yes, I fucking mind."

Before I could form a thought, he grabbed the

cigarette from one hand and returned the offending object to the pack I held in the other.

My jaw dropped at his boldness. "What are you doing?"

"My rules," he said simply, his expression tight with unmistakable determination.

"There were no rules about smoking in our deal."

"When the hell did you start smoking?"

"I don't know. When life got stressful, I guess. Give them back to me."

He held them beyond my reach as I grabbed for them.

"Do you want me to tell you I'll give them back to you at the end of the week?"

"Will you?"

He hesitated a second. "No. Not a chance, actually."

I gritted my teeth, making a concerted effort not to stomp my foot. "You're really starting to piss me off, you know that?"

He stared down at me, a smirk turning up the corner of his mouth. "You're cute when you're pissed off."

"I am *not* cute."

"You are incredibly cute. Don't sell yourself short."

I stomped my foot and groaned, trying like hell not to smile. I looked around us, wishing I could re-harness my original flash of anger. I bent down and grabbed a handful of snow and planted it directly in his face.

He jolted back and yelled. "What the hell?"

"Is that cute?"

He brushed the snow off his face, revealing a broad smile. "That's it. You're getting it now." He leaned and packed a snowball between his hands.

"You wouldn't," I challenged.

"Want to bet?"

I took a few cautious steps back.

"You better run," he warned.

He wound up and I ran, quickly finding a tree to shield me from the snowballs flying in my direction. I threw a few, landing none. This was easier when he wasn't expecting the assault. I hid behind the trunk and prepped a fresh one when he circled behind me and sank me down to the ground. I was pinned under him, my back half stuck in the snow.

I screamed, suddenly fearful of getting a face full of snow. "No, don't!"

"Are you sorry?"

"Yes, I'm sorry. Please!"

He hesitated, as if considering the sincerity of my remorse.

"Please don't," I begged.

"No cigarettes?"

"Not a drag. I promise." The choice was rash, but I was desperate. Also a tiny part of me—the part that wasn't furious about being told what to do with my own body—was happy that he cared enough to say anything at all.

He tossed away his ammo and relaxed against me. He held me in his gaze. The fog filled the air as we caught our breath.

My smile faded as the reality of our position sank in. My ass was freezing, but the pressure of his body on me, his thigh between my legs, was warming me damn quick. Before I could come up with something to say to break the sexual tension, his mouth was on me.

CAMERON. Her lips were soft. She sighed softly, melting into me the way she had so many times before. Her scent filled my lungs, a potent rush of memories with it.

I wanted to taste her.

I caught her hair and angled above her, opening her to me. Our tongues met, tentatively at first. A quiet moan hummed through her body, urging me to seek more of her mouth. She was so fucking sweet. Her hands fisted into my coat, never moving while mine roamed restlessly through her hair and along the soft lines of her face, down the front of her chest.

"Maya..." Her name left me between breaths, momentarily clouding the years that had come between us, as if no time had passed. The dream of us, of who we'd once been, was suddenly real again.

I cursed the layers of winter clothing between us. I wanted her breasts in my palms, every inch of skin exposed for my mouth to roam upon. I wanted to tease her and coax the desire out until she was trembling for it. I wanted her open for me, begging me to take her the way I'd wanted to from the moment I set my eyes on her.

"Cam," she breathed.

I pressed soft kisses into her now swollen lips, dipping inside with tiny licks, silencing her. She pressed my chest.

"What are we doing?" Her eyes were glossy, and her cheeks flushed with pink.

I blinked away the blur of the overwhelming need I had for her body. I kissed her once more, not wanting the moment to end. "We're making out in a snow bank. This is totally normal," I whispered.

She smiled under my lips.

I slid my hand down her thigh and back up under her jacket to the band of her jeans. All joking aside, I was ready to make passionate love to her in a snow bank. Overwhelmed with the urge to touch her, to claim her skin and her body in all the places I'd once been, I slipped my hand over her belly and over the soft curve of her waist.

She giggled, pushing my forearm down, and my hand slipped from her warm flesh.

I stilled. "What?"

"Your hands are freezing." She laughed, the smile meeting her eyes.

"Oh, shit. Sorry."

I went to move when she spoke.

"Don't stop."

She slid her fingers through my hair, stilling my retreat. Her tongue slid along her bottom lip. My balls tightened. Christ, I wanted this woman. My brain had no say whether it the right time or not. I needed to be inside her, and soon.

I tightened my grip on her hip. "If I kiss you again, I'm not sure I'll be able to."

"Then kiss me," she whispered.

She pulled me back down to her mouth, fisting her hands tightly, tugging at the root, a sure sign she didn't want me to stop. I had no plans to.

Time stood still. Nothing mattered but this closeness and having her in my arms. I kissed her jaw, her neck, then her mouth again until we were breathless. Nothing could stop me. Each motion heightened my urgency to have her, taking me higher.

My head buzzed, my heart raced, and I had the unmistakable sensation that I was standing at the edge of a cliff. I had no idea what was at the bottom, but I knew if I slept with her, I would go past the point of no return. I loved her once, and if I fell for her again, I'd never have her out of my system. Yet for all my wanting to wait for the right time, tonight seemed as good a time as ever. And I could show her exactly how I wasn't like any of the others who'd come before.

The thought of wiping out the memory of any other man in her life spurred me. Sucking her tongue, I lifted her against my thigh, ensuring just the right amount of friction to drive her wild. She moaned, kissing me back with all the fervor I'd come at her with. I was impossibly hard, on fire despite the cold. I couldn't stop myself.

Her small gasps and moans drove out the inconvenient fact that we were still making out in a snow bank until the sound of distant voices sobered me momentarily. I tore myself away from her lips and the frustrating exploration of her clothed body.

"Damn it." I caught my breath a minute. Begrudgingly I rose, lifting her with me.

I was an odd mixture of wet and cold and hot and bothered by the time we got vertical again. I didn't want to let her go, but frankly we couldn't get much further without public indecency.

"We should head back." She brushed the wet snow off of her jeans.

"Yeah, we should get you warm."

"And dry. I'm soaking wet."

I forced myself to ignore the alternate meaning to the comment, took her hand, and headed for the car, determined to break all her rules.

MAYA. We drove the short ride back in silence, Cameron's hand clasped around mine. The contact wasn't casual, but rather firm, our fingers laced tightly together and resting on his thigh as he steered us back to my apartment. His gaze was intent on the road, the look of determination plain on his beautifully shadowed features.

He squeezed my hand gently as I continued to stare in a tangle of wonder and worry. That simple touch was our only connection, but it was a meaningful one, like a thread between our hearts that had always existed, even through distance. Now with our reunion, that thread was tugging at my heart—hard and painful tugs that were increasingly difficult to ignore and pass off as the result of latent memories. They were the stirrings of new feelings mixed with the old.

I'd banished those kinds of feelings from my life for too long to face them calmly now. I'd had plenty of lovers. They'd been good guys, most of them, not the sex-driven devils I made them out to be. In truth, relationships might have flourished without too much effort, but as soon as deeper feelings had begun to take root, I found myself withdrawing. At first, I'd done it subconsciously, blaming it on a lack of interest or some imagined fault or innuendo. Eventually I isolated the recurring moment of fear, the moment when their rejection had the power to hurt me. And I couldn't go back there. Cameron had devastated me at the end. I'd toss back every fish in the sea to avoid feeling any of that again.

Yet here I was, dancing with the devil who'd broken me beyond repair. The threat of rejection muddled with this undeniable attraction, a pulsing energy between us that had always pulled me under, deep into the throes of our love. Is that what he wanted again? After what I'd told him tonight, maybe he really was out to prove that he wasn't like the rest. The reality was that he couldn't be anything at all if I had any hope of saving myself.

The silence between us stretched as we walked up to the apartment. No exchange was needed. I'd offered the unspoken invitation back at the park, and the dark look in his eyes had accepted. One step across the threshold and he had me pinned again. We tugged our coats off, and he roamed his hands freely across my skin where my sweater met my jeans, up along my ribs, daring to go higher. The sharp rise into my desire hit me, his own hard against me.

I wrapped my arms around his neck. He circled my waist, lifting me high and tight against him. The friction between us was enough to drive me out of my mind. Lust burned through me, threatening my resolve, my better judgment, and all the carefully constructed rules I'd learned to trust to keep my heart safe.

His mouth and hands moved over me, passionately claiming my body, the same one he'd once known so intimately. Nothing about this was tentative. Every movement held the promise of pleasure. Fuck, did I want him. In that moment, I let myself feel it all. I rode it out until I was wet with need and ready to scream with the frustration.

Our lips broke contact. I swallowed hard and caught my breath. I couldn't surrender to this. Not tonight.

Rational thought was breaking through. I caught his arm, pressuring it down.

"I'm going to go change," I said, my voice breathy, weighted with my doubt.

He stared, confusion plain on his face. I pushed him gently back so I could make my escape. I couldn't think straight with him so close, and I desperately needed to think instead of act on my raging impulses right now.

"Make some coffee or help yourself to whatever. I'll be right back."

CAMERON. Reluctantly, I let her go and she disappeared into the bedroom, shutting the door behind her. Clothes between us, and now a door. I scowled, irritated by the small things that separated us that had never used to. I shoved my hands in my pockets, not wanting to dwell on the fact that I'd personally created all the obstacles between us now.

I wasn't sure why she'd pushed me away. In an effort to distract myself, I walked around the small room, taking in its small details, wishing my frustration would ebb.

She and Eli seemed to live simply, which surprised me. Everything about Maya since I'd seen her in New York had been about keeping up with some sort of unspoken standard. The way she dressed and put herself together most of the time ran in contrast to the simple girl I used to know, but her home seemed incredibly normal and moderate. Mismatched well-worn furniture adorned the room, and the only decorations were photos of her, Eli, and their group of friends. I studied the photos, unable to keep from smiling at the ones where she was laughing and posing. She looked like she was on the other side of fun in most of them, but she was happy. A dull pain burned in my chest. I wanted to make her that happy.

I sat on the couch, willing myself to relax. What was taking so damn long? I wanted to find her in the bedroom, interrupt her wardrobe change, and promptly undress her. Press her against the wall the way I'd pressed against her moments ago, skin to skin.

Fuck all. No. I leaned forward, propping my elbows on my knees. I had to distract myself so I didn't come at her like a wild fucking animal. I couldn't risk pushing her away. We had to take this slow. I repeated the mantra, desperate to convince myself. If we had any chance of achieving *more* in the long-term sense—whatever the hell that even meant in Maya's new warped version of relationship statuses—we had to.

I grabbed the remote on the table in front of me and switched on the television, muting the volume. I dropped it back down. Next to it, a black spiral notebook sat. Several loose pages were stuffed in and beside it. The sheets peeking out were scrawled with handwriting I immediately recognized as Maya's.

As I reached for them, Maya emerged. I lifted my gaze to her. She was dressed in yoga pants and a hoodie. Her eyes were wide with concern that hadn't been there before. She walked to the table and quickly stuffed the errant papers into the notebook. Taking a few steps away, she held the book close to her chest.

"Everything okay?"

Her lips parted. Her gaze was fixed on me. "Everything's fine." Her voice wavered. She set the notebook on the shelf behind her. Joining me on the other end of the couch, she pulled her legs under her and stared at the soundless television.

She shivered, tightening her hold around herself. Something had shifted between us over the course of the past few minutes. I had no idea why. All I knew was I wanted her in my arms again.

"Come here," I whispered, holding my hand out to her.

Her gaze flickered, casting up at me from under her eyelashes. "Cam, we shouldn't—"

Before she could talk me out of it, I reached for her, pulling her close so her legs fell over my thighs, the rest of her body cradled against me.

Without another word, her body relaxed, melting into me. The shivers stopped and there was only the sound of our breathing. Afraid to speak, to bring attention to whatever had suddenly come between us, I simply held her. I'd been without her for so long, I had no right to want more, to ask for more. This was enough. For now, this was enough.

CHAPTER EIGHT

MAYA. I stared blankly at the screen in front of me. The numbers and letters blurred. All I could think about was Cameron's mouth on me, his body crushed against me. The attraction hummed between us. I'd pushed him away just in time. One more second against the wall and my already weak willpower would have snapped like a twig. If I hadn't interrupted the moment, I had little doubt we would have spent the night in my bed instead of curled up on my couch watching bad television until we couldn't keep our eyes open.

If Cameron had been anyone else, I would have slept with him without a second thought. When it came to men, I was impulsive, yet always carefully guarded. I'd been this way for years, never saying no to a vice or a pleasure that could bring me through a difficult moment right into the next. Cameron was turning into both a vice and a pleasure of the most dangerous variety.

I wanted him, and he wanted me, but as we climbed

the stairs to the apartment, a little voice that knew better had reminded me that something more was at stake—my heart, the same one he'd destroyed when he left me the first time. The same destruction I'd written about and that I really hoped he hadn't read. The thought of him looking through that window into the world of my words was exponentially worse than facing Eli's inebriated opinions.

I closed my eyes, trying in vain to lessen the torrent of emotions. Being with Cameron now was like a slow dance, and every time we met, we came closer. We touched more, laughed more. As much as I wanted to, I couldn't fight the way he made me feel from one minute to the next, which varied from massive irritation to the potent desire pulsing through me at the moment. God, what I wouldn't do to be in his arms now. One of these days I'd find myself pressed against him, begging him for more, drowning out that tiny voice of reason, and very likely barreling headfirst into inevitable heartbreak.

I groaned inwardly and crossed my legs, painfully aware of how badly I wanted him. My body remembered him, regardless of my mind's better judgment. My skin heated with the memory of his touch. Unless one of us had the good sense to stop it, sleeping together wasn't a matter of if, but when.

I jolted when the phone on my desk rang. I picked it up and my boss's predictably curt voice came through the receiver.

"Maya, come see me in my office please."

"Sure, I'll be right there."

I took a deep breath and my mind spun over what he'd want to meet me about. Kevin Dermott rarely had anything nice to say to me. Since I'd been at the company, he'd only spoken to me to note a shortcoming or highlight what he wanted me to do next. Positive reinforcement was a foreign concept to him.

I walked into his office. He was poring over some papers at his desk but motioned for me to sit at one of the chairs facing his desk. Dermott was in his mid-forties and predictably clean cut, with a crew cut of dark blond hair and a gray suit that highlighted the gray in his eyes. He was an attractive man, and I might have counted that among his qualities if he weren't such a prick most of the time. He wore a simple platinum band on his ring finger, reminding me that I wasn't the only woman who had to tolerate him.

"You were late from lunch today," he said.

"Yes, well, I—"

"I'm expecting those reports today, as we discussed."

"I'll have them to you within the hour. I'm almost done."

"Good."

Never mind that I'd worked through most of my lunch. I decided not to bother defending myself. He was in the mood to railroad me so I didn't want to spoil his moment. Instead, I sat patiently waiting for him to continue.

"The holiday party is next week. Assuming you'll be attending?"

"Yes, of course." I'd planned to attend out of sheer obligation. Sober mingling with dozens of people who I had the displeasure of working with on a daily basis was not my idea of good times. If I had anything to drink, I'd end up telling every last one of them what I really thought about them, as I was apt to do at the end of every Saturday night.

"The company officers will be there. There's a deal coming through that we'll need extra hands for, and they may be interested to know who will be involved."

"Are you saying you want me to be involved?"

He sat back in his chair and looked me over. "Despite your attitude, yes. You're one of the best people I have. This would be a good opportunity for you, that is, if you don't have other plans for the holiday. It could run into Christmas."

"I don't actually." I almost relished the idea of being able to work through the holiday so I could distract myself from the reality that everyone around me would be celebrating. Eli and Vanessa had their families, and every year I turned down their invitations to celebrate with them. Something about tagging along seemed even more depressing than waiting out the day on my own.

"Good choice. Consider yourself on the team. We're starting on the paperwork today, so plan to stay late."

Perhaps because Dermott's offer was laced with an insult, I couldn't quite celebrate it. He was giving me an opportunity, picking me among the mass of cubicle dwellers, to help with a deal that could set me apart. I reminded myself of Jia's advice. I should jump at this. Play the game.

"No problem. Let me know what you need."

A half smile twisted his features. I resisted the urge to tell him to fuck off. Instead I returned it with a perfectly polite subordinate smile.

"I will. I'll look for those reports shortly too." He straightened and shifted his attention back to his papers, scribbling his pen across some documents.

I took the signal to leave. Stepping out, I nearly ran into Jia.

"Hey, did you just talk to Kevin?"

"Yeah."

"Did he mention the Cauldwell deal?"

"He didn't mention it by name, but I assume that's the one."

"And you agreed?"

"Of course."

"Perfect."

The twinkle in her eye made me wonder if she'd been behind the whole thing.

"I'll be working on it too. It'll be great to have some friendly company. Speaking of, what are you up to this weekend?"

"Uh, I don't know yet," I lied. Our rapport was launching forward pretty quickly. I'd already told her about Cameron and how much I couldn't stand my job. I wasn't sure about confessing how I partied hard every weekend. That seemed to go against the professional progress I'd very recently made.

"I might be grabbing drinks with a couple friends on Saturday night. Maybe we can meet up," she said.

"Sure."

"Sounds good. Email me your number. I'll text you with details."

I agreed and returned to my desk, trying unsuccessfully to make sense of this new development at work. First Jia's unexplainable eagerness to be...friends? And now this new opportunity to work on an important deal. At least this would be a welcome distraction from

Cameron, who'd taken over my thoughts with a vengeance this week.

Alex was by in a matter of minutes to grill me about the meeting with Dermott, seeming shocked that I'd been chosen for this all-so-important responsibility. When he left, I reoriented myself with what I was working on. I smiled as a different kind of energy surged through me. I hated to get my hopes up, but maybe between work, Cameron, and this new health kick, I was getting my life together after what felt like years of simply living and getting by.

I texted Cameron that we'd have to miss our workout tonight. I registered a pang of regret that I'd miss seeing him, but we could probably use the space. Things had become too heated last night, and I needed some time to figure out how I was going to handle all of this tension between us.

The next evening, Dermott let us leave early, for no other reason than he had plans on a Friday night.

I poked my head into the gym's small office in the back. I was dressed, energized, and oddly eager to start tonight's torture session. I'd gone almost forty-eight hours without seeing Cameron and he was nowhere in sight.

"Where's Cameron?"

Darren looked up from the computer screen. Around him, the desk was overflowing with stacks of paper. "He had to take care of something back at the house. He said I could work with you tonight."

"Why didn't he just call me?"

"I think he probably thought you'd skip your workout."

I rolled my eyes. "Jerk."

He laughed. "He might be back before we're done. You can tell him yourself."

"You don't have to babysit me, Darren. I think I can probably figure things out for myself today. Thanks though."

I turned to leave when Darren stopped me. "Hey, what's the plan for this weekend? Cam said you guys were going out."

"Oh." I hesitated. "Yeah."

He stared blankly ahead, apparently waiting for more details.

"We usually hit up Muse. We can meet you guys for drinks across the street before we head over."

"You want us to pick you up?"

"No, I have to coordinate with Vanessa and Eli anyway. We'll probably be there around ten."

"Who's Vanessa?" He cocked an eyebrow, a gesture that instantly worried me.

"A friend. You'll meet her."

He nodded and turned back to his work. "Cool. I'll see you out there in a bit. I need to finish up this schedule."

I walked back toward the free weights. I rested my hands on my hips, noting a new sense of empowerment. Day five and though sore, I was a pro, or so I told myself. Who needs a personal trainer?

I silently commended myself for moving up a weight class in my admittedly very low-weight division. I was up to 15-pound dumbbells and pretty damn pleased with myself as I lifted them easily. Small triumphs. I caught Raina's reflection in the mirror as she approached me. She was dressed for one of her yoga classes.

"Hey, Maya. How's it going?"

"Going great, you?"

"It's been busy. Mind if I join you?"

"Of course not. Go for it." My self-esteem took an immediate hit when she grabbed a heavier set and went through her motions with perfect form.

"So Darren tells me you're Cameron's ex. Is that right?"

I set my weights down for a break. "Yeah, something like that." I hated being called Cameron's ex. The term seemed too negative when we were trying to rekindle something positive—a friendship, or something that my body definitely wanted to be more than friendship.

"That's funny."

"Why?"

"He's never mentioned you, that's all."

What the hell does that mean?

I reached for the weights again, hoping to mask my irritation with another set. I pretended to ignore her, but I followed her movements through the rest of my workout, hating her impressively toned body with every minute that passed. Cameron and she could be the perfect couple on the cover of some fitness magazine. My energy waned at the thought.

Why would she say something like that unless she and Cameron had history of their own? He didn't strike me as the type to talk relationships with just anyone, but maybe she wasn't just anyone.

Before my thoughts could run away any further, Darren returned.

"Hey, sorry about that."

"No worries. Raina and I were just catching up," I

said with an unmistakable hint of sarcasm. Was I posturing over their yoga instructor?

"Want to do some shoulder work?"

"Sure." I didn't care as long as it brought me closer to the end of the workout and hopefully farther away from Raina.

"So what's the story with her?" I tried to keep my voice steady.

"What do you mean?"

"Do Cameron and Raina have something going on?"

He laughed. "No, definitely not. Much to her disappointment."

Despite Darren's infectious grin, my earlier inkling of jealousy surged. I looked across the room, searching for her figure among the crowd. Why? So I could give her a dirty look? *Christ, get a grip.*

Unable to find her again, I finished the last set with methodical determination.

"You okay?" Darren frowned, concern wrinkling his brow.

"I'm fine," I mumbled.

"There's nothing going on with them, Maya. I can assure you that."

I managed a thin smile. "Thanks, but it's really none of my business. I'm not even sure why I asked."

Who was I kidding? Probably not Darren, master of female manipulation. I asked because I simply had to know. In that moment, nothing had been more important than finding out if he and Raina had history.

I hit the locker room and dressed quickly. The thought of her pursuing Cameron, regardless of his level of interest, pissed me off. That she might be trying to create friction between us so we didn't get too close pissed me off even more.

Five days with Cameron and I was already marking my territory—unbelievable.

Cameron walked through the front doors as I was about to make my escape. *Shit.*

"Hey, I was hoping to catch you before you left." He smiled, his eyes bright.

"Well you caught me."

I wished I could light up for him too, but I was too pissed off, too much in my own head to be cheerful for him.

"Sorry, I got held up. I had some people doing some work at the house and had to stay late."

"It's fine."

Raina passed us, smiling sweetly at him before meeting my gaze.

"Hey." He nodded casually in her direction.

"Hey, hon."

Those two little words out of Raina's mouth had me grinding my teeth. I scolded myself for caring. I shouldn't care. I shouldn't care at all. I pushed past Cameron and headed toward the front doors.

"Hey, where you running off to?" He grabbed my hand.

"I'm heading out. I'm pretty sure this marks the end of my week of torture. That was the deal, right?"

He frowned. "Is everything okay?"

"I'm fine. Just tired. It's been a long week, you know." My body weakened as I said the words. Cameron was right that working out had given me more energy, but right now all I felt was wiped out. Now I was emotionally exhausted and draining by the minute.

"Well, it's Friday. You can take it easy now."

"I plan to. I have a date with a glass of wine. I think I've earned it." I had a date with a bottle, but I figured I would omit that small detail.

His eyes turned serious. "Maya," he whispered, closing the distance between us and brushing my cheek. "What's going on? You seem upset."

I leaned into his touch, my whole body relaxing with the contact. I wanted him to pull me into his arms the way he had before, like I was already his. Why? Why did I want him so damn much? Why couldn't I keep him at a distance like everyone else?

"Let me take you out. I can have Darren cover me tonight."

"No, I'm fine," I insisted. "I have to go. I guess I'll see you tomorrow night. I gave Darren the details."

His brow wrinkled. I offered him a small smile, hoping he'd leave me be. The past day might have given me a little clarity, but now I was as mixed up as I had been the last time we were together.

He released me and I pushed through the doors, relishing the cold. I needed air. I needed a drink. This week had been sobering, literally, but in that space Cameron's presence had left me off kilter, more than usual.

The truth was that deep down I wanted Cameron to myself. When we talked about more, as much as I'd kept the possibility indefinite, that's what I wanted. Except I'd buried that person long ago. Being attracted to him was one thing, but wanting to secure that special place in his world as badly as I did was another. The way I'd reacted after my brief conversation with Raina indicated how far I'd already fallen.

CAMERON. "What the fuck did you say to her?"

I slammed the door behind us and Darren's eyes went wide.

"What the hell are you talking about?"

"Maya. What you did say to her?"

"I don't know. We did a shoulder workout."

I caught his shirt and shoved him against the wall.

"Tell me," I growled, my adrenaline spiking.

He shoved me back, confusion replaced with an anger that met my own. "Christ, get hold of yourself, Cam."

"She looked like hell when she ran out of here. You must have said something to her."

"Fuck." He shook his head and rubbed his forehead. "Raina."

"What about Raina?" I frowned and took a tentative step back, not entirely sure I was finished with him.

"Maya asked if there was anything going on between you two. I reassured her there wasn't but that Raina's got a thing for you. She seemed pissed about it for a second but then nothing. It was like she shut off. We went through the rest of the workout, and she didn't say more than three words to me."

"Fuck."

I was all too aware of Maya's ability to shut someone out from what she was really thinking. I struggled to think of what would have upset her so much. I walked away and paced a line in front of the desk.

"With your reputation, she probably thinks you were bullshitting her, trying to cover for me or something."

"My reputation?" He grimaced, the words laced with challenge.

I faced him again. "We're brothers, best friends, and we work together. She hasn't seen me in five years, and I don't think she's seen you in here once without some woman all over you or vice versa. She probably assumes I'm on the same plan and she's nothing but a new conquest."

"She isn't a conquest? You haven't had your hands all over her every time she's been here? I'm not fucking blind, you know. What makes you so goddamn noble?"

"You and I are *not* the same," I gritted out, though my anger toward Darren was waning.

"No? Because I don't want to settle down and have a litter with the first girl who gets all starry eyed after a wild night?"

We both caught our breath, a tense silence between us. This wasn't the time or the place to get into Darren's lifestyle with women. I had bigger issues to deal with. Something else—someone else—had inspired this cold attitude from Maya.

"Sorry, this isn't about you," I finally said, though it burned me to utter the words.

"Apology accepted." He straightened and his furrowed brows ironed out. "Believe it or not, I want this to work with you two, Cam. I wouldn't make things difficult between you intentionally. I hope you realize that."

I nodded. "I know. She's...shit, I don't know. It's hot and cold with her. Every time I think we're getting close to where we were, something happens, some shift between us and I feel like she's slipping away. I can't stop it because I'm afraid I'll push her away completely. It's driving me crazy."

"Yeah, I can see that." He laughed. "You haven't slept with her, have you?"

I shook my head.

"You think you're going to screw everything up with her if you fuck her, don't you?"

"It's a concern I have, yeah. I don't want to rush into things, have her regret it, and freak out." God knew, I wanted to, but she was cagey enough. The blowback from sleeping together too soon could be enough to push her away for good. The other night had proved that.

"I know you think I don't know anything about women, but Maya strikes me as the type of person who knows what she wants. Do you think it's something she wants?"

"I don't think it. I know it." She didn't have to tell me outright, her body had. Small gestures, the subtle reactions of her body, the not-so-subtle reactions of her body. I could have capitalized on any number of them and had her, but still I held back.

"Then what the hell are you waiting for? You're just giving her more time to come up with some excuse not to, to push you away like you're already afraid she's going to."

"If all I wanted was to get her into bed, I could have done that already. Maybe she deserves time to decide whether or not it's something she wants. I left her without a word five years ago and never looked back. I'm sure she harbors some doubts about whether this is even a good idea. I sure as hell have."

"Obviously not enough to stay away."

"True enough."

Darren shook his head. "If you care about her that much, Cam, you should just be with her and see what happens."

I sighed, beginning to feel as tired as Maya had looked when she pulled away from me tonight. I wanted nothing more than to track her down at her apartment and get to the bottom of this, but maybe we both needed a night to think and make sense of what all of this meant between us.

"I'm heading home. Can you cover me tonight?"

"Sure. I'll see you in the morning." He waved me off.

I walked home, more certain than I'd ever been that I wanted Maya. There was no question. She wanted me too. Nothing could convince me otherwise. As I walked back home, to what would surely be another restless night, I resolved that whatever had changed in our lives wasn't enough to keep this from working.

CHAPTER NINE

MAYA. I'd spent nearly every weekend in recent memory at the club, partaking in all manner of drunken fun. Eli, Vanessa, and I would glam ourselves up and dance the night away, rain or shine. Every weekend was an adventure. Who would we meet, and what vodka-induced debacle would we get ourselves into? Between the three of us, we'd usually be able to get a good story and a few laughs out of the night. Some nights I'd rather forget, of course. At the rate I was going, tonight could very well be one of those.

While I usually relished the inevitable air of excitement before going out, tonight was different. Bringing Cameron into my world would be strange, and a part of me dreaded it. I didn't want my world to revolve around his presence, but whenever he was near, it inevitably did. Maybe tonight he'd realize I wasn't girlfriend material and back off. Where there was drinking involved, anything could happen.

"Almost ready?" Eli poked his head in and handed me a fresh glass of wine. I eagerly accepted it. I needed to take the edge off. The edge was getting duller by the minute but my stomach was still in knots.

"Almost."

"You look hot." He smirked, looking pretty fresh himself in leather pants and a tight black v-neck. His hair was expertly gelled and his eyeliner rivaled mine.

With my free hand, I tousled my hair once more. I'd chosen a tight red mini dress and put enough product in my hair to ensure that I looked perfectly windblown and sexy for a night of gyrating. I caked on the eyeliner, eye shadow, and mascara, making a mental note to periodically check myself for raccoon eyes throughout the course of the night.

"I bet Cameron's never seen you dressed for the club."

I ignored his comment and put on some sparkly hoop earrings.

Eli leaned against the counter, staring at me. "What's up with you two? Are we still pretending that you aren't hot for each other?"

"We can't keep our hands off each other. Everything's just moving too fast."

"That's never been a complaint of yours before."

I rolled my eyes.

"Sorry, but I've seriously never seen you agonize over a guy like this. Ever."

"That's because no one else has been Cameron." I blew out a breath and fidgeted nervously with the mascara. "I almost pulled a nutty on that yoga chick at the gym. She's got a thing for him, and it hit me like a ton of bricks. We're not even officially in any kind of relationship and I'm ready to cut a bitch. It's too much."

"Whatever goes on between you is going to be more intense because you've already been in a relationship with him."

"I know that, but I thought I could keep this under control. It's not under control at all though. I'm already starting to have feelings for him again and it's way too soon for that."

"You've always had feelings for him."

"I wasn't always falling in love with him, and at least for now, I'd like to keep it that way."

"Don't you want a second chance at...you know, whatever you had?"

"Part of me wants that, I'll admit." I sighed, my heart sinking with what I was about to say. "But if I let myself fall in love with Cameron again and it doesn't work out, there won't be enough pieces of me left to put back together."

Eli's eyes softened and he held my hand, giving it a small squeeze. His silence spoke volumes. I was a hot mess on a normal day. I couldn't crawl out of that kind of misery again and possibly survive. I wasn't letting him anywhere near my heart again. I couldn't.

"What are you going to do?"

"I don't know. I feel like the sexual tension is seriously affecting my ability to think clearly about any of this."

"And..."

"Maybe I'll get belligerently drunk and sleep with him tonight. And that's it. Get it out of my system and move on." I leaned toward the mirror, rolled light gloss onto my lips, and smacked them together. What had this week been other than a series of opportunities to heighten the already acute attraction between us? Sleeping with Cameron had seemed inevitable. If I ended up drunk and wound up, dragging him to bed with me, then so be it.

"Whoa, honey, do you hear yourself? You're talking about him like he's a hookup. I think we both know he's not. You just said that yourself."

I shrugged. "Maybe I should start thinking of it that way. Maybe that's where I've been wrong. This is why I don't date, Eli. This is fucking why. Because of what we had, I let my guard down and let myself believe it could be more. But frankly, I can't handle more. It's probably best for both of us to keep this casual."

I squeezed my eyes shut, hating the flood of emotion. Why the hell couldn't I be objective about this? I'd managed to keep my heart closed off to men for five years.

The buzzer went off.

"That must be Vanessa," Eli said quietly.

I took a last look in the mirror and finished off the wine. *This will be fine*, I reassured myself. But like every other Saturday night, I had no idea what the next few hours would bring.

CAMERON. Darren and I grabbed a corner couch at the bar across from the club. We drank our beers in silence while I mulled over his words from last night. I didn't want to give him any credit, but he'd told me exactly what I wanted to hear.

I had no idea how tonight would go down, but I was determined to let Maya know how I felt. With any luck, we'd end up back at my place, and I could show her. Maybe it was risky, but sometimes our bodies did the talking better than we did. I'd never regretted a night in her bed. I didn't imagine anything had changed where that was concerned. Visions of her under me clouded my thoughts, and my cock twitched.

Darren elbowed me back to reality. Maya approached with Eli and a beautiful, leggy redhead in tow. If Maya hadn't been standing next to Eli, I might not have recognized her at all. She looked amazing, but I'd never seen her that way. All made up, her hair wild and untamed, her tight dress mid-thigh. I raked her in, highly aware that I wouldn't be the only one doing that tonight. Already I could think of nothing else but hiking up her skirt and wrapping her legs around me.

The comfortable silence between Darren and me erupted into an excited chatter among the group. I pulled my thoughts out of the gutter and rose to greet her. Sliding my arm around her waist, I pulled her close and kissed her on the cheek.

"You look incredible."

"You like the dress?"

"I love it. I'm just not sure how I feel about the rest of the world seeing you in it."

She offered a slanted smile, her body bending easily into the embrace. Something was off. She lifted her arm and gestured to the redhead.

"Cam, Darren, this is my friend, Vanessa."

Darren rose quickly and shook her hand, shooting her his signature panty-dropping smile. "Pleasure to meet you."

"Likewise." She returned the smile, blushing slightly. Her green eyes illuminated as they darted from me to Darren, her gaze lingering on him.

Maya slipped out of my grasp and dropped herself on the opposite couch, pulling Vanessa and Eli down on either side of her. Slighted by the tease of her contact, I sat back down by Darren and nursed my beer.

Eli and the girls huddled over the cocktail menu. I couldn't take my eyes off of Maya. Her dress left far too little to the imagination now that she was sitting. I imagined sliding a hand up her thigh to the flash of black panties I swore I saw a moment ago.

Darren blew out a quiet whistle. "Oh, man. I'm all over that," he murmured, too low for anyone but me to hear.

His gaze was locked on Vanessa. I relaxed, grateful she was the one who had his approval. She seemed oblivious to his lascivious appraisal, caught up in ordering when the waitress arrived. Maybe Darren wasn't going to be the best wingman tonight. Not that I really needed one, but the idea of clubbing sounded a little more bearable with him in the group. Still, I could see this going downhill fast.

I lowered my voice so only he could hear me. "How about you *not* fuck Maya's best friend and complicate things for me?"

He shot me an annoyed look. "Really? You're blocking me?" He sized her up again, tightening his jaw. "Does she have any more friends?"

"Go prowl, Darren. I'm sure you'll find someone drunk enough to fuck you."

He scoffed, seeming genuinely insulted. "Hey, screw

you, man. I'm not that shallow or desperate."

We were two sides on the same coin sometimes. I didn't like hearing about any of his frequent and meaningless conquests, and I didn't expect him to understand my determination to save the only relationship that had ever meant anything to me.

His gaze never left the expanse of Vanessa's bare toned legs. "How about I play nice?"

I hesitated, trying to imagine what he was proposing. "What does that mean? Get her to fawn all over you and then ditch her when you realize you're not allowed to sleep with her?"

"No. I'll be my usual charming self. But we'll all have a good time as friends. That low-key enough for you, old man?"

I stared at him, skeptical of what he was proposing. I'd never seen him spend time with a woman without having a very singular motive in mind.

"I'll be good, all right? I get it. I'm not big on drama either, and if you're going to keep Maya around, I don't want it to be awkward." He paused, waiting for me to give him the okay. "You know, I'm capable of interacting with women without taking them straight to bed." He was getting pissed now, which was good. I wanted him to know I was serious.

"Fine." I hoped he'd keep to his word.

By the time the three of them had finished off a round of drinks and a small tray of shots, I'd begun to realize what was off with Maya. She was plastered. She leaned lazily against Vanessa and Eli, pressed snugly between her and Eli. She laughed loudly, and while I loved the sound and the way her eyes glittered when she smiled, I couldn't shake a protective worry over her.

"Should we head out?" Maybe I could get her to sober up at the club. She claimed to have a penchant for dancing the night away.

"Let's do it!" She hopped up.

We made our way out of the bar and across the street. A sizable line had formed at the club entrance. I groaned inwardly. Standing outside for hours wasn't my idea of a great Saturday night. "I guess we're not in a rush."

"No worries. I don't do lines. Come here." Maya flagged the attention of one of the guys at the door who nodded to her.

She joined the bouncer, bounding into his arms for a hug. "Hey, Paul."

"Hey, baby. How's it going?"

"Good."

When I approached, he nodded and held out his hand. I shook it, if only to give him a reason to stop touching her. "I'm Cameron." The words came out strained because my teeth were clenched.

"Good to meet you. Friend of Maya's?"

I simply nodded. Something like that.

"Cool. You guys can head in."

"Thanks, Paul." Maya smiled and slipped a bill into his palm before disappearing into the noise of the club.

I followed, eager to keep her in my sight. The place was loud and filling quickly. Maya led the way and we found an unoccupied seated area large enough to accommodate our group. Darren immediately posted himself between Eli and Vanessa. Eli seemed to clue in to Darren's plan and disappeared a few minutes later to mingle.

A cocktail waitress approached and leaned close to Maya to take her order.

"What do you want?" Maya asked me.

"Diet Coke is fine."

She turned back to the server. "Two Jack and Cokes and a shot of Jager."

I raised my eyebrows. "Going for a strong start?"

"I'm not letting you drink soda at the club."

We settled back into the couch next to each other. I draped my arm over her shoulders, lightly grazing the bare skin of her arm. She leaned into me, tracing circles into the fabric of my pants at the knee. Her bright energy seemed to dim.

I tightened around her shoulders, bringing her closer. "What's going on in that mind of yours?"

She lifted her gaze to mine.

Before I could press her, she looked away. Her eyes narrowed over Darren and Vanessa, now pressed firmly against each other. Vanessa was laughing, and Darren was at her ear, telling her God knew what. So much for self-restraint.

"What's with them?"

I rubbed my jaw anxiously. "Hopefully nothing. He's assured me he'll be on his best behavior."

She let out a short laugh. "You'll have to excuse me if I take that assurance with a grain of salt."

"I hear you, but he did promise me."

Before she could respond, the server brought our drinks. Maya tossed back the shot and handed me one of the two remaining drinks. She'd barely looked me in the eye once since arriving. I wasn't going to endure the night this way.

"Are you upset about something?"

Maya's lips twitched slightly. "No, I'm having fun. This is me having fun." She sucked down her drink before I could even taste mine. Her eyes darted around us, never landing on anyone or anything for too long. I caught her chin and turned her to face me. Her eyes were glossy, her skin flushed and warm.

"I never know what you're thinking."

She brushed me away. "Maybe you should stop trying to get into my head. You probably wouldn't like it in there anyway."

"I think you're wrong."

She looked down at her hands and toyed with the rippled fabric of her dress. "No one else tries this hard. I don't understand why you are."

"I'm not like everyone else. I thought you'd figured that out by now."

"Maybe that's not what I want."

"What do you want?"

She sighed and worried her lip. "We should keep this casual so no one gets hurt."

"When you say casual, you're saying you don't want our relationship to mean anything. Is that right?"

She looked up, paralyzing me with a penetrating gaze. "It wasn't important enough for you to want to keep back then, so why should I want it to mean anything now?"

She could have punched me in the gut, the way her words hit me.

I ground my teeth. "I could say the same thing to you, Maya. You weren't the only one who got hurt, you know."

She rose quickly. "I'm going to grab a drink."

"Maybe you should slow down."

"Maybe you should mind your own business." She rose quickly, disappearing into the crowd.

MAYA. Jia leaned up against the bar as the bartender brought her martini. I'd texted her upon separating from Cameron. She showed up not long after, thanks to Paul's VIP treatment. I was thankful for the company since my connection with Cameron had noticeably cooled as the night had progressed. Maybe that was a good thing though. Eli was off doing his thing, and Vanessa was in Darren's clutches. Thanks to my significant buzz, I cared less and less. This was my night, and I wasn't going to let him or anyone else spoil it.

"Did you come alone?" I asked.

"Yeah, the friend I was with bailed. No worries. This place seems great. Do you come here often?"

"It's in the rotation."

"You look cute." She smiled and ran a finger down the ruching of my dress.

"Thanks, you too."

She was wearing a sleeveless blouse and skinny jeans. Her hair was down, framing her face. Seeing her so casual seemed odd, wrong even. Having her see me in my weekend club attire also felt strange, as if I were exposing myself to a world that never saw me this way. Even though we'd been inching toward friendship, Jia represented that world in this context.

"It's a little strange to see people outside of work," I said. "I imagine everyone wakes up and goes to sleep in their suits or something."

She laughed. "No kidding. You'd be surprised what you find under all those suits." She lifted an eyebrow and the corner of her mouth quirked up.

I couldn't help but laugh. I wasn't remotely interested in anyone at the office. The thought of seeing someone like Dermott under his suit was nausea-inducing, if only because I hated that bastard.

"Did you come with the ex?"

I rolled my eyes and groaned like an angst-ridden teenager whose mother had followed her to the mall. Thankfully, the sound was muted by the blare of the music. A part of me wished I hadn't come with Cameron tonight. He was on the other side of the club, probably wishing he hadn't too.

"He's here."

"You don't look so happy about that."

"I'm not exactly thrilled, no."

"I take it the reunion isn't going so well."

I shook my head. "I don't know. It's complicated." I didn't want to go into all the reasons why with Jia right now. "Honestly, I don't even want to think about it. I don't really want to think about *anything* tonight." I waved my hand for effect. "It's been a long week, and I just want to have some fun."

"I say we drink to that."

She lifted her glass, and I clinked my shot against its rim before swallowing down another ounce of sugary heaven.

I set it down and looked around. The bar was lit up in blue neon lights, its patrons laughing and talking. The music was loud, vibrating every corner of the dimly lit club. Despite my spat with Cameron, I caught myself smiling widely. This was the moment—that perfect moment when the night felt like it had possibilities. I wanted this moment to last forever. Liquid happiness and excitement mingled with the promise that I could lose myself in the music, in the fate of the night. This was my freedom.

"Let's dance," I yelled.

Jia smiled and nodded. She finished her drink, grabbed my hand, and led the way to the dance floor. We pushed through the crowd, now thick with all walks of life. The push of people gave way at a certain point. The music changed into a deep beat of a Lady Gaga song, asking someone to do what he wanted with her body. I hummed to myself, liking the sound of that. Maybe I'd drag Cameron into bed anyway. What did it matter anyway? Give Raina a run for her money. Give Cameron something to remember me by, because that would have to be it. I'd fall in love with him otherwise. That much was certain.

My head was buzzing, my limbs and soul lighter than they had been in days. God, *days*. I closed my eyes, reached for the sky, and let my hips sway in time to the consuming pulse of the music.

Someone bumped into me from behind, interrupting my moment and jolting me into Jia. I kept my balance, but she encircled my waist protectively with her arm. I could have moved back, but she held me there, like she wanted me to stay. Our faces were inches apart, our legs staggered over each other's as we moved, creating our own rhythm. Her hands slid down my dress, tracing the skin of my thigh lightly.

Her eyes were fixed on me, inspiring that breathless

feeling I had when I knew something intense was about to happen.

"Kiss her!"

I shot a glare to my right. A young guy in a white collared shirt unbuttoned at the neck and dress slacks was gawking at us with a stupid drunk grin. He wasn't bad looking, but he was soaked with sweat and surrounded by a gaggle of similarly dressed guys.

Jia turned my face back to hers, her soft finger coming down my cheek and resting on my lower lip. She licked her lip suggestively, and I knew. She was about to kiss me. And I was about to let her. The night was mine, and the opportunity was here. Something felt wrong and right about it, right enough that I blocked out the chants around us as our lips touched.

Kiss! Kiss! Kiss!

We did. Her mouth was soft on mine as our lips pressed to each other's. I took in a sharp breath. The smell of her expensive perfume infused the hot musk of the crowd around us. Her one hand grazed down my chest over my breast. The other found the tight hem of my dress, pushing it up a couple inches over her fingers as they slid up my thigh. The movement elicited some more excited howls. I smiled under her kiss. A stupid laughter bubbled up with the idea that we were putting on a real show for our new admirers. That excitement quickly dampened when I felt someone's dewy, clumsy hands on my thighs and an erection pressed hard against me from behind.

My eyes flew open. Before I could react and push him away, I heard him yell. His friends' yelled too and then stepped back.

CAMERON. I had to remind myself of my own strength when I ripped that little fucker off of Maya. He and his friends had postured for a moment, probably long enough to realize I had about forty pounds of muscle on any of them. Their strength in numbers would have been annoying, but not enough to pose a threat.

Then there was the girl, her body indecently entwined with Maya's. She didn't look like a drunk idiot though. She had a shrewdness about her and dark assessing eyes that looked me over. Slowly she relinquished her hold on Maya.

I caught Maya's wrist, spinning her to me.

"What are you doing?" I was beyond furious that she'd put herself in this position, with some—multiple—strangers' hands all over her. This was un-fucking-acceptable.

"I could ask you the same thing." She looked to her wrist, where I held her tightly.

She twisted in my grasp, and I released my grip. My adrenaline was still thrumming.

My chest expanded on a deep breath. The rush of anger had ebbed but remnants of it still pulsed through me. "Can we talk?"

"I'm dancing. I'll meet you back at the table in a little while." Her voice was clipped, irritation showing on her features.

I wasn't about to leave her. "Let's dance, then." I placed a protective hand on her hip, urging her toward me.

Her irritation gave way to something else, an emotion

I couldn't name. She seemed to consider the proposal as she stared at me. Her admirers had scattered after they shot us a few glares and offensive gestures.

Maya turned away from me, saying something to the girl. She nodded and gave me one last cool look before disappearing through the crowd. I took advantage of her absence and pulled Maya to me, our bodies close—closer than theirs had been.

Mine.

Maya hooked her arms over my shoulders, her fingers toying with my hair. We moved in time to the slowest part of the beat, turning the house music into a slow song that only we seemed to hear.

I wrapped my arms around her, bringing my mouth to her ear so she could hear me. "Who was that?" My jaw clenched, possessiveness over her body rioting through me.

"Doesn't matter."

I thought I saw a hint of embarrassment before she looked away, bringing her hands down to my chest. Her eyes flickered back to mine.

"You're full of surprises, Maya. I can say that."

"Are you jealous?" She shot me a sassy smile that riled me and made me want to kiss the look right off her face.

"Should I be?"

"No. You have no right to be." She tipped her head up, her jaw resolute. Little fucking minx.

"I want the right to be."

"Get used to disappointment," she said.

"How about I change your mind?" I brushed the hair away from her neck and dragged my lips across her hot skin. Two could play this game.

She sagged against me slightly. "You can't."

I grinned at the wavering in her voice. "Try me." I opened my mouth against her, letting my tongue dart out to taste her. A moan vibrated through her when I squeezed her ass and pressed her firmly against my thigh.

Her breasts rose and fell with quick breaths. She trailed her hands down my chest. Unable to stop myself, I took her mouth, channeling every ounce of possession into kissing her breathless. She clawed into my shirt, and the slow rhythm of the dance morphed into her grinding her supple little body against me. Suddenly I wished we weren't in the middle of a crowded room. I needed her in my bed. I wasn't willing to wait anymore, and I wasn't asking.

"I'm taking you home."

CHAPTER TEN

MAYA. Cameron loosened his hold on me to unlock the door of his apartment. I stumbled inside, my heels tripping me over the threshold. I lay on the bare floor, rolling to my back. My drunk laughter echoed loudly in the dark room. The floor was cool and so smooth. Everything smelled new. Like paint maybe.

"Where is this place?" My voice sounded very much full of wonder, like we'd just walked into some kind of amazing new place. Perhaps we had? I couldn't know, because I'd hit the wall in the cab. I'd gone from wildly horny and excitable to epically intoxicated, only able to stay upright thanks to Cameron's strong body holding me up. Oh well. I was still horny.

"This is the third floor of my building. Olivia stays on the second floor. I'm still fixing it up, so don't mind the state of things. Come on."

I couldn't see anything from behind my eyelids, nor did I care to. The floor was more comfortable than I'd expected. *Shit, I'm tired.*

Cameron caught my hand and hoisted me back to my feet, holding me so tightly to his chest that I barely touched the floor. I could scarcely move.

"Can you walk?"

I giggled a little, resting my head on his shoulder. I wanted to be wrapped up with Cameron. He was so warm, so unbelievably strong. I'd gained weight and he was still carrying me around like I weighed nothing more than a feather. His hold softened a little as he wrapped his other arm around my hips, warming the small of my back.

"You okay, hon?" He pressed a soft kiss to my bare shoulder.

I hummed. His touch awakened a familiar stir inside me. I couldn't press myself any closer so I tipped my head up and kissed him. He pulled away when I tried to breach his lips with my tongue.

"You didn't bring me here just to tuck me in, did you?"

He didn't answer me. Instead, he hooked an arm under my knees and carried me toward the only light in the apartment. He kicked the door gently and lowered me by the bed. Coming from the darkness, I squinted. Everything was too bright.

I wavered, clutching at his shirt. He caught me to him again, and I buried my face in his neck. The scent of him, spice and sandalwood, washed over me. I hummed, darting my tongue across his skin, and then sucked hard.

He pulled me back, angling away from my assaulting mouth. "You need to get some rest, Maya. You drank too much."

"Who cares?"

"I care."

"Are you trying to say you came out with me tonight and didn't plan on taking me to bed?"

He shook his head. "I had no idea what to expect tonight, but I try not to sleep with nearly unconscious women."

"Sure." I rolled my eyes, pushing away from him slightly. The sick twist of rejection mixed with all the shots I'd drunk.

"You don't believe me?"

"Whatever." I waved my hand. "You're not interested. I get it."

His bright blue eyes widened slightly. "Trust me, I'm interested."

I cocked my head at him. "Maybe Raina's still up. Miss Perfect is probably patiently waiting for you on the back burner somewhere."

A smile split his face. "Are you jealous, Maya?"

"Not in the least." Shit, he was onto me. "You can screw whoever you want to and so can I."

His smile slipped, and his eyes turned serious. "You made that point abundantly clear tonight. Who was that girl anyway? Did you even know her?"

"Her name is Jia. I *work* with her." The words that justified my earlier lip lock with Jia seemed to float in the air toward Cameron and then come back to me, sounding just as idiotic as they must have sounded to him.

He shoved a hand through his hair. "Wow."

A short laugh at his reaction escaped me, and I took a step back in my now dangerously high heels. I blinked, wanting the room and Cameron to appear to me more clearly. Fuck, I hated when I got this drunk. How did I get so far gone again? *Fucking fuck.*

I cleared my throat. "I'm not your pristine virgin anymore, Cameron, so maybe we should just call it a night. Sorry you had to witness my fall from grace tonight. What can I say? I'm full of surprises, like you said."

"Will you stop? All I'm saying is I wish you'd value yourself more. You're out on the dance floor dressed to kill, with all these strangers grabbing at you. Are you trying to bait yourself?"

"You were out there grabbing me too. What does that say about you?" I poked at his shirt, my fingertip stopping abruptly against the rock hard muscle beneath.

"I'm not a sex-crazed stranger. I've been inside you, Maya. I've loved you. Does that give me no license to touch you, especially when you want to be touched? Wouldn't you rather it be me than someone you don't know from Adam? Or is this part of your weekend routine? Go clubbing and pick up some random guy, or girl, to fuck."

The sorry way he looked at me when he said the words made me ill. I loathed the idea of being judged by someone who had no right to judge me. Tears pricked my eyes as a vile mix of embarrassment, shame, and outright rage coursed through me.

"I'd rather have a random string of one-night stands who took what they wanted, gave me what I needed, and didn't judge me in the morning than be looked at the way you're looking at me now, like I'm some kind of slut for dancing and looking good doing it. Fuck you and whatever self-righteous horse you rode in on."

I had every right to be as sexually liberated as I damn well pleased. I clung to that tenet as I tried to pick myself self-esteem up off the floor. I spun, vaguely aware of having dropped my purse somewhere on the way in. I needed to find it and be on my way.

"I'm going home." I scanned every surface, making my way farther into the spacious mostly finished bedroom. The small tableside lamp cast a warm light over the white bed, off the white walls and warm wood floors, sparsely covered with a few pieces of old furniture. This was where Cameron slept every night. I closed my eyes a second with the thought that he'd spent hundreds of nights here, so much closer to me than I ever thought he was.

"No way. You're drunk. You'll stay here, and I'll take you home in the morning." His voice was rough.

I found my tiny purse and spun back toward him. "I'm not so drunk that I can't take a cab home." I kept my voice steady. My anger was giving me new clarity, thank God.

"At this hour on a Saturday night, no. It's not negotiable. Here." He reached into his closet and tossed a white T-shirt on the bed. "You can wear this to sleep in."

I scoffed at the cool delivery and his assumption that I'd stay simply because he demanded that I do. "You can't hold me hostage here, you smug prick."

He crossed his arms over his muscular chest, his jaw setting with a ghost of smile, as if challenging me. He was a smug prick.

My growing irritation was sobering, but my head spun a little as I appraised the large bed beside us. The thought of finding my way home was unappealing, possibly more so than relenting to his demands. I stiffened my spine so I wouldn't lose balance on my heels as I considered it.

"Where are you sleeping?" I asked, trying to sound uninterested.

"Here, with you." He nodded toward the bed.

I laughed. "Like hell you are. I'll sleep on the couch then."

I peeled off my tight dress and kicked my heels across the floor, too pissed and inebriated to care about being naked in front of him. Clad in my tiny black thong, I circled the bed and reached for the T-shirt. He caught it before I could, tossing it back into his closet.

"Make yourself comfortable."

"Are you going to give me that damn shirt or do I have to parade around here like a naked marionette?"

The corner of his mouth lifted and he caught his lower lip between his teeth. "Will you calm the fuck down?"

"I will not."

I went to move around him into the closet when he circled me around the ribs and tossed me back onto the bed. I propped up on my elbows and opened my mouth to protest. The words caught in my throat when he tugged off his shirt, revealing the awe-inspiring details of his anatomy that I'd try to imagine so many times before.

Sweet Jesus.

His pectorals were flat and sculpted, the skin tight and pinched where they met the nook of his arms. *I want to lick him there, and over light disks of his nipples.* The walls of my sex clenched at the thought of my mouth on his skin, tasting every delicious inch of him. Because every inch was delicious. I knew this from experience. The pack of taut abdominal muscles flattened into the most pronounced vee I'd ever seen. Jesus Christ, did he live at the gym? No one—no one real anyway—looked that good.

My heart thumped rapidly. With the quiet determination of a man who had every intention of getting what he wanted, he crawled onto the bed after me. Catching my ankle, he lifted my leg and began a slow trail of kisses from my calf to my knee, repeating the journey on the other side.

I snapped my mouth shut to suppress a gasp at the contact, wishing I were sober enough to find the right words to stop him, to play a little hard to get. I could tell him to fuck off, but that seemed like it would backfire. Plus I was already a quivering mess at the way he was coming at me, like a predator hunting his prey. I was mad as hell, but I still wanted him. Possibly more than I ever had.

His journey took him higher, pressing hot kisses along the way. He took a hard suck of soft skin of my inner thigh, centimeters from the throbbing flesh of my sex. I moaned and let my head fall back. He inched his hand over my hip and belly, splaying his open hand between my jutting breasts. I lifted my head to gaze at him. His eyes were dark, so serious they took my breath away. With a little pressure, he flattened me to my back and wasted little time stripping me of the last tiny barrier of my clothing.

CAMERON. I stood at the edge of the bed a moment too long, simply staring. The worry that she'd run off or protest if I stopped was overrun by the overwhelming desire to capture this moment in my mind in case I lost her again. She was as perfect as I'd remembered. Small and pale, like the tiny broken creature she'd become. Heaven help me, I couldn't have her tonight. Not like this. I had to rein in some sort of control over the animal that wanted to spread her out and fuck her senseless straight into the morning. Hours of fucking her wouldn't be enough. Once I was there, tight inside her again, I'd never want to leave. Tonight wasn't going anything like I'd planned, but I was determined that she vividly remember the inevitable moment. In the meantime, I'd sate her and try like hell to keep my resolve.

Her chest labored with breaths, the swell of her breasts tightened with the motion. Her nipples pebbled into taut little rosebuds that begged for my mouth.

"What are you doing?" Her voice was wispy, her body naked and at my mercy.

I licked my lips, transfixed on the hint of glistening flesh between her legs. "I'm hungry."

"I thought you didn't want me."

"Quite the contrary. I want you, and I have every intention of having you."

"You're still dressed," she whispered.

She teased the pads of her toes up my thigh. I became acutely aware of my erection straining inside my jeans, where it would safely stay until she was fully satisfied. I didn't trust myself.

I caught her traveling foot and replaced it on the bed. "Open up, baby."

After a moment's hesitation, she lifted her knees slightly and parted, baring herself for me. I lowered to her, spreading her with my fingers. I was nearly drunk on her scent before I even tasted her. Memories flooded me. I suppressed a groan when I met the wet rush of her sex with my lips and then my tongue. *Fucking hell.*

I forced myself to go slow, lavishing her with deliberate strokes. I purposefully neglected the taut bundle of nerves that could take her over the edge far too quickly. Even as my resolve hung in the balance, I committed to make this last. When I flickered my tongue over her clit, she arched off the bed.

"Oh God," she whimpered.

She sifted her fingers through my hair and tugged it by the roots. The sting only spurred my hunger. She bucked into me, damn near forcing me over her. Forgetting myself, I tongued her mercilessly. I plunged two fingers inside of her, bathing them in her wetness. I massaged the sensitive spot that would set her off like clockwork. She tightened around me almost painfully, her thighs tensing over my shoulders.

"Cam, oh fuck. I'm going to come. Don't stop."

A growl escaped me, rumbling through my chest, past my lips, and against her quivering flesh. I gripped her bucking hip with my free hand, forcing her down. She seized around me, letting lose a string of cries that broke in time to the shudders that rocked her frames. Jesus Christ, what I'd do to have another part of myself inside of her now, buried in that warm heaven between her legs.

Unable to take my mouth off of her, I spread kisses over her hips, the swell of her belly, over her breasts and along her collarbone. In seconds, she was writhing beneath me again, tugging feebly at my belt.

"Take this damn thing off."

I hid a smile and entertained the thought of letting her struggle with it or removing the obstacle myself. I could be inside her so easily. She was more than ready. It would be good, drunk or not. No time between us had ever been anything short of fulfilling. We fit. We always fit, and making her come was addictive, which is why I couldn't stop tantalizing her even now. I could do this all night and drive us both to the brink of madness.

"Cameron, please. I can't wait any more," she pleaded.

"Sure you can." I kissed the line of her neck, licking and sucking the salt from her earlier exertions. I rocked into her, cursing myself for wanting her lucid when the time came. But I couldn't be like any self-serving brute she'd brought into her bed since me. I wanted to worship her, love her, and I wanted her to feel every minute of it.

"What are you waiting for? I need you now." She bucked her hips against me, having given up on the belt.

I breathed in the heady scent of her body with the floral aroma of her hair—one last intoxicating breath of Maya. It had all become too much, and I was losing control. "I want to make love to you, Maya."

"Then do it, for God's sake. I'm dying here."

"I want you to feel everything. I want you to remember everything."

She pulled me back, capturing my face in her frail hands. Her eyes were glossy, hooded with desire. My jaw set, resisting the urge to kiss her more. Slowly, with every ounce of resolve I possessed, I pulled away.

CHAPTER ELEVEN

MAYA. I woke after what seemed like only a few hours. However much time had passed, it wasn't nearly enough to sleep off the damage I'd done. Soft light poured into the room through the beige curtains. Cameron wasn't there. I should have taken his absence as a hint to leave, but I was in no condition for my walk of shame back home.

Exhausted and supremely hung over, I tossed back and forth. My legs tangled in the soft white sheets that were my only protection against the violent chills and waves of heat that tormented me. I cursed myself, hating this physical torture I'd brought onto myself. I'd overdone it again. I tried to quiet the self-loathing and prayed I could sleep it off soon. But I couldn't relax enough to ignore the tight fist of my stomach around its contents and my body's instinct to toss them.

Flashbacks of the previous night rushed through my mind, and my body heated every time I remembered my own stupidity. I kicked off the sheets again, realizing I was naked. Last night... Oh God. Cameron's mouth on me. His words last night were framed by an otherwise blurry night of fun and bad decisions. I couldn't imagine what he must think of me now. I cringed inwardly and another wave of nausea hit. Fuck.

I got up quickly. I found Cameron's T-shirt on the floor and put it on. I rushed into the attached bathroom and knelt at the toilet. After only a little coaxing, my body finally rejected the night's libations. I wished the regret would go with them. Breathless and shaking, I rose. I found a toothbrush in its package in one of the drawers and used it to wash away the terrible tinny taste of all the alcohol I'd poisoned myself with. I scolded my reflection in the mirror, wiping the smear of mascara from under my eyes. *What a fucking wreck.*

I padded back to the bedroom and considered Cameron's large fluffy bed for a second. Then I dove back under the covers, unwilling to leave their comfort for the outside world yet. Hopefully he'd be gone a while longer. I curled my body into a fetal position, burying my face into the pillow that smelled like him. I grabbed another and squeezed my arms around it, only a little guilty of wishing it were him. I inhaled deeply. A soft musk mingled with the cool subtle scent of his soap filled my lungs. If I hadn't felt so wretched, I might have considered this heaven. My body instantly relaxed, and I fell into an exhausted dreamless sleep.

When I came to again, Cameron's arm was wrapped around my waist, his body loosely curled around my backside. By the change in the room's light and my faint hunger, I guessed it was late afternoon. I blinked away the fog of sleep and the room came into focus again. White and unadorned except with basic furniture, the space seemed plain by contrast to the remodeled bathroom where floors and shower were marble and every fixture shone. I tried to remember what he'd said last night about fixing the place up.

Memories from last night were hazy, but the vision of his body hovering over mine, rocking into me, had me tingling all over again. As if last night had unlocked the most potent memories, thoughts of how sex had been with him plagued me. I kept shaking my head, trying to physically dislodge him from every thought.

His arm tightened around my waist and his erection strained against my ass. As promising as that was, I needed to get out of here and embark on my walk of shame before his proximity clouded all of my better judgment. I shifted, inching carefully from his grasp. He groaned and pulled me closer than I'd been before.

"Good morning." He nuzzled my neck, kissing me softly there.

My nipples went hard, a shiver running across my skin. I bit my lip, tensing against the riotous response of my body.

He turned me to face him. His mouth curved into a sleepy smile as he propped up on his elbow. Even in a relaxed state, his abs looked ridiculously impressive and defined. No sane woman could resist him. My breath left me for a moment as I took in all his beauty again. I didn't want to go, but I really should before I did something stupid. I'd already hit the quota for the weekend, and I was sober now. I had no excuse.

"How do you feel? You slept a long time."

"Better," I said. The sexual energy that pulsed through

me seemed to obliterate the last of my wretched hangover. All I could think about now was him. My body came to life, as if I'd been waiting my whole life to be wanted the way his look told me he wanted me now.

I took an unsteady breath. "I should go now though. It's getting late."

"Maya, we need to talk." His hand traced a lazy path up and down my thigh. Whether he was killing time or trying to find the right words, the motion was driving me insane. I was still pantiless and all too accessible to his roaming touch. "You didn't tell me why were you so upset the other night."

"I wasn't," I lied.

"You mentioned Raina last night. Darren wasn't lying. There isn't anything between us and you need to know that."

"You can see whoever you want, Cam. I have no claim over you."

"Yes, you do." His voice was soft, his eyes relaxed but more serious than they had been a moment ago. "You're the only one who's ever had claim over me."

I heated under his gaze. He brushed his hand over my cheek where the color no doubt had come to the surface. That simple touch had me wanting more. I fisted my hands to keep from reaching for him.

"I wanted you last night. It took everything I had to stop, but I couldn't stand the idea that you'd regret it in the morning because you were drunk. Or worse, that you wouldn't remember it at all."

"I remember." *Most of it.* I bit my lip at the hazy but intoxicating vision that passed behind my eyes. How his mop of inky black hair had moved between my legs, and how his piercing blue eyes had hunted me the way they hunted me now. I'd come like a rocket, so weakened with the release that I'd begged for more, for all of him.

"So do I. But now I want more."

The soft rasp of his voice paralyzed any thoughts I'd had about fleeing. His lips parted, his tongue traveling over his bottom lip. The overall effect was brain-frazzling and willpower-crippling.

Sealing the moment and dispelling any lingering reservations, he kissed me, a soft but demanding kiss. I answered, eager for his taste as much as I knew it would be my undoing.

I could sense the determination in his touch as he gently kneed my legs apart and positioned himself between them. He tugged his shirt over my head, leaving me naked and exposed in a matter of moments.

The sharp lines of his face took my breath away. The skin over his cheeks tightened as he looked me over. There was determination in his movements, in the quiet domination of our kiss as his lips crushed against me again, his palms sliding over my skin, reclaiming every expanse of my body he'd once known so intimately. Once upon a time.

Our lips rushed over each other's. His erection throbbed through his boxers against my belly. The rise and fall of his chest matched my own anxious breaths. My skin heated with a searing desire that stamped out any remote thoughts of shyness.

Still, doubt crept in, tainting the moment, when I only wanted be lost with reckless abandon.

"We shouldn't do this."

He stilled. "Tell me why, Maya. You push me away,

but you've never given me a good reason."

My lips parted, but I couldn't speak. The words lodged in my throat. He had to know what was at risk, for both of us.

"I care about you too much," I whispered.

Understanding softened his eyes. My throat thickened. I squeezed my eyes closed, unable to meet his gaze to say what I needed to say.

"You broke my heart. I—I want to be strong and pretend like it didn't destroy me, but it did. I can't do it again. I still have feelings for you, but—"

"Maya." He caught my face in his palm, silencing me. "We'll make it right this time."

I tried to look away but he wouldn't let me.

What he wanted seemed impossible in the face of what we'd been through. As much as I wanted it too, the reality of the situation hit me. I thought I could keep things between us casual, give in to the attraction, even revisit some of those old feelings—the good ones, the ones I could handle. But whatever forces had taken over this week had not inspired manageable, casual feelings. No miracle could piece me back together if I got invested again only to have him leave. How could I give him that chance?

"Everything is different now. We've changed."

"We've both changed, but a day hasn't gone by that I haven't thought of you or wanted this. Most days I wished I'd never met you if it meant taking away what missing you so badly did to me. Believe me, I don't want to go through that again either, but I can't get you out of my head." He hesitated, and the last words lingered. "I love you, Maya. I've never stopped loving you."

My heart beat heavy in my chest. The pressure of his body on mine suddenly robbed me of the ability to breathe properly. His words echoed in the same deep place where I'd buried my ability to love a man, to give both my body and my heart to another person, trusting he'd cherish and protect it. Of all the stupid decisions I'd made in this life, I hoped sleeping with Cameron right now wouldn't be one of them. I had a hard time saying no to anything I wanted this much, and I'd never wanted anything or anyone more than this.

"The question is do you want me? Do you want this...with me?" A flash of doubt passed over his eyes.

"I do, but I'm scared." *Of falling in love with you all over again. That you'll leave me again.*

My pride kept the confession silent, but my heart ached and swelled, a painful testimony of how deep these feelings for Cameron ran. Except doubt now colored the love I'd once succumbed to in simpler times, with innocence and abandon.

But that didn't lessen how I wanted him now. Deep down, I wanted to lose myself in this love. I saw it, a tangible earthly thing that I could hold despite its sharp edges, jagged with the shattered pieces of our hearts. I couldn't deny its compelling force, even knowing how I'd bleed if I let him inside and he hurt me again.

"I'm scared too, but I want you more than I'm scared to lose you again." His eyes never left mine, never letting me question for a moment his intentions. They were the same eyes that bored into me when he'd asked me to marry him.

I closed my eyes, squeezing them tight to keep the tears locked out. How could he do this? Break me open with his words. And I came apart so easily.

"Say yes," he whispered, his breath dancing across my lips.

He laced our fingers, raising my arms high above me. I was powerless, spread for him, a prisoner to the craving. The sharp ache that overtook my senses and better judgment last night was back with a vengeance. I weakened in the possessive embrace, letting the warmth of his body envelop me.

I might have been scared as hell, but every cell of my being wanted to be with Cameron right now. I longed for the slow tease of his lips across my skin, the wild vigor of him thrusting inside of me. I was on fire, and desire was winning.

"Yes."

Then his lips were on me. Eager and urgent, he took my mouth. I met him fully, surrendering to my choice. My lips tingled, swollen from the passion of his movements.

Awakening stirred through me as his mouth roamed over my shoulder to my neck, nibbling and sucking. I gasped, bowing into his body. The heat of our naked bodies sliding over one another warmed me. A wild fever licked over my flesh everywhere we met. Already, I ached for him. A deep, wet ache that only he could satisfy.

He caught my breast in his hand, squeezing the soft flesh tenderly. He licked over one, then the other, grasping and sucking. I shifted anxiously beneath him, still powerless and pinned.

He released a hand, feathered his fingertips through the folds of my pussy. I gasped, lifting into the motion, eager for his intimate touch.

"You're ready for me." His blue eyes were dilated, hooded with lust.

I tightened around an exploring finger teasing my inner flesh. "I need you." Yes, this was need. We'd surpassed want. I had to have him, even if falling this deep broke me again. Anything seemed worth it.

I reached for him, coaxing his boxers down to reveal his thick, hard erection. I bit my lip, trailing my fingers over the hot flesh. Squeezing him gently, I was overwhelmed with wanting him, the promise of the pleasure he could give me. He kicked his boxers off and leaned over to the bedside table. He ripped open a condom packet and rolled it on. I regretted that we'd have anything between us, but this wasn't the time I wanted to spend discussing our sexual histories.

Then he was there, notching the head of his cock against me, exactly where I'd wanted him for days. I squirmed, eager to hasten the penetration, but he had my arms bound again, our fingers tightly interlaced. I arched impatiently, hooking my heels into the backs of his thighs to urge him closer. He pressed inside me only by the tip.

"I've wanted this"—he exhaled as he pushed in—"for so long."

"Hurry." I tightened my fingers through his, breathless with want.

He held me in his gaze as he slid deep, deliberate, and slow. "I want to feel you. It's been too long." The rumble in his voice vibrated through me.

"Cam…" I whimpered. I could have been praying, for all the power this man held over me, how at his mercy I was. When he was fully inside me, I swallowed over the sudden urge to cry. Something about the deep connection of our bodies in this moment had me unraveling. I loved this man, even though I couldn't say the words now. I loved him so much I could scarcely breathe.

He lowered, sealing our lips with a possessive kiss. He retreated slowly and thrust again. I shuddered at the exquisite sensation of him filling me, over and over. He made his presence known as my body stretched to accommodate the invasion, a bittersweet pleasure that I'd come to love, to crave.

He moved a hand to my hip, lifting and angling me so he could deepen the penetration. Immediately I let my free hand roam through his hair, down his chest, clawing at his waist as he pumped into me. His hips ground against mine as he claimed me in the most intimate way possible.

The tip of his cock massaged me from the inside, hitting a sensitive spot. He filled me so completely, there was no missing it. Pleasure coursed through me like lightening every time he grazed it, satisfying the sweet ache.

Every motion brought me closer to the edge. The rhythmic friction, the tight grip of my flesh encircling his had me coming apart at the seams. An orgasm was within reach and the tease of the sensation had me spasming, my pussy clutching against him to heighten the impact of every stroke. I cried out, my head rearing back on the pillow.

"Fuck." His forehead dropped to the bed beside me, his breath on my neck. "Maya...you're so sensitive."

"I can't help it. You feel incredible." My breaths came fast, my mind reeling with desire. "Please don't stop."

I caged him to me tightly with my thighs, desperate to know his strength as he let go.

"Hard, Cam. Please I want you deep."

He growled in my ear, taking my earlobe in his mouth. "I'll bruise you."

"Then bruise me. I can't wait anymore. I need all of you."

He found my mouth, the intensity of his kiss a prelude to what would come. My words set him off, spurring a rugged pace. I clung to him, my body wrapped perilously around his unyielding frame. He moved with fierce drives, his muscles rippling under the heated flesh as he powered deep.

I wanted to cry out, but I was already at the edge. My voice and every limb were paralyzed by the climax as it ripped through me. A violent heat exploded from my core and finally brought air to my lungs. With it, a thready cry tore from me, the last of my resistance going with it.

Through the blur of my release, I stayed with him, ready to see him over the edge. His jaw tensed, and his eyes closed. He cursed. Burying his cock until it reached the very end of me one last time, he froze.

"Maya."

A guttural groan escaped as he came. He collapsed over me, his cock pulsing inside me with the aftershocks that trembled between us.

He encircled me in his arms. His heart beat against my chest, proof of the stampede of energy that coursed through us both. Pressing breathy kisses over my skin, he soothed the wild rush. I threaded my fingers through the damp strands of his hair. Every small touch seemed right and true between us.

Bliss, an intoxicating contentment, washed over me. I chased after the memory of the pleasure. I opened my eyes when he shifted over me. He rested on his elbows, a lazy smile lighting up his face.

I smiled in reply. "What?"

"Nothing like make-up sex five years in the making."

I laughed. A tired heaviness inside me lifted, making room for his warmth, this simple happiness. My soul was lighter, stripped for the moment of my emotional defenses. As if by a light shining through the clouds, a dark memory from our past brightened. I remembered this. This had been our love.

CAMERON. We lay there for a long time, drifting in and out of sleep. I had no desire to leave or move if it meant putting unnecessary distance between us. I had her, and I had no intention of letting her go.

Her back was to me, her body barely covered by the sheet. Her chest moved with a steady rise and fall that told me she was sleeping. Somehow, between last night and this afternoon, I'd completely missed that she had a large tattoo on her back. I moved the sheet enough to reveal all of it. I traced the black ink that marked her skin, the flesh raised slightly beneath my fingertips like a scar. I wondered what this meant—a sketch of jagged branches drawn at the small of her back and a flock of stark black birds taking flight up the side of her torso.

What did it mean? As much as she'd changed, Maya didn't strike me as the type of girl who'd mark her body without it having meaning. She didn't strike me as the type of girl who'd have a tattoo at all, but she was surprising me left and right. This new Maya was still a mystery to me.

Inexplicably, I wanted to kiss her then. I pressed my lips to her shoulder and down her arm, slowly and gently so I wouldn't startle her if she woke. With every brush against her skin, I breathed her in. The velvet softness of her skin was intoxicating. No woman had ever felt so soft. The curves of her body called to me like no one's ever had. My fingers itched to claim them again, to pull her up against me, over me. I wanted to sheath my cock in the warmth of her tight little body. Already I wanted her again. Hours wouldn't be enough.

She'd given herself to me. Never had I felt so gutted, so desperate to possess someone physically the way I had with her. We'd danced around our attraction all week, and I'd begrudged Darren's seedling of advice, however inspired, to give ourselves over to what we wanted. Now we would see how it played out. I hadn't planned to tell her I loved her. I'm not sure I'd even admitted it to myself. But something had transformed between us and the words had simply rushed out.

Everything was like that with Maya. A familiar impulse, a craving I had no good sense to resist because I'd indulged it already. My body and mind refused to go without the best thing I'd ever experienced, the embodiment of her love.

I idly traced my fingertips over a tiny black bird, its wings outspread over the back of her rib. Maya stirred then. She looked over her shoulder with those beautiful brown eyes.

My chest tightened almost painfully, like the wind had been knocked out of me. "You're beautiful," I whispered.

She frowned slightly as she turned, a confused smile turning up her mouth. "I doubt it."

She lifted the sheet up to cover her breasts. I tugged it back, even lower than where it originally was. I caressed her skin, obsessed with every curve and contour of her body.

"You've never looked so gorgeous. I like you like this. No makeup, your hair wild like this. The 'just fucked' look works for you."

She shook her head with a smile. "Yeah, right. I'm a mess."

"A beautiful mess." I kissed her. With my hand, I followed the arc of the design that I could no longer see on her back. "What does this mean?"

"What?"

"The tattoo."

She hesitated, her eyes now more alert. She linked her arms behind my neck. "That was amazing, earlier," she murmured, bending toward me. "I'm not sure how I managed to go without that for so long."

Her breath warmed my lips. She darted her tongue out, licking my lower lip before seizing it between her teeth, biting down gently. I groaned, and she licked over the sting of her bite. My cock stirred back to life, ready for her. I grasped her hip, barely resisting the urge to push into her right then and there.

What the fuck? The tattoo. My brain shifted back. She was avoiding the subject, but I pressed. "Tell me about it. When did you get it?"

She relaxed back into the bed. Her eyes were somber now, darker, as if she were remembering something unpleasant. "A long time ago."

"And?"

She sighed, seeming to give up some resistance on the subject.

"It was a dark time in my life. Without you and…other things that were happening."

I lifted an eyebrow. "So you commemorated it with a tattoo?"

She frowned and looked away. "It's not like that. I guess it's hard to understand." Her body tensed in my grasp and a coldness began to creep between us. I caught her chin, turning her to face me once more.

"I don't, but I want to. Help me understand."

Her lips set firmly, resistance back in place.

"Please," I urged, tracing the bow of her mouth.

She took a slow breath. "I think there's something cleansing, even cathartic about getting ink. The decision, then the pain and the healing. Not just physically, on the skin. On the inside, it helped me heal. I remembered running my fingers over it the same day, feeling the beginning of a scar. It was kind of a rush, but something about it gave me strength when I needed it."

"It's enormous. It must have hurt like hell."

She shrugged. "I knew it would hurt, but I'm not sure if the experience would have been the same without the pain."

I nodded, trying to wrap my head around what she described. I'd put myself in harm's way to deal with my demons, but never to commemorate them.

"It probably sounds strange, but getting the tattoo was

like a rite of passage for me. Having it and remembering where I was emotionally at the time doesn't make me sad. It reminds me that I can survive, that I came out of a difficult time in one piece."

Maya's lip trembled and she fidgeted with the edge of the sheet. She hadn't opened up like this to me before, maybe ever. More and more my vision of Maya, who she was in her soul, began to resolve with the memory. The brown-eyed, blond-haired angel I used to love had changed, her bright flame both darkened and intensified at once, as if she'd walked into a long, cold shadow on her path and had spent the past four years trying to outrun it.

"Sometimes you don't seem happy. I don't have much to compare it to, but were you so much unhappier then than you are now?"

"Markedly. I'd lost you, I…" She swallowed hard and bit her lip, reddening the already rose-colored plump of flesh with the tip of her teeth.

Tension rippled through me with the unpleasant memory of how I'd left her. Wanting to forget it as quickly, I kissed her shoulder. I breathed in her subtle scent, reveling in the warm, petal-soft skin beneath my lips. Maya's soul was encased in this body—warm impassioned flesh. Marked with dark symbols, her body held secrets to her past. I wondered what other truths I might uncover from it when she wasn't pushing me away from her innermost thoughts.

I resisted the urge to let my mouth wander, to coax out the cries she'd given me earlier. I couldn't ignore the premonition that more dwelled below the surface.

"You said other things… What other things were

happening?"

She gave me a gentle push away. Resistant at first, I leaned back, giving her room to sit up. She moved her legs over the edge of the bed and rose quickly before I could pull her back down to me. She found her dress on the floor and slipped into it, the tight fabric hugging her everywhere.

"Where are you going?"

"I have to go home. Eli is probably wondering where I disappeared to."

She had a valid point. In fact, I wondered why her phone hadn't been ringing off the hook. She'd been gone for almost an entire day, and we'd never let anyone know we left. She could have been anywhere, with anyone. Maybe they assumed we would end up together last night, but then again, maybe this was routine.

Memories from last night played in my mind. The one with another women's mouth on her shot to the forefront. I fisted my hand, bristling at the display they'd put on, how I'd nearly pummeled their onlookers.

"You disappear a lot on Saturday nights?" The question came out before I could think about its implication or temper the meaning and disappointment that laced every word.

She shot me a cold look. Motionless, she stared, and regret rooted in my gut. She grabbed her purse and pulled on her coat.

"Bye, Cam."

CHAPTER TWELVE

MAYA. I took a cab back home. I wanted to put distance between us quickly.

I hated the judgment in his voice. Especially after what we'd done. I'd exposed myself physically and emotionally, only for him to fling my bad behavior at me.

I stewed the rest of the day, and my phone remained ominously silent. Maybe now that he'd gotten fucking me out of the way, we could get back to reality. Anger circled around the raw vulnerability I had when I was with him. I wanted to wipe it out, bury it deep. But how could I when he had me pinned that way, stripping me with his own honesty? He'd said he loved me. If he'd been anyone else, I wouldn't have believed him. I believed him. I had no doubts that he was falling as hard and fast as I was.

Yet, the hours of silence had me unsettled. I had no idea what he was thinking now, and I hated that I was on the defensive now. I sat with the rejection, slowly turning it to self-assurance, that I could stay ahead of this. I wasn't going to let him run my heart into the ground this time. I couldn't go through that again. I wouldn't deny loving him, but I'd just dipped my toe in it. I wasn't drowning in it yet. I could still save myself.

He called on my commute to work the next morning. I ignored it, and the handful of texts that followed. He'd let me sit with my resentment a little too long. Just before lunch, my phone dinged again. Compulsively I searched for it, too eager for another inquiring text from Cameron. Instead, it was Jia.

J: *Pop into my office before you head out.*

A nervous heat prickled under my skin—a mixture of shame and embarrassment that I was going to lose my job for my atrocious behavior. I tried in vain to focus on work as the last thirty minutes ticked by before I was supposed to meet Vanessa for lunch. Finally, I couldn't take it anymore. I knocked quietly on Jia's door. I heard a muffled voice inside. Hesitant, I opened it. She was sitting at her desk, her fingers flying over her keyboard. She paused when I entered.

"Come in. Shut the door."

I obliged, taking a seat in front of her desk. Her office was small, not nearly as opulent as Dermott's. Still, it was an office, a space away from the communal drone forces of the bullpen, with a desk and a sitting area to the side where she could meet with people.

She finished up her email and turned my way. I rolled a number of apologies and excuses over in my head, unsure which to use because I didn't know how bad all of this was on her scale of inappropriate behavior.

"Jia, I'm sorry about the other night. I got so drunk, I really wasn't thinking clearly."

She frowned. "Do you think that's why I asked you here?"

My eyebrows shot up. "Well...yeah. I mean—"

"Seriously, don't give it another thought, Maya. We were having fun. I had a blast. I mean, I wouldn't go shouting it off the rooftops at the Christmas party, but it's nothing to worry yourself over."

"Okay. Thank you, for your discretion, I guess."

"Likewise."

She gave me a smirk and straightened some of the papers on her desk. Relief flooded me, followed by an unexpected uneasiness. How could she possibly think this was acceptable? I didn't even think it was appropriate. Making out with one of the female VPs of the company in front of a pack of horny guys wasn't exactly reputable behavior. It fell into the kind of impulsive behavior that only drunk-me could talk herself into. Though I'd never admit it out loud, I'd *still* known it was a bad idea under all the alcohol I'd imbibed. I'd possessed enough control at that point to know better and act differently.

Stunned by her nonchalant attitude, I sat silently, waiting for her to continue. "What did you want to see me about then?"

"This is about the deal. We'll probably need you to stay late all week. Hopefully it doesn't run into the holiday, but it might. You okay with that?"

"Sure, that's fine." I nodded.

"Great. I just wanted to make sure, because I don't want Dermott getting pissy if you can't come through on this. If you can't, I can find someone else to chip in."

"I don't have any family to go home to, Jia. I have nothing to keep me away from finishing whatever needs finishing." I regretted the admission as it left me, but I figured blunt honesty might work here. Family obligations were the number one excuse during this time of year. I figured I would assure her that wasn't an issue.

"Okay, good. That's settled then." She sat back, her pen resting against her full lips. "How did things go with the guy anyway? You two disappeared pretty quickly."

"Cameron. Um, they're fine."

Her lips lifted into a coy smile, her eyes glittering. "He's the jealous type, isn't he?"

"Seems that way." I couldn't exactly judge him for it.

"Well, I hope it all works out." Her voice was soft, a little more cautious than it had been. No doubt she could read the angst all over my face when I spoke about Cameron. "You have plans for lunch?"

I glanced at my watch. "Actually, I do. Maybe tomorrow?"

She nodded, dismissing me with a wave. I grabbed my purse and headed to the elevators with the rest of the cubicle crowd. I stalled in the lobby downstairs and spotted a stressed-out redhead walking my way.

"You look pissed," I said as Vanessa approached.

"Same stupid fucking shit," she spat.

I cringed for her. At least as of late I had a little bit of opportunity to look forward to. Vanessa was locked into a seemingly never-ending cycle of running around after Reilly. He expected her to look happy doing it too.

We pushed through the revolving doors without a word. As soon as we were outside, my eyes zeroed in on Cameron. He was leaning against the street sign, his legs crossed at the ankle. Shit, why did he always look so good? I groaned inwardly as we walked his way.

He smiled and leaned in, kissing me on the cheek. I tensed, all too aware of our very public setting. Also, I was still pissed with him and his insinuations.

I took a safer step away. "Vanessa and I were headed to lunch. Do you need something?"

"Can I join you? My treat?"

He shot me a sexy smile that had my brain short-circuiting. I wanted to stay mad, but he was making it difficult.

I looked up to Vanessa. She shrugged, not seeming to care. I sighed, and we walked together to a nearby cafe.

"How's corporate America doing today, ladies?" Cameron said as we settled down at our table with sandwiches.

I nodded to Vanessa. "You want to field that one?"

"Pretty simple, it sucks. Reilly seems to think that coordinating the entire fucking holiday party is my personal responsibility."

"Ugh, I wish I didn't even have to go." I cringed at the thought.

She glared at me. "You better go, because I'm busting my ass on it."

"I will. Dermott insisted that I go anyway."

"Who's Dermott?" Cameron asked.

"My boss. He's a prick. Only a few notches below Vanessa's boss, who is in the top echelon of corporate pricks."

"Sounds like you two are living the dream."

Neither of us could argue with that. Such was our life.

"When's the party?"

"Thursday night." Vanessa said before I could. "You should go with Maya. Would probably make it more tolerable."

I fought the urge to snap at her. She was on edge, and she had no idea what was going down between Cameron and me.

"Sure. If Maya wants me to, of course."

"I'm not sure if bringing an ex-boyfriend to the holiday party would really make a great impression."

He noticeably grimaced. The dig had met its mark. Maybe he didn't like that "ex" title either. A pang of regret hit me, but Vanessa spoke before I could smooth it over.

"Actually, being attached tends to work in your favor. I think I read somewhere that being married with kids makes you look more stable or something when it comes to promotions."

I rolled my eyes. "Well, I'm not sure I'll be able to swing that in time for the party. Thanks for the tip though."

Cameron laughed. Our eyes met for a second. I didn't like what I saw there. Possibilities. Promises. Dreams we'd given up on. Vanessa's phone rang, interrupting our brief moment.

"Hello?" Her whole posture had changed, her shoulders high and tense. Her eyes were seemingly fixed on some detail beyond our table as she listened. "Yes, I'm at lunch."

A man's sharp voice could be heard even muffled through the phone. She worked her jaw, rolled her eyes, mouthed the word "fuck" a few times. Then she plastered on a disgruntled smile. "Sure, I'll take care of it right away." She ended the call and gathered her purse. "Sorry, guys. I have to run out and take care of something for Mr. Wonderful."

"Reilly?" Cameron cocked an eyebrow.

"You guessed it." She pushed up from the table, her shoulders sagging. Then she brightened slightly. "I'll see you at the party then?"

He shot a questioning look my way. I tapped my foot nervously, feeling cornered by how this was playing out. I couldn't refuse without major awkwardness. "Fine," I relented.

He looked up and smiled. "I'll be there."

Vanessa bid a quick goodbye and took off, trashing her half-eaten lunch on the way. I fidgeted nervously with my watch, wishing the long hand would move a little faster for once. I picked at my lunch, secretly wishing I'd gone to Delaney's by myself instead. I could use a drink.

"I called," he finally said.

"I know."

"I texted too."

I nodded, my gaze skirting past him.

"Do you want to talk about why you're avoiding me?"

"Because I'm not rushing to the phone every time you want to talk to me doesn't necessarily mean I'm avoiding you. It means I have my own life. Don't make the mistake of thinking I'm your girlfriend now just because we've slept together."

He nodded slowly. "Are you this cold with everyone you sleep with, or am I getting special treatment here?"

I sighed. I wasn't going to like wherever this

conversation was going. I'd underestimated how awkward things could be with Cameron. This is why I didn't date, why I never let things go further than sex. I'd never had to justify emotional distance with someone I'd slept with. Of course Cameron broke all of those rules simply by being Cameron.

"I don't usually have to be, because the terms are clear from the outset."

"What are our terms, then?"

"Honestly, I have no idea, because they keep changing. We went from friends to—"

"Wait, this is friendly?" He leaned in, eyebrows high, and gestured between the two of us. "This isn't how I imagine friends interacting."

"Which is why this is a bad idea." I threw my hands up and leaned back, wishing he could get on board with my doubts.

"I want to know why you feel the need to shut me out? Where's the Maya I used to know? We were never like this, *ever*."

I let out a short laugh. "I hate to be the one to break it to you, but the Maya you used to know is gone. If you're holding out for that person to resurface from all of this, let me spare you the expense of waiting."

"I don't believe you. I think you're hiding, and whatever you're hiding isn't gone forever."

I crossed my arms against my chest. I hated his words. Every fucking one of them.

"When did you get so goddamn stubborn, Maya?"

I locked my jaw and glared at him, unwilling to give him anything. Except he was right. We'd never fought like this before. We disagreed and bickered sometimes.

But we'd never been on different sides. Now, when we weren't lusting after our memories together, we were fighting over them. Our relationship had become a battle, one that I was petrified of losing. He was digging too deep, trying to uncover a side of me I had no wish to unbury and willfully give to him.

"This isn't what I want."

He paused a moment, staring, as I dug in for the next round.

"No offense, but you have no fucking idea what you want until I start kissing you, and then I can guarantee that we both want the same thing."

"This isn't about sex. Trust me, I wish that's all it was."

He stilled. "Really?" His voice was too quiet.

"We can't possibly keep this simple."

"Why do you keep trying to when you know it's impossible? I'm never going to fit into one of these frankly impossible categories that you place men into."

Anger surged and I leaned forward. "This is me. This is my life. You can't march in here and tell me who to be and when to love. If this is how it's going to be between us, we should move on and save ourselves the heartbreak."

"Wouldn't a heart be required for heartbreak?"

Heat flooded me, dampening my hands, and suddenly the room seemed too warm.

"You're right. I'm honestly not sure I have any left to break. You did a pretty thorough job of it the first time around."

I tossed down my napkin. Sickness twisted in my stomach, annihilating any remnants of my appetite. I grabbed my things and made my way out the door quickly. I took brisk steps toward the office, anxious to return. Cameron caught up with me a few seconds later.

"Maya, wait."

He caught my elbow, spun me to him, and pulled us out of the sidewalk traffic. I didn't pull away. Deep down I didn't want the physical distance between us as much as I needed the emotional space from him.

When my eyes met his, concern and frustration were written all over his face. "Why do you keep running away from me?"

"Why did you come here?"

My voice wavered unsteadily. I brushed away his touches, but he tugged me closer until we were chest to chest. He circled an arm around my waist, keeping me close.

"I came here because I missed you. I needed a minute to think, but I could feel you slipping away again. I didn't want to wait around for days to talk to you, to know where things stood between us." He sifted his fingers through my hair, thumbing my cheek.

"Is this really worth it? I mean, really? Haven't we been through enough?"

He tipped my face to his. I opened my eyes, finding his burning intensely into me—steely and unmoved. "Stop with that bullshit, Maya. We are worth it. *You* are worth it. What we had, saving any of it is worth it. I can see that now."

I shook my head. "I don't know."

"Enough with the doubts." The sharpness in his voice surprised me. "Enough with all of that. Figure it out in your head right now, because I'm not going anywhere. If you want to run, you need to know I'll be right behind you."

"But—"

"No buts. We're doing this. I can't promise it'll be easy, being without you has been hell, so really it can only get better from here. I'm not letting you go this time."

I struggled for breath and for the right words. He wasn't giving me an inch. Physically and emotionally, I was in his clutches. I steadied myself against the tornado of emotion ripping through me, doubt among them. My lip trembled and I shivered, neither from the cold.

His voice softened when he spoke again. "I can't undo what I did. But you need to know that I love you." Sadness flickered behind the blue depths of his eyes. "You'll never know how sorry I am for what happened between us. For what it did to both of us. And if I have to spend the rest of my life making it up to you, I will."

I opened my mouth to speak. Resentment, regret, and a deep soul-piercing love—a soundless rush of emotion pulsed through me at his words. The damn broke, and the tears fell faster than I could stop them. I was breaking open. Everything was coming to the surface now, and I was bubbling over.

"What if it doesn't work?"

"It will," he insisted.

"You can't know that."

"All I know is that I love you, Maya. That needs to be enough."

"Stop," I begged. Everything he said ripped open another wound, exposed some raw feeling that I'd buried long ago. But I clung to my anger. I didn't want him to be sorry. I wanted him to be terrible and smug so I could go on hating him, hiding my heart away in the safe place

I'd always kept it.

"I meant it when I said it. And I know you still love me too." He tightened his hold, gravel in his voice betraying the heart in his words. "You don't have to say it, but I see it in your eyes. In fleeting moments before you try to pretend you don't feel it, I see it."

Small sobs escaped me, and I didn't care who saw me now, breaking down like the kind of girl I never thought I'd be again on a busy New York City sidewalk. What the hell was this man doing to me?

He hushed me, kissing me sweetly. I weakened at the contact, breathless as I kissed him back.

"It's going to be okay, I promise."

I grasped at his coat, pulling him impossibly closer. Relief and embracing the love I felt for Cameron was on the other side of this. Deep down, I knew it. The person I wanted desperately to run from was the only one who could put me back together.

CHAPTER THIRTEEN

CAMERON. "It's starting to look good around here. Maybe you should keep Liv around after all."

Darren walked around the room casually, his hands in his pockets, as he perused the day's progress. Olivia shot him an annoyed look, pushing back the dark hair that fell from her ponytail before she rolled more paint onto the wall.

I hid my grin. Ribbing her never got old. "Yeah. It's starting to feel like a real place now. End is finally in sight."

The past few weeks I'd made real progress on the remodel. Olivia was good motivation, buzzing around, micromanaging, nagging, and ultimately helping with the finer details that pushed a lot of my good intentions into actual moving projects. Floors, windows, molding, getting the second floor kitchen finished up, and now we were finally getting around to paint and the final touches.

"We're hitting the third floor next week, and then we

should have everything perfect by Christmas," Olivia said.

Darren nodded. "Yeah, are we having Christmas morning here or what? I haven't been very good. I don't think Santa's going to bring me anything."

Olivia didn't answer, rolling the last section of the wall in silence.

"Liv, did you have plans?" I asked.

"Actually, I think Mom and Dad might be coming down. Might be nice for them to see the place fixed up."

Darren and I exchanged a look that was full of *fucking great*.

He let out a short laugh, but I could tell he wasn't too amused. "Smooth, Liv. Way to drop that one. How long has that been in the works?"

She shrugged.

"You realize that's this weekend, right?" My voice betrayed my growing irritation at the thought of their visit.

"We'll be done by then." She plastered on a cheerful look and walked over to where we both stood with our arms crossed. "We just need to get some new furniture and spruce it up a little bit. I know Mom's a stickler for details, but I'm sure she'll be impressed."

I held up a hand to silence her. "I don't give two shits about the state of this place and who it impresses. I want to know why you thought you could invite them here without talking to me about it? This *is* my house, you know."

"So you keep reminding me." Her sharpened tone matched my own. "I know you have your issues, but they are still our parents. We can't cut them out of our lives."

I laughed. "Are you kidding me? You're the one

193

who couldn't get away from them fast enough. It's been weeks, and you're missing them so much you need to invite them here?"

"I didn't invite them, okay?"

I paused, trying to imagine any other scenario. "Well, I certainly didn't. They know where I stand."

She looked down at her bare feet and bit her lip. "I may have let it slip that you were seeing Maya again, and Mom might be a little concerned."

I let the words sink in along with the sheer disbelief of what I'd heard. "You've got to be kidding me."

She looked back up, her eyes wide and innocent. "She thought it would be a good idea to come down here and see all of us anyway. Once she'd decided, I couldn't talk her out of it. Believe me, I tried. But they've made plans, so we might as well get used to the idea and make the most of it."

I shoved my hands through my hair and paced a wide circle through the room. Having her come live here was a terrible idea. What the fuck had I been thinking? Darren was a pain in the ass, but he couldn't hold a candle to Olivia right now.

"Don't be mad at me," she pleaded.

"In what world would I not be mad about this? First, you're pulling some over-protective bullshit at the gym over Maya, and now I have to deal with *them*? I spent three years dodging bullets and hoping a roadside bomb didn't kill me or mangle me beyond hope. Do you really think I need you people hovering? Do you really think you are somehow protecting me at this point in my life? Because if so, you need to realize that my relationship with Maya and any inherent threats that may come with it cannot possibly come close to the dangers I've seen and faced. You do not have a fucking clue, Liv."

I took a deep breath. Olivia seemed small under the wrath of my words. But her jaw was set firmly, determination still lingering there.

"She's the reason why you were there," she said, her voice low.

I clenched my teeth, forcing myself to take a minute so I wouldn't lash out again. I kept my voice steady but clear. "That's where you're wrong. I joined the Army to get the fuck away from them and make a life that wasn't dependent on every door they opened."

"We both did." Darren took a small step forward.

If anyone knew where I was coming from, he did.

I halted my pacing and stood in front of her again. "Listen carefully. The place will not be ready for Christmas. Beyond that and more importantly, I'm not ready. We'll get together when the time is right, but you deal with them. You made this mess, you fix it. Tell them we have other plans, or whatever. I don't honestly care what you tell them, but it's not happening until I'm good and goddamn ready to see them."

"When will that be? It's been nearly a year."

"I'll let you know."

MAYA. The week seemed short and long all at once. The days ran into each other. I couldn't remember being this taxed since maybe finals week in college.

The non-stop work was energizing in its own way though. Working side-by-side with Jia had been eye opening. I may have seen a softer side to her, among others, but when it came to work, she was ruthless. She was appropriately polite, mainly to her peers and the higher ups like Dermott, but she didn't linger on niceties. She took command over the aspects of the deal that fell into our laps, and as soon as we worked through them, we tackled more and expanded our reach and dominance over what was happening until it became clear that we were both pivotal in its completion.

Dermott's jerk tendencies had lessened significantly, and I caught knowing looks from Jia from time to time. She must have recognized the change. If she'd planned things to play out this way, she'd done a marvelous job. I still hated him, but he'd become much more tolerable, especially considering how much time we'd spent working together lately.

As thrilling as the new possibilities at work might have been, I was exhausted. Another long day crept into the night. My eyes were fatigued from staring between a computer screen and the spreadsheets for hours, and I would have killed for some fast food. I'd texted Cameron earlier, begging him to bring me some when the group dispersed for dinner.

"Let's break for dinner," Dermott finally said.

Jia rose next to me. "Sounds good. You hungry, Maya?"

"Famished, but Cameron was going to swing by. He's been waiting for me to get a break."

"Sure. You want us to bring you back anything?"

"No, thanks. He's bringing me something."

She leaned down, speaking quietly so only I could hear her. "You can use my office."

My eyebrows shot up.

"We'll be gone at least an hour. I'll make sure of it." She winked and nodded for the other men to join her as she led the way out of the conference room.

I waited a few minutes until they'd gone before venturing into the reception area. Cameron was reading one of the dull financial magazines they offered. A black V-neck sweater accentuated the firm muscles of his arms and chest, revealing the well above his collarbone. I compulsively wanted to lick it, all the way up his neck and... *Shit.* I felt the familiar twinge low in my belly. My gaze wandered lower. His jeans strained against his thighs, his long legs outstretched in front of him.

I tore myself away from trying to name all the muscle groups under his clothing and locked in his cool blue stare. My stomach leaped, and I recognized that under the fatigue and the hunger, I really had missed him, every gorgeous inch of him.

After our emotionally charged last meeting, I was eager to smooth over the rough edges from our conversation. We'd both hurled some rough words at each other. He'd hurt me, and I'd landed a few too. Maybe we were saying things we'd wanted to say for a long time. Now they were out there. He still wanted me, despite all my faults. I still wanted him, despite our painful history. Just as I was ready to start over, the deal at work had taken over every spare minute of my life.

Seeing him now was a reward in a class of its own. I smiled at the new feeling of him being mine. He stood when I approached. I pressed up on my toes and kissed him. My stomach growled on cue.

"Tell me you brought me dinner."

"I did." He held up a brown paper bag, suspiciously

void of fast food branding or grease saturation.

I wrinkled my nose, suspicious. "Come on. We can eat in Jia's office."

He frowned slightly. "Jia?"

I ignored the embarrassing remembrance of our indiscretion and hooked my arm in his, leading him through the office and into Jia's smaller one. I shut the door and locked it behind us.

"What did you bring me? Something good, I hope."

"A sandwich that will change your life. All organic."

I rolled my eyes and groaned. "Oh my God. You're trying to kill me, aren't you?"

"You're going to like it. Stop complaining." He sat on the small couch in the corner of the office and I joined him.

No sandwich had come close to changing my life, and nothing organic had ever tasted as good as the processed full fat version. My stomach growled again as he pulled out two foil packages. Too hungry to argue, I unwrapped mine without any further assessment and took a big bite.

"Wow, this is actually really good." The sound was muffled through my chews, and I quickly covered my mouth with my hand. Chicken, avocado, some kind of sauce that was blowing my mind. I couldn't place it. I'd never been much of a culinary connoisseur.

"Told you." He smiled. He loved being right, I could tell. "How's work going?"

"We're getting close. We're going to wrap up early tomorrow anyway because of the party, so that'll be a good break. Are you still coming?"

"Are you asking me out on a date?"

I smiled. "Yes. I need reinforcements, anyway."

"I don't need to rough anyone up, do I?"

I laughed, swallowing the last bite of my sandwich and washing it down with one of the fruit juices he'd brought. "I hope not. Shouldn't be quite that bad. Although if Reilly lays into Vanessa in front of me one more time, I swear I'm going to deck that guy."

"Scary, but I can see you following through on that. You're so feisty now."

My face heated. The way he looked at me reminded me of a different person, someone innocent and still pretty scared of the world. I sat back on the couch. I closed my eyes and let my head roll back, a new wave of fatigue hitting me.

"Where'd you go?"

I lifted my gaze.

"I was joking, but you got all quiet on me. Did I say something awful again and not realize it?"

"No." I caught his hand. "I don't know. Sometimes when I'm around you, I get glimpses of how my life used to be. People change. It's inevitable. Sometimes it makes me sad, though."

"What makes you sad about it?"

"I was kind of naïve back then, in a lot of ways, but there were possibilities. I felt like the whole world was open to us, you know? Life wasn't always perfect, but in some ways it was."

"I feel that way too."

"What if we can't get that back?" I drew faint circles in his hands, over the rough calluses on his palms. " What if I'm not what you really want, because I'm so far from the person I used to be?"

He hooked an arm around my hips and scooted me

onto his lap.

"You're everything I want, okay?" He toyed with a strand of my hair. "You surprise me, and I like that. Just because we've changed doesn't mean we're any less good for each other. We've both lived a lot since then. Give us time to figure it out before you go thinking the worst, okay?"

I feathered my hands over his chest, over the broad curves of his muscular body. He mesmerized me all over again. I'd lived enough and seen enough these past few years to believe no one could really get under my skin anymore. I'd never been so wrong.

CAMERON. Her hand curved behind my neck and her tongue breached my lips. Her need passed into me with every soft touch. Every tiny lick and nibble was met with more wanting, a flame aglow that had grown in heat and intensity since we'd been together last.

My arms tightened around her. My tongue sought hers, delving deep, kissing hard, probing into the wet depths of her mouth. She moaned quietly, tightening her grip on my hair. I let my hands wander, over her ass and thighs, over the sheer dark fabric of her blouse where her nipples jutted out. I let the point slide over my palm as I cupped her breast through the thin barrier of her bra and clothing. She shifted her bottom against my lap, increasing the pressure on my cock.

Already, wildly erotic visions of what I could do to her passed through my mind. I was vaguely aware of their inappropriateness given our current setting, but I missed her so much it hurt.

My body ached to be with her. That much was certain. But something happened to my heart when she was with me, pressed close the way she was now. Some chemicals were likely firing off in my brain, reminding me what real happiness felt like. Happiness, bliss even, seemed to find its way to me when we were together, in the peaceful pockets of time when we weren't fighting or driving each other crazy rehashing the past and the terms of our future. Now that I'd explained I wasn't going to negotiate anymore when it came to our relationship, I hoped the peace would replace the tug of war of finding my way back to her heart.

I drew a hard line with my fingertips up between her thighs, finding her most sensitive spot through her pants. The repetitive motion elicited a gasp. Her lips left mine suddenly, parted with jagged breaths.

With restless hands, she grabbed at the bottom of my shirt. "Take this off."

Her eagerness was seriously affecting my ability to think clearly. "Are you sure?"

"Do it."

I pulled it off. When I could see again, she'd slipped off my lap and onto her knees on the floor in front of me. Her hands slid up the inside of my thighs over my jeans, cupping over my semi-hard cock. I blew out a slow breath, struggling to regain control over my brain and better judgment.

"This probably isn't a good idea. Anyone could walk in."

"The door is locked. Plus, that sandwich didn't quite hit the spot."

She licked her lips seductively, and my balls ached in

response.

"What are you saying?"

"I want you in my mouth. I've been thinking about it all day. Indulge me."

"Christ. When you put it that way, how am I supposed to say no?"

"Don't." She lowered her head, trailing hot breathy kisses along my erection that warmed through my jeans. I ground my teeth, losing my resolve.

She had my belt undone and jeans unzipped a second later. I lifted as she pulled them down just enough to free my cock. Circling it with her hand, she stroked gently. Her other hand moved higher, over my stomach and the muscles that tightened in anticipation.

She flicked tiny licks across the head. Her skin flushed and her lips shone as they spread over me. I was already hard, but my cock grew as it disappeared from view into the hot silk of her mouth.

I exhaled sharply, withholding a string of curses at the sensation.

She took more of me with each stroke, gentle grasps becoming firmer, drawing me up with her mouth and hands. Each motion, every expert flourish of her tongue brought me closer to the edge.

She released me suddenly, her hand replacing the pattern of her mouth. Her lips were swollen and her breaths came hard. Her eyes gleamed, reflecting our desire.

"Everything okay?"

"You're just so fucking impressive. Your body, everything."

A stupid grin split my face. I laughed quietly. "I'm

not sure what's swelling faster, my dick or my ego."

She smirked. "I think I know."

She disappeared behind a sweep of hair as she lowered over me again. She was everywhere, her hand stroking the base of me as I shafted her mouth. Her tongue did something crazy that I couldn't completely identify. The slow graze of her teeth put me on edge. Then a hard suck, over and over, until I knew I couldn't take much more.

"Fuck. Like that, baby."

I groaned, fisting my hand in her hair, guiding her motions now. I wanted to throw my head back, close my eyes against the heightened sensations, but I was transfixed on her. I pushed her hair back, wanting to see her face. I couldn't leave the sight of her and the selfless carnal way she was pleasing me.

She gently dug her nails into my thigh, and I arched into her mouth. When my head hit the back of her throat, I lost all control. My abdomen and thighs clenched almost painfully. My hips seized with the force of the climax. I released into her mouth, now soft and accommodating. I leaned back, holding my head in my hands, dizzy in the sudden darkness. Her tongue slid gently over my head, the light touch enough to jolt through me.

I leaned forward, caught her arms, and urged her up beside me. Her movements didn't stop then. She spread soft kisses across my shoulder, my neck, her tongue sliding over my skin the same way it'd just tantalized me before.

I pulled back, desperate to stop the reeling in my mind.

"Stop. I seriously can't take it. You're driving me crazy."

She laughed quietly. "Best blow job ever?"

I leaned my head back, still struggling to catch my breath. "Definitely. You fucking own me."

Her lips turned up into a pleased smile, delight glittering in her eyes. She had the appearance of a smug feline. I pulled her tight to my side, our lips nearly touching. I slid my hand between her thighs again. She brushed me away.

"Let me touch you. I want to see you come."

She touched a finger to my lips. "Tomorrow."

"I can't wait that long."

"Yes, you can. Tomorrow, I promise, you can make me come all you want."

CHAPTER FOURTEEN

CAMERON. She'd lied. *Tomorrow* was eaten up with another long workday that stole her from me. We'd agreed to meet at the Christmas party, but at the last minute, I decided I wasn't having that. I needed to see her before sharing her attentions with a group of stuffy strangers.

Eli opened the door and met me with wide-eyed surprise. "Hey, Cameron. She's in there getting ready." He motioned to the bedroom.

A quiet surge of satisfaction went through me as I passed into her bedroom. Fucking finally. Maya stood in front of a long mirror on the wall, in her partially zipped up cocktail dress. She stared at me in the reflection of her dresser mirror as she put her earrings in.

"What are you doing here? I thought we were meeting there?"

I tossed my coat onto the bed and came up behind her.

"Not my style. Plus, I wouldn't want anyone to think you were just using me as your stand-in boyfriend to help increase your chances for a promotion."

Her red lips curled into a smile. "That begs the question. What do we call you? I'll likely have to introduce you to a few people."

I traced my index finger down her back and over the clasp of her bra, only a little tempted to unhook it. I was early, after all.

"Let's see. How about impressive? I like the sound of that. Of course, I was having some pretty intense thoughts about your lips when the words came through them."

I bent to her, pressing a kiss to her neck. Her quickened pulse flickered under my lips. The floral scent of her perfume filled my lungs, a dizzying potent aroma that brought back so many memories. She shivered under my touch, the small reaction tempting me further.

I straightened, reminding myself not to get too far ahead of myself. "Want me to zip you?"

"Please."

I obliged, regretting that we weren't moving in the other direction. She spun to face me. Her gaze darted over me, her lips parting slightly.

"You look good too," I murmured, having a strong sense of our mirrored appreciation of each other tonight. "Delectable actually." I leaned into kiss her, but she evaded me.

"You're going to get me all wound up before we even get out the door."

"Fine by me," I muttered, unable to keep my hands from exploring every curve of her body over the satin of her dress. She caught my roaming hands, but I only pulled her closer, eliminating any doubt as to the effect she had on my body.

"Seriously, what are we calling you?" The words wavered as she spoke them.

I traced a faint line across her cheek and down her jaw. "I think boyfriend will do for now."

My eyes fixed on her plump pink lips and the wicked things she could do with her mouth. I traced the lower curve. At the sight of her tongue's movement, impulsively I pushed my finger inside. Her lips closed around me, her tongue laving over the sensitive pad before giving it a hard suck.

My grip on her tightened, my arousal pressed fiercely into her hip. "Fuck me, how long is this thing?"

She hummed, her mouth curving into a grin as I retreated. "A few hours, max."

"I'll be counting down the minutes until you're under me."

"Eager, are we?"

"That's simply not the right word."

"Desperate?"

"Possibly."

"And what are you desperate for?" she whispered, brushing her lips against mine.

Fucking hell. She was going to regret asking me that.

I kissed her hard, delving into her mouth, mimicking the motions I wanted to lavish upon her elsewhere.

"I'll tell you exactly what I want. I want you dripping wet, in my mouth, coming until you think you can't come anymore."

"Oh," she breathed, her chest laboring for air.

"Then you're going to beg me to fuck you."

She closed her eyes, biting her lip. Her hips shifted restlessly.

"Hard and repeatedly." I growled. "I didn't nearly get my fill of you the other night. We have catching up to do."

She exhaled sharply. Her once steady gaze now clouded with the animal need that pulsed through me too.

"Promise?" Her lip quivered slightly as the word left her.

"I can't promise I won't take you right here and now unless you get us out of here and save me from myself."

MAYA. He steered the SUV casually with one hand and kept another firmly on my thigh, tracing the sensitive skin above my knee.

I flexed my fingers, rubbing them nervously against the smooth leather seat. I tried to focus on the road ahead, the ebb and flow of evening traffic. They did little to block out the visions his dirty promises conjured. I'd been trembling I wanted him so badly, but at least he'd had the strength to get us moving.

He'd taken my breath away by merely entering the room. Dressed in a black suit, he was irresistible in a whole new way. Now I fought the little voice inside my head proposing we turn around, skip the party, and go straight to bed. Dermott would have my ass if I even considered it, and somewhere I remembered I would be letting Jia down too, after all she'd done for me.

"Are you nervous?"

"Maybe, a little," I admitted. I'd never come to these

things with any intention other than to chat with the few people I already knew. I'd never considered it a networking event with opportunities for advancement.

"Are you worried about me being there with you?"

"No, I'm glad you're going. I wasn't lying about needing reinforcements." The thought of having him by my side was reassuring, even though he'd likely feel more out of place than I usually did.

"You'll do fine." He gave my knee a little squeeze.

We pulled up to the hotel awning, and the valet helped us out. The ballroom was already filled with hundreds of people. I hoped to spot a friendly face when I saw Vanessa speaking heatedly to someone who appeared to be part of the hotel staff.

Her countenance became friendly when we approached. "You came!" She pulled me into a small hug and gave Cameron a kiss on the cheek.

"How's everything going?"

"Good so far, I think."

Before I could ask her anything else, Jia slid up beside me.

"Maya." She leaned in and air-kissed my cheek. "You look amazing."

The relief of seeing her among the crowd dissipated when I remembered the last time Cameron had seen us together. I tensed under both their gazes. Jia glanced expectantly up to Cameron whose tall frame towered over us. Somehow he looked even more imposing and impressive in a suit, though deep down I knew it wasn't his style at all.

I cleared my throat, trying to find my voice. "Jia, this is Cameron. Um, my boyfriend. Cameron, Jia is one of the VPs in my office." The last bit of information was unnecessary, but I wanted the introduction to sound more formal somehow. Christ, this was awkward.

Jia held out a hand and shook his. "Cameron, it's a pleasure."

Cameron's jaw twitched as he nodded wordlessly.

"Would you mind if I stole Maya from you?" His eyebrows shot up.

She hooked her elbow into mine with a smile. "We have some mingling to do."

Cameron looked to me, as if for the okay to release me into her custody. I gave a reassuring smile.

"I'll be at the bar if you need me."

I squeezed his hand slightly before Jia pulled me away, effectively breaking our contact and launching me into the activity of the party.

"Champagne?" She caught a flute from a passing tray.

"No, thanks. I'm fine."

"You sure? You seem nervous."

"I am a little, but I'm fine." Tossing one back would help my nerves considerably, but I needed to stay straight tonight. My willpower was on track, and I had Jia to help me through this.

"So Cameron? You're official now?"

I fidgeted nervously with my clutch. "Yeah, I guess so. We're figuring things out."

She took a slow sip from her glass and glanced back at the bar where he stood, his broad back to us. I sighed inwardly at the thought of taking that suit off of him tonight, revealing the man beneath.

"He's a little intense."

"He can be," I said. I liked it, though. I craved it.

When he looked at me, as if he were looking straight into my soul, nothing else mattered. No one had ever seen me the way Cameron had, known me the way he did. No one.

CAMERON. Maya moved from group to group, Jia by her side. I knew nothing about this world, but I hoped for Maya's sake that all was going well. Her work didn't seem to make her very happy, but perhaps that could change with the right connections. I turned back to the bar, regretting that Jia might be one of those connections. Something about the woman turned me. Her sharp brown eyes seemed to quietly assess me each time we met, like she was trying to figure me out. Wisely, Maya didn't speak of her much, but I knew they were spending more and more time together at work.

I heard a woman's sultry voice behind me. "Cam."

I turned. Jia greeted me with a slanted smile.

"Jia." I regarded her coolly. "Where's Maya?"

"Talking to some people. I thought I'd give her a few minutes to fly solo."

She canted her head at me. My skin crawled. Maybe I shouldn't have disliked her as much as I did. Then again, last time I'd seen her, she'd nearly had her tongue down Maya's throat.

"Maya looks beautiful tonight," she purred, glancing over her shoulder.

She did, her pale skin glowing against the black satin of her dress. Jia turned back, her gaze traveling over me suggestively. I shifted my weight, wishing she'd leave. I didn't know anyone here, but she wasn't exactly what I would consider a friendly face.

"You clean up nice too, Cam."

She traced a finger along the lines of my jacket. I resisted the urge to brush her hand away, reaching instead for my glass to take a deep swallow of the amber liquid. Maya didn't need any drama tonight. I had promised to be supportive.

"Did you have fun the other night?"

I shrugged. "Can't say I'd do it again."

"No? You two left early. That couldn't have been all bad."

I avoided her eyes, unwilling to take the bait.

"We should go out sometime, the three of us. It'd be fun."

Her lips curled into a seductive smile, her tongue wetting her lower lip. The gesture fueled the growing irritation I felt in her presence.

"What are you two doing later?"

I took a deep breath, wondering how long this line of questioning was going to last. "Going back home, I imagine."

"I live close by. You two should come by for a drink."

I narrowed my eyes at her. "No thanks."

She leaned in closer, and her perfume wafted over me. "You don't need to pretend with me, Cam," she whispered, brushing the side of her body against me gently.

From the outside, her proximity might have seemed normal, casual even, but everything about the way she moved around me seemed charged with intent.

"Whatever you're implying, Jia, I'm not interested,

and neither is Maya. I can assure you."

She cocked her eyebrow and glanced back to Maya. "I'm not so sure about that. She might be a little more curious than you give her credit for. Could be fun."

I tensed. I couldn't care less how anyone's sexual orientation fell, but I'd be damned if I was going to share Maya's affections, or body, with anyone. Jia could paint a picture that would be anyone's fleeting fantasy, but I'd be the only one in Maya's bed.

She slid her hand up my arm, squeezing me slightly. "Relax. You're overanalyzing this. You could do whatever you wanted with us. Have us both or just watch. Wouldn't you like to watch another woman make her come?"

I would have dragged Jia out of here by her hair if the thought of being jealous of another woman making advances on the girl I loved hadn't struck me as too odd to act on. I drew a slow breath, gathering my self-control. I wanted nothing more than to shove her off and take Maya back home, so I could show her again exactly how I'd be the only one to please her.

"I appreciate the offer, Jia, but with all due respect, that's never going to fucking happen."

She laughed quietly. "I'm not a threat, you know. You're taking it too seriously."

I straightened, facing her fully, so she'd understand that I wasn't remotely susceptible to her feminine wiles. "You want to fuck my girlfriend. I'm taking that seriously. But Maya thinks of you as a friend, so I'm going to say this politely, *once*. Put the idea right out of your head or—"

"Or what?"

I breathed through my teeth, suppressing a growl. "I'm sure there are people here who'd be interested to know what you're trying to do."

She narrowed her eyes at me, the sultry softness of her posture stiffening slightly.

"No need to make idle threats, Cameron. I get it." Her throat worked on a swallow as she glanced down at her champagne flute. "You're possessive, and rightly so. She's lovely. I can see that she's special to you."

"You're right about that. She's very special to me, but I'm not making idle threats."

"Who's making threats?"

Maya joined us, distracting the laser focus I'd had on making my point to Jia. Maya frowned, looking between the two of us. No one looked too pleased, but of course she was none the wiser as to why.

Jia plastered on a more genuine smile. "I was just asking Cameron if you'd like to have drinks later, but it sounds like you two have plans. Anyway, it's just as well. I have to catch up with some people. You two enjoy yourselves. I'll see you tomorrow." She leaned in and kissed Maya quickly on the cheek, flashing a sly glance my way before disappearing into the crowd.

I clenched my teeth and fought the urge to take Maya into my arms, the only place where I could keep her safe and out of reach of the people who only pretended to care.

"What the hell was that all about?"

"Let's get out of here. You made an appearance. They don't expect you to network all night, do they?" I wanted to get out of here before I actually made a scene. The lengths I was willing to go for her sake continued to surprise me. As much as I wanted to protect her, in the same breath I was perilously close to jeopardizing any progress she was hoping to make at work. The last thing I wanted was to become a hindrance in that part of her life—of any part of her life.

"Sure, we can go. Are you going to talk to me though?" Her beautiful features strained with concern as she brushed her fingertip over the frown that marred my brow.

I took a breath, willing myself to relax. I turned into her palm, kissing it gently and keeping her hand locked in mine. "We'll talk on the way home," I said, moving us toward the cloakrooms.

I didn't really want to get into the dirty details of Jia's proposal on the drive home, but the more time went by the more pissed I became. By the time we stepped into her apartment, my words came out more harshly than I'd wanted.

"That bitch is trouble."

Maya jolted, freezing in place while I paced the small path at the foot of her bed.

"Jia?"

"Yeah."

"You're upset because she invited us over for drinks?"

"She doesn't want drinks. She wants to orchestrate some sort of fuck fest between the three of us, and I'm not interested. You need to keep your distance from her."

"Oh?"

Her voice was quiet—too quiet. I came closer and took her hand, as if that would be some lifeline, some way for her to understand the reality of the situation without getting upset with me.

"She's manipulative. You can't trust her, Maya."

"How do you know?" She slipped out of my grasp, her eyes intent on me.

I shook my head, shoving my hands through my hair, wishing she could have seen the look in Jia's eyes when she made the offer. "I just know."

Maya shivered and took a step back, staring at her shoes.

"What's wrong? Are you cold?"

"You should go."

"Why?"

"I have a long day tomorrow. We need to finish this deal before the holiday if we can."

"The deal that Jia's managing."

She reached for my coat and handed it to me.

"Maya."

"Thank you for coming with me tonight. I appreciate your support. I really do."

I tossed the coat away and took a step closer, our bodies so close I could feel her warmth. She was flush against the wall now, trapped. Her frustration radiated, mixing with the sexual tension that was damn near palpable by now.

"You can't tell me what to do." The edge to her voice softened a bit.

"No?" I raised my eyebrows. When it came to Jia, I had different thoughts on the matter.

"All you've done since we've been together is tell me what to do, what not to do, and now you're telling me who I should be spending my time around. What makes you think I need someone like that in my life?"

"You need someone like that in your life because no one's telling you the truth. And when you do stupid shit, I'm going to call you out on it. If you want to call that me telling you what to do, fine. But I'm not going anywhere, and I think you know that."

Her glaze flickered to mine, and for a split second, I saw all of her vulnerability. The soft scared girl lingered for a moment before an impassive expression took over.

"I think you're forgetting who you're talking to."

"You're doing it again."

She frowned. "What?"

"Hiding," I murmured. I traced the hard line of her jaw, the pulse of her neck, cupping my hand behind her nape. She pulled it away, a new fire in her eyes. I caught her palm, pressing it firmly against the door, then the other as she reached to push me off.

She glared at me, her nostrils flaring. I fought the urge to smile. She was so easy to rile these days. Despite the firm set of her perfectly pink mouth, her chest heaved. Her eyes shifted restlessly over me. Our lips nearly touched. My fire matched hers now, stoked with frustration and the need to fuck her, to possess her. I held her gaze, daring her to look away, to hide.

"So defiant."

"Never what you expect."

"No," I admitted. "I wasn't expecting fighting with you to turn me on, either." I licked my lips, eager to taste her. But I held back, prolonging our stay in this tense middle ground.

"If fighting with me turns you on, then we have a serious problem."

I smiled and released her from my hold, gliding my

hands down the sides of her body and curving them over her ass. "Agreed. Then again, you could always put that spark to good use." I pressed us closer.

"You should go," she breathed, her eyes closing.

She could have said *fuck me now* for all the strength her words held.

"I made promises. I intend to keep them." I caught her thigh, hooked it over my hip, and pressed her against the wall with a quiet thud. She gasped, her hands fisting in my shirt. I bridged the small space between us, sealing my mouth to hers. Our tongues tangled in a heated rush. I could taste her fire, the white-hot desire between us. I lifted her, wrapped her legs around my waist, and carried her to the bed.

CHAPTER FIFTEEN

MAYA. He'd stripped us down in seconds, sinking me onto the bed beneath him. He rested his hard body between my legs. His caresses were firm, almost calculating, and so slowly rendered that they filled me with an intoxicating anticipation. His lips teased a slow path across my skin.

Goddamn it, he owned me too. I loved him and fucking hated him, how he never gave me the room I needed to run. I grasped feebly at his shoulders, pushing him away and pulling him to me at once.

He moved over me, undeterred. Skin against skin, he worked me over with his tongue, his lips, and the edge of his teeth until I was trembling, mindless with all the ways I wanted him.

"Beautiful…perfect."

The love in his eyes when he said the words gutted me. The lusty rasp in his voice had me desperate, as desperate as he'd been earlier.

"And mine. You're mine. Every feisty inch of you." His fingertips dug into my ass, grinding my sex against his cock.

"Stop." I pushed at him again. His words were killing me.

"Never stopping." He dropped his lips to mine again, nibbling and sucking my lower lip. "Never leaving."

The thought of him leaving cut through me, an old wound exposed. Everything wanted to pour out of me when he said things like that. I wrapped my arms around him, trapping him against me.

"I don't want to think about any of that. The things you say... I can't handle it."

His caresses slowed as I spoke. "I can't tell you you're beautiful? That I love you so much it hurts?"

Fucking hell. I squeezed my eyes closed.

"Just...just want me, Cam. It doesn't have to be about our past or how we feel."

He paused. "Are you trying to tell me to shut up and fuck you?"

I held my breath at the crude delivery, my body arching into his infinitesimally, a silent answer. "Something like that." A jagged breath left me.

Is that what I wanted? Something that meant a little less, so my heart didn't explode from everything he was telling me right now? I tightened the hook of my leg around his hip, urging him to me.

His body was frozen against mine. Hesitation and lust swam in his eyes. Yes. I wanted raw and intense. I wanted to be fucked, to disappear in the blinding surge of sensation that I'd known not so long ago.

"I'll fuck you, Maya. Within an inch of your life if

that's what you want, but you need to know there's more between us than that. I've lived that kind of life, believe me. A warm body is just that, a warm loveless body. You'll never be that for me."

His lips feathered over the wild beating of my chest, my heart pounding against its walls. I blocked out the sounds. My jagged breathing. My heart. His voice.

"I'll take your body, but I want your heart, Maya."

My nipples tightened, grazing against the hard planes of his chest as he slid lower, his arms tightening around my waist. He lashed the hardened tips of my nipples with his tongue, his eyes holding my gaze seductively. His heated breaths tantalized my wet flesh. He placed an open mouthed kiss on my belly, pinpointing the enflamed coil that tightened there. Heat shot through me and I wanted him everywhere at once. Over me, inside me, fiercely taking me until I lost all sense of myself, until I forgot what those words meant.

As if in reply to my silent longing, he grabbed my hip, jerking me lower until he hovered over me. I went wet at the hint of his strength. God, the things he could do to me.

I lifted my hips until the heat of his condom-clad erection slid between the slick folds of my sex. I closed my eyes, clenching my jaw, the tension seizing all of my senses. "Now, Cameron."

"Look at me."

My eyes flew open at the sharp command of his voice. Before I could speak he drove into me so suddenly that I whimpered at the fullness. I opened my mouth but words caught. He took my nape with his other hand, leveraging my body so firmly that when he thrust again, I swore he hit the very end of me.

"Is this what you want?"

"Yes." I gasped, sucking in a sharp breath as I tightened.

"Every inch of me driving into you?"

"Oh God," I moaned. I wrapped my legs around his strong thighs as if I could possibly control his strength with my own. The first of what was sure to be many orgasms took its hold, the slow ember of desire now a wild heat rushing over me as he powered into me.

"I'll fuck you this way until you beg me to stop. I'll make you scream, and you'll feel the memory of me inside you tomorrow. Is that what you want?"

"Yes… yes…" The slow tremble that vibrated through me transformed into a violent shuddering at the uncensored promises falling from his beautiful lips. My physical reaction was answer enough. I kept my gaze trained on his, but struggled to maintain the contact as he found an intense rhythm that was quickly short-circuiting my ability to think beyond my instincts.

He kissed me passionately, tenderness giving way to an urgent fucking of my mouth. I gripped his hair tightly, arching in time with his violent undulations.

"This is me, Maya. Fucking you, loving you."

He lifted my hips a few inches off the bed, driving into me at an angle that had the room spinning. I cried out, dragging my nails down his arm, unable to control the climax that had taken me over, heart, mind and soul. Our bodies melded together, my pussy tightened down on him. I clung to him, my hands slipping against the sweat on his skin.

I couldn't let go, every part of me entwined with

him. He kept on, burying himself deeply one last time with a strangled groan, my name on his lips. The sound echoed off the walls, disappearing like the lightening of our release.

I shivered at his breath on my neck, the aftershocks of the orgasm flitting through me with the slow return to coherent thought. That had been intense, but he'd certainly delivered on his earlier promise.

He kissed me softly, brushing the hair back from my face.

"Tell me you love me, Maya."

My jaw tightened. The words rooted in my gut somewhere, tied up by all the confused emotions surrounding our new relationship. I wanted to tell him, but even in this warm post-coital bliss, something held me back. Pride, maybe. Saying it meant forgiving everything he'd put me through, handing over my heart for real. Fully entrusting him with it again. In a way, I already had, but I needed to be able to hold something back, even if it was those three little words.

He held me in his gaze, his blue eyes tired and full of emotion. "Why can't you say it?"

I relaxed back into the bed, running my finger along the stubble of his jaw.

"Answer me."

"I'm not ready." No words were truer. I wasn't sure when I would be, but I couldn't give in to his simple request.

He brushed his thumb over my lips. "How about I make love to you until you do?"

My lips went dry, and I licked them. He captured one, sucking it into his mouth, nipping and soothing until I moaned. I tightened my hold around him, and he kissed me deeper, like he was pouring every ounce of love he felt into me.

CAMERON. She'd already left for work when I woke up. I put my suit back on and found my way into the living room. Eli poked his head out from the kitchen.

"Hey." He waved.

"Sorry, I was just leaving."

"You want some coffee?"

I hesitated, unsure whether I wanted to risk a post-mortem with her roommate. He seemed good-natured but Maya was giving me enough grief. Coffee sounded good though, and necessary. I'd kept us up most of the night. My body and brain were sluggish, but not enough to regret it.

"Sure, that'd be great actually."

I tossed my coat down on a chair while Eli tinkered in the kitchen.

My gaze caught on the black notebook resting on the bookshelf. I remembered the way Maya had grabbed it from the table, holding it close to her chest like something precious. Eli appeared beside me then with a large steaming mug.

"Thanks, man."

"Sure. I figure we all need a little boost this morning."

I rubbed my forehead. "Uh, yeah, sorry." The apartment was small, and I had little doubt we'd kept Eli up too. I'd gotten all manner of dirty words pouring from Maya's lips last night and into the morning except the one admission I'd really wanted from her. God, was she obstinate.

"Whatever." He shrugged and settled back onto the couch. "Things getting serious with Maya, I take it?"

I moved my coat and sat down in the chair. The steam rose in tiny billows from my cup, disappearing into the air. How could I answer that?

"Getting there. She sure as hell doesn't make it easy."

Eli smirked. "She's a pain in the ass."

"You're not kidding."

"You love her though."

"I'd like to think that was enough. She's..." I blew out a breath. "I have no idea what the hell goes on in that mind of hers, Eli. I thought I knew her. I did. I mean, I knew her. Inside and out. The looks, the gestures, I could read her like a book. That's not all gone, but this fucking warped philosophy she has on relationships is all new."

Eli took a sip of his coffee and regarded me silently.

"She's been through a lot."

I nodded. Eli would have known the whole story. Hell, he probably knew more than I did. Who was I to complain? I'd created this whole damn mess.

"No need to remind me. I put her through hell and I probably deserve all of this."

"Maybe you do, but maybe you both deserve a chance to make this work again. If you can figure out how to make that happen without hurting her again, you have my blessing. She's my best friend, and I can see that despite everything, she's happy with you. That's all I want. To see her happy."

"I'm trying. She doesn't make it easy."

Eli stood up and came closer. My grip tightened around the mug. I hoped he wasn't going to try to hug me or something. He leaned over and grabbed the notebook off the shelf. He handed it to me, his lips in a tight line.

"Tell her I gave it to you, I'll hunt you down, and they'll never find the body."

We shared a wordless stare before he disappeared into his bedroom. I set down the coffee cup and contemplated what I might find between the covers of the book. The notebook was light in my hands. Curiosity and pure desperation to find some clue to Maya's carefully guarded thoughts spurred me. Carefully I opened the book, flipping through the nearly filled pages. Page after page of words, poems, doodling. I closed it again.

I stood up and paced the room. If this were anything like a diary for Maya, what I was about to do was unconscionable. Could I do this? Maybe just one page... could one page tell me something? Anything about this woman I was falling hopelessly in love with again.

I sat back down. I finished my coffee and let the minutes pass. Finally I opened the book and began to read.

Yes.

Every day, no stone unturned
A promise of more
Happy days and long nights,
Of love and living,

If I'd said yes.

Picket fences, cherub faces,
every dream realized
if I'd said
yes.

Second chances play out in a dream,
because I couldn't
say yes.

With shaking hands I turned the page. There were dozens more. I could barely make out the words because the meaning behind the poem I'd read was swimming through my mind. *Jesus Christ.* I brought my hands to my face.

I'd spent days trying to dig deeper, to find out who Maya had become. A surge of hope spurred me on every time I got a hit, and now this. A fucking avalanche of feelings. And I wasn't reading into this. I'd spent the past several hours trying to fuck the feelings out of her, and this notebook held the truth. Some of it, most of it maybe.

I stood quickly, unable to speak or formulate a single coherent thought. How could I possibly after reading that? I paced the room, wishing Maya were here so I could hear the truth straight from her lips. Would she ever give me that much? I wanted to search those fathomless brown eyes for some acknowledgement of what this meant, of everything we ever felt that had gone unsaid. The dreams I'd only shared with her, the plans we'd made for our future that could only be realized with her, no one else.

I replaced the notebook on the shelf, grabbed my coat, and rushed down the stairs. Stepping outside, I relished the painful, sobering burn of the cold air filling my lungs. I looked in the direction of my apartment and took the first steps of what I knew would be a very long walk in the opposite direction.

MAYA. Tonight was Christmas Eve. The team had thinned out until only Dermott, Jia, and I remained. We'd finished, just under the wire. As much as the holiday didn't mean much to me, I'd hoped we could wrap up and finish early. I was exhausted and wanted to go home to Cameron. Last night had been intense. Exhausting and intense. We never used to fight, but this new version of us did. I fought and he fought harder. Then he silenced me with the kind of passion that I'd never known, the kind of wild crazy love that took us straight into the dawn. He was relentless, tireless, like he was breaking me down in his own way.

Whatever he was doing to me might have worked too. I couldn't think about anything else. He was like a really good drug that I'd had the good sense to stay away from until now. He was in my blood, and fuck if I didn't need him again already.

I sank back into the club chair in Dermott's office, trying not to think about how I'd rather be rushing back to see Cameron than taking a minute for a celebratory drink now that we'd finished.

"Scotch okay?"

Jia's lithe figure swayed toward the bar in Dermott's office.

"Sure." I sighed. I scanned the room, appraising the size and decor—dark woods, clean lines, and an impressive view of the glittering night sky. I tried to imagine myself here, sitting behind the enormous executive desk or looking out over New York from our forty-third floor vantage. I couldn't imagine it. Perhaps the prospect was simply too far from the reality I was living. It certainly didn't align with any dreams I'd had for my life before coming here.

Yet this was what I was working toward, wasn't it? Jia was, and she was taking me along with her. Would respect and a title make all this worth it? The long nights, the years of being passed over? My tired delusions about my professional future were interrupted when Jia lowered an engraved tumbler into my grasp. "Here, drink up."

"Thanks."

She stood across from me, leaned against Dermott's desk, and sipped her own. She seemed softer, younger. How, I wasn't sure, because we'd just wrapped up a marathon workday. She smiled as I assessed her silently. There may have been an inkling of mischief in her eyes, but I was probably seeing double at this point.

"Tired?"

I closed my eyes for a second. "Glad to be done, I suppose."

"Cheers to that." She raised her glass and I met it with a clink.

I took another slow sip, appreciating what I knew had come from an expensive bottle. I swallowed, savoring the smoky burn.

"You did great this week, by the way."

"Thanks, you too."

"I wasn't sure what to expect, but now that I've worked with you, I can see what an asset you'll be. I think everyone can see that now."

"You think so?" I beamed a little.

"Absolutely. And if they can't, I'll make certain they do."

"Thank you, Jia. This was an amazing opportunity. You went out of your way for me. I realize that, and I hope you know that I appreciate it."

"I'm happy to have done it. Perhaps you could return the favor sometime."

"Of course." To repay a gesture such as hers would go without saying. She'd taken a risk for me, not knowing me, and I would do whatever I could to do the same for her one day.

As I committed to that in my mind, Jia held out her hand to me. I hesitated. She curled her hand up toward her, urging me to take it. Once I did, she gave me an upward tug. I stood, taking an unsteady step closer until we faced each other.

"What?"

She hushed me, placing her finger on my lips.

"I want to finish what we started the other night."

My eyebrows shot up. Before I could speak, she moved closer, bringing her mouth to mine. Shocked by her boldness, my lips parted instantly to suck in a breath. She took the chance to kiss me deeper, seeking out my tongue with her own. Catching my cheek in her palm, she coaxed me closer still.

"What are you doing?" I gasped, breaking our

contact.

"I'm kissing you."

"I know. I'm not sure why."

"Because you're beautiful, and I'm attracted to you." She traced a line down the buttons of my blouse. "And Dermott wants to watch us."

I went wide-eyed, my heart racing with panic and confusion. I hoped I'd misheard her. "What?"

Her brow wrinkled. "Maya, do you want to be promoted?"

"Obviously."

"Then, relax." She started on the top button of my blouse. "We'll make it fun, okay?"

"Jia, I can't do this." I jolted back, out of her grasp. Her hands fell down.

"Is this about Cameron?"

I fumbled for an answer, thoughts whizzing through my mind. "Maybe."

"He never needs to know. Plus, you can't let him tell you what to do."

"This is insane. Kevin will be in here any minute."

"He will, and we're going to give him a good show. You'll like it, Maya. Then he'll do his thing, but don't worry, that never lasts too long. You'll be all blissed out from me making you come to even notice anyway." A dark smile curved her lips. "You do this and we might both get promotions."

"Are you fucking kidding me?"

She rolled her eyes, her sultry voice hardening again. "He's bored."

"He's *married*."

"Oh, who cares? You think half these guys don't fuck

around? Anyway, he's never seen two women together. We're hot, we like each other, and he gets off. Everyone wins. If we're lucky, he'll come in his hand before he can put it in either of us."

My mouth opened wordlessly.

"Ladies." Kevin's voice echoed through the room as he entered "Don't let me interrupt you." He closed the door behind him and loosened his tie, tossing it to the side. Undoing the first few buttons of his shirt, he sat leisurely on the adjacent chair. His legs were wide and casual, and he bit his lip. He gazed up at us with an obvious hunger. The sexual voyeur who I used to think of as my boss was now waiting with waning patience for Jia to start the show.

"Where do you want us, Kev?"

He nodded to the desk. "Right there. I want to fuck her on it after."

My heart beat rapidly, my head swimming in a sudden dizziness. This was too much. For starters, I wasn't drunk enough to remotely consider this. Secondly, this was my job, my livelihood we were talking about. I didn't gamble with that.

With no signs of hesitation, Jia started to unbutton her silk blouse while I tried to get a handle on the proposition she'd just landed on me. In a matter of moments she'd slipped off her skirt and stood before me, clad only in dark lavender lace under-things, her thighs decorated with lace topped stockings. She went for the buttons on my blouse again and pulled me into another kiss. Her lips were rougher, more demanding this time, blinding my ability to think clearly.

This wasn't happening. This could not possibly be

happening. Jia was beautiful, a friend, sexier than I'd given her proper credit for. Sure we'd had our moment at the club, but I hadn't really thought of her like this. We'd just been having fun before, but this was far beyond the boundaries of our friendship.

I darted my gaze around the room, wishing someone could save me from this totally fucked up situation. Dermott readjusted himself, his eyes never leaving us. A wave of nausea hit me. This was eleven shades of wrong. I tensed, resisting the urge to push her off of me even though that's all I could think of doing.

"What?" she whispered.

I shook my head slightly, hoping the motion was imperceptible to Dermott. She hushed me again, her frown disappearing with a slow, sexy smile. She slid her hand between my legs and pressed against me through the fabric of my pants.

"I won't bite, I promise," she whispered.

I took a step back, leaving her at the desk. With shaking hands, I fumbled with my buttons, trying to pull myself back together.

"I'm sorry." I shook my head. I couldn't find the words to say anything else. I turned and left. Rushing toward my cubicle, I struggled with the last buttons on my blouse. The office was empty except for the cleaning crew that hadn't made its way to our part of the floor yet.

I went to my office to grab my purse and stopped suddenly when Cameron was sitting at my desk. He was doodling on a notepad, his legs outstretched, filling up the small workspace with his large frame.

He looked up with a bright smile that quickly faded as he assessed me. A second later Dermott was there, unaware of Cameron's presence. He looked irritated and somehow determined. Before he could speak, Cameron rose.

"What's going on here?" Cameron's voice barely hid a rage that I sensed was growing rapidly below the surface.

Dermott straightened. Cameron was wearing a thermal henley that highlighted the strength of his chest. A detail that was no doubt noted as Dermott quickly recovered himself.

"Nothing at all," he rushed. "Maya, I just wanted to let you know that there may be a few minor details left on the documents that we need to clear up tomorrow. I'll email you if anything comes up."

I stared at him, nodding slightly. Was I going to play along with this? Dermott turned back and disappeared into the darkness toward his office where Jia was probably still getting dressed. Or not. A wave of guilt hit me that I'd left her there to fend for herself.

I fastened the last button on my blouse, threw on my coat, and reached around Cameron to grab my purse.

"You want to explain what the fuck is going on?" His jaw worked, and his eyes were wide with the anger that rolled off of him now.

"Let's get out of here." My voice was quiet, hiding the embarrassment of being caught in the midst of this totally fucked up situation.

We hadn't left the block before he stopped us. He turned to face me, leveling his eyes with mine.

"Talk. Now. I need to know what the fuck went down in there."

I searched for the right words, failing because I was still trying to figure it all out myself. I hated how it looked on the outside. He was obviously furious. I had no hope of explaining this one away as a non-sexual late night rendezvous.

I eyed him warily. He looked even bigger and broader in his coat. If I didn't love him so much, his sheer size might scare the hell out of me.

"It was nothing," I insisted.

"Like hell." His breaths came slow, billowing in the cold air. "You need to tell me what the hell happened in there before I lose my fucking mind."

I sighed, looking around nervously. I didn't want to have this conversation with him, now or ever. I wanted to pretend this whole thing had never happened. I squeezed my eyes closed and decided to go with the truth.

"Jia came onto me."

When I opened my eyes, a confused grimace pinched his features. "Jia? I don't understand."

"She and Dermott wanted me to…" I shook my head, trying to shake off the uncomfortable new memory. "I don't know. Let's talk about this later, please."

"No. Why was your shirt unbuttoned?"

I threw my hands up. "She unbuttoned it!"

"You didn't say no?" He shoved his hands through his hair, his jaw working anxiously.

"Well, not right away. I didn't know what the hell was happening! She kissed me out of the blue. I was confused."

"Did you enjoy it?"

I gasped. "What kind of question is that?"

"I don't know. Are you, like, a lesbian?"

"Oh my God, did you get concussed in the military? Kissing a girl doesn't make me a lesbian. I was stunned by

235

what was happening. Not like I fucked her. Jesus."

"Would you have?"

"Did I? I ran out of there and the decision, which wasn't really a decision, probably cost me my job. I'll be shocked if I don't have a pink slip on my desk when I go back next week. Why were you there anyway?"

"It's Christmas Eve. I thought you'd finish up early and we could get dinner. I guess that's shot."

I dropped my head in my hands, exhaustion taking hold over my mind and my body at once. "I'm sorry you had to see any of that. I have no idea what to make of it. Dermott..." I groaned and fought the surge of panic that welled at the very real possibility that I could lose my job over this debacle.

"Dermott, your boss?"

"Yeah."

His eyes narrowed and his breathing slowed, the overall effect being predatory, and not in the seductive way I loved. I dropped my hands in my coat pockets, glad I could hide the dampness accumulating in my palms. The whole situation was wreaking havoc on my nerves.

"So if Jia was unbuttoning your shirt, what was he doing?"

I tapped my foot roughly against the pavement. I hated this. I hated everything about this conversation. No matter how I relayed the truth, he'd be furious, with them and very likely me too. No one was good enough for Cameron, not even me.

"Maya. Talk. Now."

"He watched," I blurted. "Until I ran out. Everything happened really quickly. They had this planned out, and

I think I ruined it. Maybe...maybe she thought I was going to be more receptive to something like that because of that night at the club. I don't know. She said if I did it, we'd both get promotions."

I laughed at the incredulous notion that I'd fuck a friend on my boss's desk for a promotion. Heaven help me.

"Mother fucker." The muscles in his jaw bulged and he pivoted in the opposite direction.

"No, no. Stop."

"I'm teaching that asshole a lesson."

"Cameron, no!" I screamed.

He stopped, allowing me to circle in front of him. I put my trembling hands on the panels of his coat.

"If I don't lose my job over this, it'll be a small miracle. Let's not hasten the inevitable, okay? Let them fire me first, okay?"

"Did he touch you?"

"No, I promise. He never touched me. I ran out of there as soon as I figured out what was going on."

"Christ, Maya." He gritted his teeth and pulled away.

I weakened at the separation. The waves of his rage were rolling over me, crushing me. "Why are you angry with me? This wasn't my idea!"

"I warned you about her, for starters. Secondly, did it ever occur to you that drunkenly making out with someone from work might have perpetuated this?"

He held my gaze. Anger was there, but also disappointment. A sickness rooted in my gut as I followed his unspoken thoughts.

My lips tightened into a firm line and I avoided his eyes. Those eyes that crushed me with the simplest, purest

237

look of disdain. I inhaled a shaky breath, but it wasn't enough to restore what that look had taken away.

"It did not occur to me because I haven't had a moment to even make sense of it, and here you are, attacking me, turning this into something that's my fault."

I stepped away quickly and hailed an approaching cab.

"Where are you going?"

"I'm going home. Alone."

I hopped in, shut the door, and locked the door before he could reach for the handle.

"Drive," I ordered the cabbie.

"Where to?"

"Delaney's on Pearl."

CHAPTER SIXTEEN

CAMERON. I sat in the dark quiet of the room, listening to the seconds tick by on the new clock Olivia had hung on the wall. Everything was perfect, I guess. Furniture, fucking throw pillows, even art on the walls. Somewhere in Olivia's world, pleasing our parents still mattered this much.

It was past one o'clock in the morning. They'd descend on the house in a matter of hours, yet I couldn't bring myself to sleep. Maya had made it clear that she didn't want me coming after her. I'd promised not to let her run anymore, but the guilt had overrun the frustration. I'd reacted without giving it a second thought, without considering for a moment what all of it meant for her personally. I'd been a complete asshole for freaking out on her, for passing judgment too quickly. She'd already walked out on me for that before. Apparently I had to learn that lesson more than once.

I jerked when the phone rang. Maya's number came up.

"Maya?"

"It's Vanessa. Are you home?"

"Yeah, why what's up? Is everything okay?"

"It's Maya. She's..."

I stood quickly. "What's wrong?"

"She showed up at my apartment about twenty minutes ago. She nearly fell out of the cab. I'd have her stay here, Cameron, but my parents are going to be here in the morning. I just don't want her to be uncomfortable when she comes out of it. I'm sorry—"

"It's fine. Text me the address. I'll be there as soon as I can."

I hung up, rushed downstairs, and jumped into the SUV parked on the street.

When I arrived, Vanessa came out front to flag me down. She was in her pajamas, her arms wrapped around herself.

"Where is she?"

She led me inside and through a hall to a small bedroom. In it Maya was sprawled across the bedspread, passed out. Her face was obscured by the tangled mess of her hair. Her limbs were limp and outstretched in different directions.

"How much did she drink?"

Vanessa chewed her lip, her eyes never leaving Maya. "I'm not sure. She said she came from Delaney's. It's this bar near the office that she goes to sometimes."

"I've never heard of it."

"I doubt she'd bring you there. It's kind of a seedy joint. I wouldn't be surprised if they served her whatever she wanted for as long as she wanted. That could be a lot. She doesn't really know when to stop when she gets going."

"You think?" My voice was clipped, dripping with disappointment that she could allow her friend to carry on this way.

Her shoulders slumped a little, betraying her guilt. "I'm sorry for bothering you with this. Usually Eli is around to help, but he left town to visit his family. I didn't know who else to call."

"I'm glad you called. But what the fuck, Vanessa? How can you two watch her keep doing this and not say something?"

She crossed her arms, hugging her body. She avoided my eyes.

"This ends tonight."

Her gaze shot up to mine.

"If I find out she gets like this again with you or Eli, you will personally answer to me."

"I can't control how much she drinks. She's an adult."

"Then don't go out with her."

Not waiting for a response, I went to Maya. Unable to rouse her with words and determined nudging, I scooped her into my arms.

"Can you open the car for me?"

Vanessa nodded, moving quickly ahead to lead me out. I laid her down in the back seat, covered her with my coat, and switched the heat on high. Despite all the movement and negotiating her position, Maya never woke.

"Should I take her to the hospital? She's not

responsive at all." I held my hand over her heart. A steady beat matched the slow rhythm of her breath. At least she was breathing.

"I know this seems bad, Cameron, but I think she's okay. I mean, she'll feel like shit in the morning, but this isn't the first time this has happened."

"Apparently." I pushed down a host of other scathing remarks and shut the door. "Good night, Vanessa."

"Merry Christmas." Her voice was sad, with a hint of sarcasm that a little part of me appreciated. *Merry fucking Christmas.*

I drove to Maya's apartment. I carefully arranged her in my arms and managed to find her keys in her purse, gaining us entrance. Her body tensed as we entered her bedroom, and I thought I heard a moan muffled into my chest. I lowered her onto the bed and switched on the side lamp. She squinted, covering her eyes with her hands.

"Cam, is that you?"

"Yeah, it's me."

She rolled onto her side and hummed, a drunk happy sound. I undressed her, tugging her clothes off with all the finesse of a child undressing a ragdoll. Afterward, I stripped down to my boxers and slid into the bed beside her, pulling the blankets over us.

I brushed the hair back from her face. "You okay, baby?"

The slits of her eyes opened, seeming to focus on me. Confusion then recognition passed over them.

"Why do you do this to yourself, Maya?" I whispered. I brushed her cheek, watching her slip back into sleep.

She opened her eyes, finding me again in the fog. She reached for my hand, feebly pulling it away from her face and down to her chest. "Cam... I love you. Even though this'll never last. You and me. I still love you. I want you to know that."

"Why are you saying that?"

"I'll fuck it up. Somehow... The way everything's all fucked up now. And you'll leave again."

Her lips wrinkled into a sad line, one that made me wonder if she'd been crying tonight. Her eyes were red and swollen, as if she had been.

My jaw tightened, my teeth gnashing against the unexplainable jolt of pain that shot through me with those words. If what I'd done to us years ago was the root of her sadness, of whatever had brought her this low, I knew her more intimately than anyone. After all, I'd brought the same torture onto myself. I'd lived with it. I'd survived it too.

I kissed her gently. "I'm not leaving. I'm going to take care of you, okay?"

She closed her eyes. A sad smile faded as quickly as it arrived, and she slid back into unconsciousness. I watched her, studied the motion of her breathing until sleep finally beckoned me too. I fought it, filled with an irrational fear that as soon as I closed my eyes, I'd lose her again.

MAYA. I'd been ill for hours before it struck me that today was Christmas. Too embarrassed to have him see me this way, I'd begged Cameron to leave me alone to purge all my horrible stupidity in privacy. Over and over, the waves of sickness came, and then the tears. I couldn't remember much but I knew it wasn't good. I'd woken up in bed with him, to the worried look in his eyes. He hadn't been anywhere in my memories of the night, which wasn't a good sign.

A while later he knocked on the door. I stirred from a merciful respite on the soft padded rug on the bathroom floor.

"Maya, are you okay?"

"I'm fine."

I rose, painfully slow to avoid the terrible rush of blood to my already throbbing head. No part of me wanted to see my face. I feared one look at myself would send me right back to the toilet, so I kept my eyes downcast as I washed my face and brushed my teeth again. I toweled dry and emerged, walking past him and back into the bedroom.

I sank into the bed, pulling the covers up around me as if they could protect me, save me somehow. He sat by my feet, silent and still.

"Can I get you anything?"

"No," I rasped. "Thank you for...taking care of me last night."

"How do you feel?"

"I feel like I'd probably rather be dead than as hung over as I am right now. It hurts to talk." I wasn't exaggerating.

"I didn't rule out death last night."

I closed my eyes. The reality of how fucked up I must have been last night sank in. "I just drank too much."

"No, you drank at a bar without anyone you knew around you and then blacked out and fell out of a cab which, thank God, dropped you in front of Vanessa's house. How you made it that far in the state you were in I'll never know."

Tears threatened again, causing the thrum in my head to grow louder and stronger.

"Please." The plea came out in a whisper. "You can't make me feel any worse than I already feel."

"I'm not trying to make you feel bad. I'm trying to make you understand what you put me through. And Vanessa. Do you have any idea?"

His voice was strained. I could sense the unleashed anger from last night coming through each word, but that was what had set me off to begin with.

Against every instinct, I opened my eyes. The way he looked at me, with so much hurt and worry, destroyed the last part of me. I swallowed over the nausea that threatened anew. My body was still very much at war with itself.

"I'm sorry. You don't have to stay here with me. I'm sure you want to be with your family. It's Christmas after all."

"As angry as I am, no, I'd rather be here with you." He tossed a small wrapped package next to me.

"What's this?"

"A present. One of them anyway. I didn't really come prepared for Christmas morning when I was running after you last night."

The edge of his voice stoked my guilt again. I wanted to reach for the simple wrapping of the gift but felt as undeserving of it as anything.

"Open it."

I looked up at him, my eyes brimming with unshed

tears. "Are we breaking up?"

He winced. "No. Why are you saying that?"

A quiet laugh rasped from me. "Because I'm a fucking mess, that's why. I don't understand why you would want to be with me like this." I waved a hand over my sad, sick, torn up self.

"Well, thank God you're not always blackout drunk. I happen to really enjoy you when you're not. I'm invested in that part."

"And what about the rest of me."

"We'll talk about it when you're not feeling so rotten." He gestured toward the package. "Open your gift."

I reached for it, untying the twine and carefully revealing a notebook hidden inside the paper wrapping. My fingers grazed the soft brown leather of the cover. I flipped through the pages, sepia tinted parchment.

"This is beautiful."

"For your writing."

I looked up too quickly, my headache resurfacing immediately.

"This is too nice." *Too nice for my words.* "Thank you."

"You're welcome."

He took a deep breath, full of relief and exhaustion, it seemed. I wondered how late I'd kept him up, how scared I'd made him.

"Maya, I'm sorry too…about last night. I shouldn't have let you leave like that."

"You're sorry?"

"I overreacted about Dermott. I mean, I'm not excusing his or Jia's behavior, but I flew off the handle and you didn't deserve that. I'm sure you wouldn't have done this to yourself if I hadn't been such an asshole."

"It's not your fault I drank so much. I can find an excuse to do that any day of the week without your help, trust me."

"Why?" His gaze found mine. "I can't promise to understand, but at least try to explain what possesses you to do this."

I let my forehead fall into my hand. Why? Why did I do this? Time and again, after swearing to myself that I'll never drink again. After I punish my body so terribly, the way I had last night.

"Sometimes I need to make everything go away for a little while." I closed my eyes against the reality that I was faced with now, but I couldn't escape it. "When I'm in the moment, I'm happy," I muttered, all too aware of my present and overwhelming lack of happiness.

"When all you're trying to do is cover up feeling miserable, it's an artificial kind of happiness, wouldn't you say?"

"Maybe. The relief is what's addictive, whether it's real happiness or not. I'm afraid that feeling will stop, that reality will creep back in, and I'll start feeling miserable before I'm ready to deal with my life again. So I drink more, and then at some point, I don't realize what I'm doing. I get too far gone, and…yeah, sometimes I black out."

"And someone catches you when you fall."

I nodded slowly. "Vanessa and Eli are always around, which is probably why I called Vanessa."

"I know they're your best friends, but it's not their job to make sure you don't get murdered or taken advantage of by someone."

I frowned, unable to rationalize that he was overreacting. "It's not like I haven't taken care of them too. I've held Vanessa's hair back plenty of times."

"This isn't college, Maya. You're an adult. How long are you going to keep doing this?"

My face heated, my frustration rising to the surface. "You know what, I'm suffering for it enough. I don't need you judging me. Trust me, this isn't how I wanted to spend Christmas." I pressed my fingers to my temples, willing away the pain that came with the force of my words. "What time is it?"

"Almost noon, why?"

"I should head out soon."

"Where are you going?"

"My grandmother. Not like she'll miss me, but I should go so she isn't alone on Christmas. Now that this deal is done anyway."

"Where does she live?"

"A home, a few hours outside the city."

"Let me drive you."

"It's fine. I usually just rent a car." I groaned inwardly at the thought of doing absolutely anything in my current condition, let alone coordinating the last minute details of this trip.

"You're in no condition to drive. Plus it's supposed to start snowing soon."

"I'm not still drunk!" I snapped.

He stood up. "I wouldn't be surprised if you were, honestly. Even so, I can't imagine you feel well enough to drive. I'll take you. Go get cleaned up, and maybe we can get some food into you before we leave."

CAMERON. The snow started not long after we left. I registered immediate relief when the city skyline was in our rearview, as if we'd passed out of a noise and chaos filled bubble and entered another country, *the* country. It happened every time I left, and every time I found myself eager to reenter the bubble upon my return.

Maya had fallen asleep against her coat. She'd barely eaten, but her color had returned a little. She was on her way to better, at least.

A couple hours had passed when the phone rang. I answered quickly to silence it. Olivia. "What's up?"

"Where are you?"

"I'm with Maya."

"That's great, but Mom and Dad are here. Everyone's wondering where you are."

"Well, you can tell them I'm with Maya. They'll love that. We're going to visit her grandmother."

"What? Where? Are you driving?"

"Yes, I'm driving, and I probably won't be back until late. So feel free to be merry without me."

"Cameron, you can't leave us here with them." Her voice had degraded into an angry whisper.

I suppressed a laugh. In a way, I was devilishly happy about her current predicament. On the other hand, I did feel a pang of regret that I'd abandoned her. There were strength in numbers, and usually between the three of us, we could keep any one of us from being fully sabotaged by the onslaught of their judgments and snide remarks. Our army of three had been reduced by one, but we wouldn't have needed an army at all if she'd kept her mouth shut.

"You made your bed, Liv. Deal with it. Send my condolences to Darren."

"They are going to freak out. You need to get back here."

"Tell them to get a hotel, and I'll be back later. Maybe we'll have a chance to visit before they go. I'm sorry, but there's no chance I'm coming back right now."

"Fuck you," she snapped before ending the call.

I dropped the phone into the drink holder and focused ahead.

"Who was that?"

Maya had straightened in her seat, her tired eyes looking to me from under her dark lashes.

"Olivia."

"What's going on?"

I shrugged, not wanting to get into it.

"Here's a teachable moment, Cameron. You lecture me about shutting you out, and that's exactly what you're doing to me right now. If I'm going to learn by example, you might want to rethink the silent shrug and tell me what's going on."

"You must be feeling better. You're starting to piss me off me again."

She turned to look out the window, and I caught her smile in the reflection of the window.

"Fine. My parents are visiting. Olivia invited them, sort of."

"What's that mean?"

I wasn't about to tell her that both Olivia and my parents had pegged her as the scapegoat for my mostly self-imposed deployments.

"They're nosy, and they wanted to check in on us.

Once they make up their mind about something like that, it's difficult to sway them."

"You still hold a grudge against them? They paid for your school. They've given you so much."

"That's not what it's all about, believe it or not. They've done a lot for me. I don't take that for granted. I really don't, but we don't see eye-to-eye about what's important in life. That makes it really difficult to spend time with them without some sort of argument erupting."

She rested her head on her hand and stared impassively out the window. "I guess I wouldn't know."

"What makes you think I want to be dependent on them any more than I did when we were together? The pressure to do exactly what they did, but more and better and to the letter was too much then, and they haven't let up much since. My father doesn't negotiate, and my mother is obsessed with what the rest of the world thinks about her. Not a lot of wiggle room for me to fit into that world."

Maya had been one of the only people who really understood my situation back then. She'd been the one who made me believe that somehow I could make it all work even when my plans ran in such contrast to what my parents had planned and wanted for me. Had she forgotten all that?

"At least you have a world. It would have been easy for you to step right in to help your dad."

"Of course it would have. But that's not what I wanted."

"Maybe I'm bitter. We don't all get to do what we want."

I caught her hand. "You could. What do you want?"

251

She shrugged. "I'm too busy to even think about what else I could want. Not to mention that I have to support myself."

"Couldn't you support yourself doing something that made you a little less miserable?"

"I don't know, Cam. It's a little late for dreaming."

"Why? You can't afford to be happy?"

She was silent for a long time. When she turned to me, her eyes were thoughtful and serious. "Are you happy?"

I shifted my focus back on the road, not sure how to answer that loaded question. I gave her hand a squeeze, hoping she realized that my happiness was beginning to rely on hers. If I had any chance at happiness, we needed to figure things out between us.

As I struggled for the right words, she pointed up the road to a sign partially obscured by the falling snow that read *Laurel Estates*.

"The place is up here."

CHAPTER SEVENTEEN

MAYA. The home was well off the beaten path, a few miles outside of the quiet main street of the nearest town. We could have landed on another planet for how different it was from our usual surroundings. The sky was darkening quickly with the late afternoon.

We walked in and were greeted by a receptionist.

"Ruth Jacobs, please."

The petite middle-aged woman manning the desk smiled. "You are?"

"Her granddaughter, Maya."

"Ah, of course. Just sign in, and I'll show you to her room."

I did, and she rose, gesturing for us to follow her.

"She's been doing well lately," she said in a quiet tone, "but if she gets agitated, just buzz us and we'll come rescue you."

She offered a smile that was both hopeful and

sympathetic as we paused outside of the room.

"Thanks." I looked up to Cameron. "Did you want to come in?"

"I can go grab some coffee or something. I don't want to confuse her since she won't know me."

"She won't know me either, but that's fine. I'll come find you when we're done."

"Who is that?" My grandmother's voice called from inside the room.

I turned toward the sound, hoping today's visit would go better than the last. I mouthed a goodbye to Cameron before entering quietly.

She was sitting in a chair by the window, her lower half covered with a well-loved blanket that she'd crocheted decades ago. Her hair was pure white, cut short but curling at the ends. Behind her glasses, her eyes were a soft light brown like mine, like my mother's too.

"Hi, Grandma." I spoke softly and smiled widely as if we'd been friends all our lives. This usually worked better than starting out with awkward reintroductions that we'd only need to make again in a few minutes. I kissed her and sat in a chair across from her, leaning in so she could see me clearly.

"How are you?" she asked, playing along.

"I'm doing really well. I've missed you."

"You too sweetheart. Did you say hello to Gus? He's working in the yard."

"Not yet, no." I chose not to remind her that my grandfather had died years ago, not long before my mother disappeared entirely. Not to mention the grounds surrounding the facility were covered in a growing layer of snow now.

"We were about to go play cards with the Smiths," she said, fingering the top button on her sweater. She straightened, as if she meant to take off for her social event at any moment. She always had an air about her, like she wanted everyone to know that what she was doing was important, even if it was weekly game nights with the Smiths. I struggled to think of something I'd want my grandchildren to know to elevate myself in their eyes. I couldn't think of anything.

"Yeah? That sounds like a lot of fun. The Smiths are sweet people." I vaguely remembered them from visits when I was a child.

"We go every Friday, you know."

I smiled and nodded, letting her chatter on, telling and retelling the news that she thought was current and worth sharing. Gus's arthritis had been bothering him, never mind the cancer that had slowly been working its way through his organs the last time we could share a coherent conversation. On top of that, Bernice Smith had insinuated that her zucchini bread was superior the last time they visited. I offered my support and scoffed at the audacity of her lifelong friend to outdo her in the baking department, only a little jealous that on my current track, I might never know how to bake anything.

She glanced outside for a moment. I studied her face. She seemed unchanged from the young grandmother I'd remembered playing dolls with when my mother was away working. Lynne had always tried like hell to make ends meet. Back before alcohol had stripped away her will to fight and survive, for us.

I'd given up trying to bring Ruthie up to speed on anything I was doing. Our brief and irrelevant talks had to be enough, and I hoped they gave her some comfort. I wasn't sure how much the people here entertained her, but she'd always been talkative before she started losing her faculties.

She faced me again, her eyes searching mine. I was about to speak, to pick up where we'd left off when she frowned.

"Are you my daughter?"

I shook my head. "I'm Maya, your granddaughter."

"I don't have a granddaughter."

"I'm Lynne's daughter, remember?" I hated bringing up my mother's name in front of her, but sometimes it was one of the only ways she'd remember me.

Her cheek twitched and her hands twisted a mangled tissue in her lap. "I know who you are," she muttered, her voice lower. "I told you not to come back here. I don't have any money for you."

I sighed inwardly, sending up a silent prayer that I could turn her back. "I'm not Lynne, Grandma, and I don't need your money, okay? You're confused."

"Don't tell me I'm confused," she snapped. "I know who you are. I'd know my own daughter. Stop trying to trick me."

"Lynne hasn't been here to see you, has she?" I held onto an irrational hope that my dementia-riddled grandmother could unlock the mystery of my mother's sudden disappearance.

"Gus was always giving you money. We should have kicked you out when that boy knocked you up."

I sat back into the hard plastic back of the chair, fighting the urge to snap back at her. She was a child in her mind, even less. I took a deep breath, making myself believe it.

"Do you want to do a puzzle? They tell me you like to do them."

"That's enough! Stop trying to trick me. You don't fool me, you little whore. I told you not to come here anymore, and here you are. You're embarrassing us."

She shook her head violently, muttering a string of obscenities. Ironically, I'd never heard her curse until she'd gotten so bad that a home was the only safe place for her. I looked around the room, as if anything here could help me. She started shouting at me again, and I rose, warring with the part of me that wanted to defend myself and my mother against the harsh unfiltered judgments spewing from her.

As I was about to step out to get a nurse, the door swung open and Cameron's frame filled the doorway. My body relaxed at the sight of him. His eyes flashed to mine and then Ruthie's. He came closer, handing me a small foam cup and continuing toward her.

"Hi, Ruthie. Did you want some tea?"

She brightened immediately, as transfixed on his beautiful face as I'd been a moment ago. "Why, yes, thank you. I take mine with cream."

"This one has cream." He handed her the cup carefully before sinking down into the chair I'd occupied earlier. His shoulders shrugged slightly, as if he were trying to make himself seem smaller and less imposing in front of this frail woman.

"Do I know you?"

He smiled and introduced himself, holding out his hand to grasp hers gently.

I took a step closer, wondering if I might be able to

reintroduce myself now that Cameron's presence had officially dazzled her. Her focus turned back to me, her wide-eyed approval unchanged. I pulled up another chair by Cameron's and sat tentatively.

"Is this your husband?"

My jaw fell agape as I searched for an answer somewhere between the truth and what Ruthie would want to be the truth. Never mind what I wanted to be the truth. I couldn't begin to grasp the magnitude of my feelings about that yet.

"No, Grandma. He's a friend."

Her hopeful eyes softened a bit as she glanced between us. She sighed and took a sip of her tea. "That's a shame," she murmured. "He seems like a sweet boy."

She looked up from her tea, captivated by Cameron again. "Is this your wife?"

He laughed quietly, and shook his head. "Not yet, Ruthie." He leaned in and whispered, as if sharing a secret between them. "Do you think I could convince her?"

The wrinkles at the corners of her eyes deepened and she answered with a coy smile. Meanwhile, I tried my damnedest not to reveal the wild reaction that my body was having to their outrageous conversation. My hands stiffened and trembled around the flimsy cup, threatening to compromise its stability around the lukewarm contents.

"I think so. You seem like a wonderful young man, but you have to promise me something."

"For you, Ruthie, anything." He teased her with a crooked grin.

"You must promise to take care of her."

"Of course."

"Because she's my only granddaughter."

I'd managed to keep my frail emotions from flying all over the damn room for the next twenty minutes. Eventually, Ruthie let us know she was tired and going to take a nap. We both kissed her goodbye and left before she had a chance to wonder if we were coming or going. I walked ahead of Cameron, pausing at the reception area. The same nurse looked up from her reading.

"How was she?"

"Wonderful, actually. Thank you for taking such good care of her. She seems well."

"That's what we do."

"I have a question, though."

"What's that?"

"Has anyone else been here to see her?"

She hummed and thought for a second. "Let me check, sweetheart. One second."

A few agonizing minutes passed while she sifted through files in a cabinet in the back of the office. She returned with an opened file. "You're the only one who's visited her since she's come in, except last month."

She set a sign in sheet in front of me, turning it so I could read the name scribbled by her finger.

Lynne Jacobs.

My heart stopped. My trembling hands covered my mouth and the whole world seemed to stand still in that moment.

"Maya, are you okay?"

I reminded myself to breathe when Cameron's hand warmed the small of my back. I nodded quickly, thanking the woman for her help. We stepped outside. Snow had started coming down hard.

"We need to head back now," I said, walking briskly to the car.

"The roads are getting bad."

I clutched my hands together, trying to still the tremble. "I need to get out of here. Cameron, I can't stay here."

"Hey, okay. Relax." He tucked the windblown strands of my hair behind my ear, brushing my cheek as he did. "Is there a place to stay around here?"

I shook my head. I couldn't think. I couldn't deal with any of this now.

"Cam...just, whatever. Let's get out of here."

He guided me to the other side of the car. "Get in. I'll be right back." He ran back into the home and returned a few minutes later, revving the engine to life.

"What are we going to do?" I barely recognized my voice, it was so quiet.

"There's a bed and breakfast down the road. We'll stay there and everything should be clear in the morning."

I nodded. Laurel Estates disappeared in a white haze, and before I knew it, we pulled into the drive of a large Victorian house, its windows illuminated with warm light as darkness descended on the stormy day. I followed Cam inside and the host led us to our room on the third floor, which seemed to be empty of guests. I didn't imagine Laurel Falls was a major destination, but every town needed someplace to stay.

I dropped my purse and coat on the antique chair in the corner of the room. The room was quaint, containing a queen-sized bed and some simple furniture. I walked around restlessly. Outside the snow swirled through the air. Those could have been my thoughts, the flurry of emotions that whipped through me now. I wanted this storm to end. I was at the end of a cold hard winter, and I wasn't sure how much more I could take.

My mother's name scribbled on the roster of visitors flashed through my mind again and again. She'd been here. There was no other feasible explanation. Weeks ago, after years of nothing, she'd been here to see my grandmother. Had she really asked for money? Why didn't she try to find me? Why hadn't she come to me if she needed help? That's what I'd been waiting for this whole time—a chance to help her. Where was she now?

A hopeless pain filled the hollow place in my chest. The anxious tremble had graduated to a penetrating shudder, and I couldn't stop its course through me. I was unraveling. I surveyed the room, aware that we likely lacked some of the common amenities of a hotel room. The basket near the coffee maker held nothing but gourmet teas and coffee. They were of no use to me now. I opened the small mini fridge and relief filled me when I saw it was stocked with both caffeine and beer.

I grabbed one of the beers. When I stood, Cameron took it deftly from my grasp, his lips set in a disapproving line.

"What the fuck?"

"I need a drink."

"You've got to be kidding me. After last night, how can you even consider it?"

"I'm stressed out, okay?"

"About what? Seeing your grandmother?"

"No. You wouldn't understand." He wouldn't because I'd never tell him.

"Then explain it to me."

"Just..." I groaned, wishing he would back off and leave me be. "I need to take the edge off. I can't possibly get far-gone. There are only a couple beers in there."

He shook his head. A mix of sympathy and certain disappointment tightened the muscles of his beautiful face. I couldn't have felt any worse.

"You're talking to the man who carried your unconscious body up two flights of stairs last night. If you think I'm letting you get anywhere close to drunk tonight, you're sorely mistaken."

Panic rose, tightening my throat. The walls were closing in on me—Cameron's judgments, my past, and the painful certainty that our future was doomed. Everything pressed down on me until I could scarcely breathe. I pulled on my coat and side stepped him.

I moved for the door.

"Wait." He blocked my exit, staring down at me. "Why are you running off?"

"Let me go." I could barely hear my own voice—a small and sad testimony to how I felt in my soul.

He grabbed the lapels on my coat, opening it at the chest and taking it off as swiftly as I'd put it on moments ago. "You're not going anywhere."

"Like hell I'm not. Let me go." I wrestled out of his grasp, my coat flailing to the floor. My shoulders shook with the effort to hold myself together.

"You need to stop this shit, Maya."

The abrasiveness in his voice sent a chill through me. I pushed at him, anger overpowering the pain that pulsed through me. I felt the brunt of the effort to move him away in my wrists when he didn't budge.

"Who are you to judge me?" I pounded my fists on his chest, resorting to my last and only effort.

He caught my wrists, holding them gently but firmly enough that I couldn't wrestle free or deliver another blow.

"I'm not judging you, goddamnit. I'm loving you. I give a shit. I'm sorry if no one else cares enough to tell you no, but I'm not going to watch you fucking drown yourself in booze."

"I'm not asking you to do anything, except get the hell out of my way. This is my life, and if I have to water it down now and again, that's none of your goddamn business."

"You're staying right here with me, so knock it off." He loosened his hold on my wrists so I could step back.

I struggled to catch my breath. My adrenaline surged, every nerve alive. Anxiety and the steady pain I wanted so desperately to stamp out pulsed through my veins. Cameron was here witnessing all of it, fighting my impulses like some fucking warrior. I didn't need a warrior. I didn't need this brand of love.

"If this is you loving me, I'm not interested. You don't know anything about me."

His jaw tightened. "Because you give me *nothing*. You won't let me in. I have to sneak around to learn anything about you. The poems... Christ, Maya, there's so much more there that you never give me, that you never give anyone."

My brain scrambled to catch up to his words. Then a different kind of pain hit me, like I'd been publicly gutted. Raw and exposed, I was on display for all to see.

"You...you went through my things?"

He shrugged, but the motion wasn't casual. His posture was on edge, like mine. "They were sitting out. I read some of them."

"That's why you got me the notebook." My eyes burned with threatened tears. "I can't believe you'd... How could you read something so personal and think that was okay?"

A slow tear journeyed down my face. My hand went to my mouth to stifle the sound of my shock. His betrayal—because that's what it felt like—weighed down the already crushing pain I was struggling against. What had he read? And God, why? Why had he pried? I scolded myself for being careless, for writing any of it down in the first place. Foolish, stupid words because I couldn't keep my fucking emotions in check.

He sighed and rubbed his eyes with the heels of his hands. "The words... I think I know what you're trying to say with some of it, a lot of it. I feel the same way. I want what we could have had. I need you to believe that it's not too late for that."

"It is."

His eyes dimmed. "We can fix this. Together, you and I. It doesn't have to be like this. This crutch... You don't need it."

A painful laugh tore from my throat. "A crutch... Right. Don't worry, I wouldn't ever ask you to be that for me."

"Maya. I didn't..."

His eyes squeezed shut, and I knew he remembered. Those terrible last words that he'd delivered, that well-aimed blow to my heart.

"I wish I could take everything back from that day,"

he whispered. His shoulders sagged, his head bowed with defeat.

"You left me, Cameron. And now you want...what? My heart? The adoration that I once gave so freely? You want the satisfaction that after breaking me, you've saved me? There's no saving me, okay? I can't give you the person I used to be, even if I wanted to, because she's all gone now. And, yes, sometimes I need to drink to put it all away. I don't know how else to explain it to you, but right now, that's what I need."

I moved to the loveseat and sat. I circled my arms around my belly, leaning into the dull ache. I shivered, suddenly cold, a bone-deep cold deep in my soul that he'd never be able to fathom.

Visions of my mother haunted me anew. I'd kept her full of life in my memories. I never let myself visit the reduced person she might have become after all these years. She was still young, vibrant, and beautiful in my mind. I loved her with the selfish, greedy, and consuming love of a child. Her life had always been for me, and then suddenly, it wasn't anymore. How could I feel anything but a devastating kind of rejection from it all?

That she'd reappeared under my radar cut through me. Years of worrying and taking responsibility for her disappearance were thrown in my face.

I hated her. I hated her as much as I loved her. She'd become an abstract, because she'd ceased to be real. The pain twisted in my gut, sore from my earlier sickness but still wanting the relief I so craved. Effectively trapped, all I could do was cry. I let the tears flow, praying silently for relief.

Cameron crouched down beside me, his hands on

my knees then moving over my legs and up and down my arms, warming and soothing me. He hushed me until I caught my breath, wiping away the tears as they slowed. His touch was tender, melting my earlier rush of anger. How could he do that? With a touch, he could take me someplace else, bring me out of the dark confines of my mind, the emotional wasteland that my life had become.

I shook my head, grasping his hand in mine. I squeezed it, wishing he could take it all away somehow, every last shred of it. But why on earth would he want to?

"How could you possibly want to be with someone like me?"

I chanced a look in his eyes, afraid of what I'd find. The calm shadow of his blue eyes and the firm set of his jaw made a face void of pity, but full of something else, something unfathomably deeper. I couldn't name it, but it rippled off him like a heat wave and seized my heart. I parted my lips and sucked in a sharp breath between them.

"I want to be with you, Maya, because we belong together. You may not believe it, but you're strong and you're beautiful, and we may fight like hell, but you're mine. And now I want you to fight for us, for the girl who used to dream with me, who made me believe we could do anything together. I've never known what the future held, but I've never been able to stop imagining you were the person I'd go into it with.

He took a silent breath, his features softening slightly. "Please, Maya. I'm begging you to talk to me. Something happened back there. Tell me. Don't keep me in the dark."

I squeezed my eyes closed against a new wave of tears.

I was losing it. His words cut through me, past the skin, right down to the bone, right down to the weak, scared, motherless person I hated to be.

"Maya," he whispered, grazing my cheek with the warmth of his touch.

"My mom visited Ruthie a few weeks ago." I shook my head. "There are things you never knew about me, Cameron."

"Tell me." He rose and sat beside me, his arm around me.

I brushed away the last of my tears and took a steeling breath.

"My mom and I... We never had much, but we had each other, you know? It wasn't easy for her, raising me on her own, and when I left for school... Everything pretty much went to hell after that. She was always kind of a mess anyway, but without me to hold her down and give her a reason to stay put, she spiraled out of control. Boyfriends, drinking all the time, and though she'd never admit it, I figure drugs finally entered the picture. I couldn't quit school though. I mean, I seriously considered it. But this is what we'd worked for, a better life, and I couldn't just let it all go. I was determined to finish and get a good job, like we'd talked about, and I was going to get her out of whatever mess she'd gotten herself into. But I was too late..."

"What happened?"

"You left, and then...she left. Disappeared. I figured she'd moved again and hadn't given me her new number, but days turned into weeks and weeks turned into months. I never heard from her. I filed reports. Nothing."

"Christ, Maya. You never..."

"You were gone, but even if you hadn't left, I'm still not sure I would have told you. You and Olivia, I never wanted either of you to know that side of my life, that part of me that was so far from perfect."

"I'm pretty sure perfect means something different for you than it does for me."

I shrugged. He tossed that word around too much. I wasn't Olivia. I wasn't the kind of girl you couldn't wait to introduce your parents to.

Cameron tipped my chin, locking me in his stare and interrupting my self-defeating tirade.

"Did you think you really had me fooled into thinking you were like everyone else? I knew things weren't all roses for you. I didn't know exactly why, but I'd figured one day you'd tell me. I didn't think it'd take five years though."

"I couldn't tell you." I drew in a jagged breath at the memory. "Even when I was about to lose you, somehow I couldn't muster the strength to tell you."

I looked into his deep blue eyes. They seemed to light up the darkening room.

"You weren't the reason I said no that day. I knew I needed to stay close, to take care of my mom. I couldn't bear the thought of explaining to you then how marrying me would mean signing on for that part of my life too. But I wasn't going to let her just slip away and out of my life either." I shrugged. "She did anyway. I lost you both, trying to be the perfect girl for you and somehow take care of her too. I ended up with nothing."

A sad laugh escaped me. I thought back to that dark time when all the purpose of my life had been ripped from me. Now my two reasons for living were back, in some way. I was still floundering, lost and fucking it all up. No closer to fixing anything than I had been the day Cameron left me. The tears dried cold on my cheeks and the heaviness was back, a thick suffocating kind of pain that only knew one outlet. I stared down at my hands tangled together to still the fretful tremble. Fuck all, I needed a drink.

"I need it to go away for a few hours, Cam. Everything will be better in the morning, I promise. I'll be better. I won't be like this."

He gathered me close. My forehead fell to his chest, my body even weaker in the strength of his embrace. I wanted to disappear in his arms, to curl up into a protected little ball and forget the rest of the world. But I worried that wouldn't be enough to stave off the kind of pain that plagued me now.

"Please," I begged, praying Cameron would take pity on me.

"I'll make it go away, okay?" he whispered, pushing the hair away from my tear-stained face. "Just stay with me."

I looked up at him, desperate and so very lost. He held my cheek. His arm wrapped possessively around my waist.

"I want you, Maya. Your heart may be broken, but I still want it. And I may not deserve it, but I'll wait for it, as long as I need to. In the meantime, I'm here. For tonight, let this be enough, just you and me."

I exhaled a jagged breath and his mouth was on me, inhaling my relief. He kissed my lips, my cheeks, my eyelids, his fingertips tracing his path. Angling over me, he cradled my face in his palm, commanding me with his kiss. I responded the way he knew I would, hungry for the sweet taste of his tongue. We tangled and tasted, seeking more of each other until we were both breathless.

"Maya?" He pulled back, his eyes dark and serious. "Let me be the place you go to forget and wash it all away. I can take you there. I know I can, because nothing has ever made me feel the way I do when we're together. No drink, no woman…no rush, risk, or cheap high does what being with you does. I want to make love to you until we can't remember who we are. I want you drunk on nothing but us tonight."

My heart beat loudly, a steady reminder of how I loved him, a state of being well beyond my control now. The picture he painted, I wanted that. I wanted to forget everything that had brought me so low and start over with him. I longed for the words that only our bodies could speak, for the force of a physical connection that might transcend everything that had come between us.

A simple nod was all I could manage before he lifted and lowered me to the bed. He covered me with the warm heaviness of his body. The relief was almost instant. My limbs weakened in his embrace. He kissed me, nipping and licking my lips apart, seeking my tongue and sucking gently. I moaned, my hips responding beyond my control.

He rose, unfastened my jeans, and pulled them down my legs. I sat up and tugged off my shirt, reaching next for his. He kicked off his jeans and came to me quickly, claiming my mouth.

My hands were restless. I grazed the muscles that bunched and released as he moved over me. I arched. I wanted him closer still. Impossibly close, until he was inside me, making me his. His hot skin burned against me, the twining of our bodies hungry with need. The sensations crept over me until my head was spinning with desire. The piercing pain of my reality ebbed, faded into the darkening room, until there was only Cameron.

"I love you." The words fell from my lips before I knew what I was saying, what it meant, what I was giving up with the admission.

He slowed, his lips barely touching mine. The look in his eyes—intense and full of all the love I felt in that moment—branded me.

"I've waited a long time for that."

"I was scared. I still am. I'm so afraid you're going to leave, that you're going to break me. Saying it...it's like giving you the last little piece of me, the part that I can't afford to give anyone."

I paused, frozen with a fleeting apprehension that quickly disappeared. He caught my cheek and leveled our gazes.

"Someone could drag me to hell, and I'd crawl back to you, Maya, for a chance to make right everything that was ever wrong between us. Even I can't tell you what's happening with us. I've never felt this way. But believe me when I tell you I'm not going anywhere. I swear to you."

With a sharp exhale, he crushed his mouth against mine. I moaned into the kiss, meeting his fervency, his love, his commitment. The way he kissed me was deep, devouring, as if he'd had his own demons seeking release.

CHAPTER EIGHTEEN

CAMERON. I tried in vain to slow down. I moved over her, tasting every inch of her. Her hands fisted and released anxiously by her sides. Her body shifted eagerly below me, a reflection of the longing that coursed through me too. I battled with it, wanting to take my time and love her slowly.

"Maya," I murmured, tucking a strand of hair behind her ear to gain better access to the sensitive skin below it and unfettered access to her neck. I reveled in the smallest reactions of her body. The way goose bumps raced across her skin when I was there, sucking and licking, breathing her name over and over, like a mantra, like an echo in a dream. She shivered. I pulled her closer, wanting to give her all the warmth and comfort she desired.

Seeing her so upset had overwhelmed me. I wanted to banish the memories and the circumstances beyond her control that gave her an ounce of unhappiness. I wanted to flood her darkness with light, with love. I rolled the word around in my head, analyzing what it meant in the context of having the only woman I'd ever loved in my bed again, in my arms, opening her heart and body to me.

Her shaking hands skimmed over my shoulders and down my chest. I caught them and kissed her fingertips. Then I bent to her, grasping her breast before sucking the tip into my mouth. Pulling them into long taut points, I teased each peak with my tongue and my teeth until she cried out and her thighs tightened fiercely around my hips.

I moved to kiss her shoulders, all the way up her neck to her ear, enticing more tiny shivers from her. She gripped my waist, urging me closer. I wanted to bury myself in her. My patience was waning.

"Are you on the pill?"

She blinked rapidly, as if she needed to regain her focus to answer the question. "Yeah."

I grazed her throat with my hand, pausing a second over the steady pulse at her neck. I moved south until my fingers crept to the top of her thighs, teasing down over the soft cotton of her panties where she was soaked through for me. With a little pressure she reacted, bucking into my hand. I slid the fabric to the side and slipped my fingers through her moist folds. She gripped my arm and gasped when I pushed inside her. My cock ached to be there, ravaging her. I'd be there soon.

"I want to be here, Maya, coming inside you…"

"I've always been safe, Cam. You're the only one."

I kissed her hard, swallowing her promise. She moaned, arching into my chest. I trusted her, and she trusted me to bring her through this.

Trust, the benevolent warrior fighting the misgivings that had plagued us, pulsed between us now. Trust and this love that even she could no longer deny perhaps was the bridge that would take us from who we were to who we'd become. Maybe it could be enough to undo all the hurt we'd caused one another.

"I want to make love to you, but you need to tell me if it's too much right now."

"I need too much." She ran her fingers up my chest, shifted her body against me, charging my already full erection further. "I need this. Make me forget everything. All I want is this moment between us. Make it last as long as we can."

I caught her mouth, kissing her tenderly. A small moan hummed through her tiny frame as I licked her tongue, sucking softly, and then deeper, exploring her mouth. When she opened her eyes, her half-lidded gaze met my own. My heart twisted painfully.

"I could kiss you like this forever. You're so sweet and soft." I brushed my knuckles over the blush of her cheek that grew darker with the words.

"I'm going to need something stronger than a kiss."

I laughed quietly. I tugged off her panties, lowered, and wasted no time pressing into her. Anxious, I wanted to sheath her in one fierce thrust. But I wanted to experience every second of this decadent moment, draw it out as she pulled me deeper.

And she felt amazing, warm and snug around me, the only place I'd ever wanted to be.

I'd wanted this from the beginning, but we'd had too many hurdles between us to broach the subject of our sexual histories before. It was almost worth avoiding altogether, except for the exquisite rush of our bodies being joined now with nothing to separate us.

The mere thought of her being with other men filled me with a fiery jealousy. In a rash need to claim her for myself, I rooted deeply, as deep as I'd ever been. She gasped. Every muscle tensed, locking me to her. When my eyes went to her, her mouth had fallen open, harsh breath heaving her chest. Her lip quivered. She pulsed around my cock as I held myself deep within her.

"You okay?"

"God yes."

"Did I hurt you?"

"It's impossible for you to hurt me. You know my body too well. You always have."

I released some tension, though I was still coiled tight, ready to spring into loving her passionately.

"This is what I want, Maya. Nothing between us."

"This is what I want too. I want you, us. Please don't stop."

She dug her nails into my ass and I jerked against her, spurring the first of a series of thrusts that had her unraveling quickly in my arms. The rush of pleasure took hold quickly.

"Cam, oh God."

The way she was clenched down around me, slick and yet possessive, I couldn't stop. Instead I sped up, driving deep, the delicious friction between us taking us both out of our minds. We came together, an explosion of heat and riotous emotion. I jetted inside her. I cursed, marking her as I held her hips firmly in place.

I wanted to fill her, to possess her fully this way

always. In my mindless state I dared to imagine that time hadn't come between us. What could this feel like, to come inside her with the hope that we could make a life between us, with this love? A love that was growing stronger by the day, rooting itself in our lives despite all the doubts.

I exhaled heavily and rested over her. Crazy thoughts. Falling in love with her this time around was taking hold of me in different ways. The thought was intoxicating, if severely premature.

She sagged beneath me, catching her breath. I thrust again gently and she contracted, her delicious grip rippling over me. I was wrecked and still hard, but I hadn't meant to come so soon. I had plans to do a lot more.

I pulled out and lay on my side next to her, our bodies touching. Her head fell to the side to gaze at me. All noticeable signs of worry and her earlier stress had vanished.

"That was incredible."

My lips curved into a wry smile. "I'm just getting started."

I ran a flat palm over her breasts and her belly, and then lower. She quivered when I touched her. I tucked my knee under her thighs as they fell apart. I nudged them farther until she was spread for me.

Sifting through her soft curls, I traced the seam of her pussy. She was wet, dripping with my release. I bit my lip. My cocked surged to life quickly, the ache in my balls returning with the need to do it all over again. I resisted, holding her in a heated stare while my fingers found their mark. I stroked through the lips of her sex, teasing the soft inner flesh until I was inside her again. Curving carefully into her wet heat, I found her G-spot and gave it gentle rub. She jerked at the slightest touch.

"What are you doing to me?"

I withdrew, putting my thumb to work over and around her clit. Then slid inside again, teasing her inside and out. "I'm going to make you lose count of the ways I make you come tonight."

Her whimpers and the erotic sound of the rapid penetration into her wetness were the only noises around us. Her skin, slick with sweat, heated against me. She shifted and squirmed, like she might wriggle free in her increasing restlessness. I lifted to my elbow and lowered over her, pressing her back down with a hard kiss. I pumped harder, more vigorously and with less restraint, until she came apart. Our lips broke contact and her loud throaty cry filled the room as she seized around me.

When I withdrew she was shaking, her limbs draped boneless across the bed. I might have taken mercy on her then, but I was hard and ready for her again. I was going to fuck her until she begged me to stop.

"One more, baby. Can you get up on your knees?"

Her eyebrows rose slightly. "No fucking way. I can't move. Who are you, Hercules?"

I laughed and turned her to the side, spooning her from behind.

"I'm not letting you off that easy."

I kissed over the dark designs down her back, her shoulders, the long line of her neck. Then I drove into her again. As limp as she'd felt a second ago, she was tight around me now.

I withdrew slowly, mesmerized by the vision of

feeding my cock into her again. Her skin flushed all the way up her back. Tiny circles reddened her hips where I'd marked her. I became impossibly harder at the sight of them. I thrust deep, relentlessly taking our bodies where we desperately wanted to go, again and again.

"Love the way you feel. I'll never get tired of this, being this close to you, Maya," I rasped into her ear. I breathed her in, savoring every part of this moment together.

"You're so deep." She covered my arm as I wrapped it around her, drawing her against me. Her pussy was still tight from her orgasms, still responding when I drove in her.

Inspired, I slammed harder. Her breath caught in a strangled moan. She shifted her hips and leaned away so I was able to go deeper, until I was certain I was hitting the very heart of her.

I rooted, again and again, driving steadily, chasing my own desire. I was lost in her, never wanting this closeness between us to end. I was so ramped up I could almost taste it. She'd be sore tomorrow, but I didn't care.

I was taking her past her boundaries tonight and losing my own damn mind in the process. I grabbed the meat of her ass in my hand, assessing the ample flesh there. From this vantage—and all others for that matter—it was fucking perfect.

I gave it a hard smack, watching at the print of my hand surfaced in a pink outline. She cried out pressed back against me, her pussy crushing down around me. I smacked her again, driving deep as I did. She cried out, a thready wavering sound. Her outstretched hands grabbed fistfuls of the sheet.

"Come, Maya. Give me everything."

She fell apart with a broken cry, her body rigid in a state of perpetual climax, taking me down with her. I burst inside her. An almost painful release matched the tight fist of hers. I held us there, joined, wasted, until we slipped into sleep.

When I woke, the room was dark save for the moonlight pouring into the window. We'd fallen asleep this way, our bodies tangled. I think. I couldn't remember falling asleep. I rubbed my eyes, reminding myself that I hadn't been drunk but the night was hazy. Flashes of everything we'd done flooded my mind. I don't think I'd ever fucked a woman quite as thoroughly as I'd fucked Maya tonight. If she hadn't been completely out of her mind with desire, I sure as hell was. We'd damn near blacked out afterwards. If that didn't rival a night of heavy drinking, I didn't know what could.

My eyes adjusted to the darkness. Maya was curled beside me. Her body seemed small and peaceful in the quiet of the night. I turned down the covers and carefully positioned her closer to me, covering her up as I did. She hummed and reached for me, nuzzling into my chest, her skin cool on my own. I wrapped my arms around her, cocooning her until her own body heat emanated against me.

I brushed her hair back, staring in wonder. Despite everything that had gone on between us these past weeks, I was still amazed that she'd come back into my life at all. Like a wish that I hadn't realized I'd been making for so long had finally been granted. I'd never been so deeply grateful for it until tonight.

Tonight, something had changed. Somewhere

between fucking her and loving her and not giving her anyplace else to run, I'd found the soul of the girl I knew. Underneath the crutches and the don't-give-a-shit attitude, she was there—my Maya.

Any concerns I'd had about the emotional risks of falling for Maya again were quickly brushed aside by the fear of what might become of her if she kept on this way. Deep down she needed me as fiercely as I needed her. Knowing that she did bound me to her in a way that I'd never felt before. I was going to put her back together. I'd unbreak everything I'd broken and bring her back to me if it was the last thing I did.

MAYA. We pulled up to my apartment. The car idled, but I couldn't bring myself to get out. Too much had happened between us on our brief trip. He'd peeled back a layer of my life that I'd always kept hidden. In the small room of that house, in a nowhere town so far outside the buzz of city, my universe had tilted. I stared out the window at the snow-covered rails leading up to my brownstone apartment, and somehow, none of it seemed real.

"Stay with me."

I turned to face Cameron, questioning him with a look.

"Maybe it's just me, but I don't want to be away from you right now. I feel like you're going to disappear on me or something. The very thought of it is driving me a little crazy. Give me some peace of mind and come stay with me for a while."

"I'm not going anywhere," I promised.

"Prove it."

"But your parents are visiting. I'll be intruding."

"They left. Darren texted me that the coast was clear. There's Olivia, but she's usually pretty good about keeping to herself. And she's going to have to get used to the idea of you being around anyway, so we might as well break her in now."

"I don't want to cause problems, Cam."

He laughed, his eyes glittering. "Well, you do. You're a royal pain in the ass."

I scoffed, slapping his shoulder. "You're no picnic either."

He caught my hand, giving it a meaningful squeeze. "I know that. I was only half joking. Come stay with me, though. I miss you already. It's kind of pathetic."

His lips quirked up into a smile and my heart melted. I sighed. I didn't want to say goodbye any more than he did.

"I don't have to be at work for a couple days anyway. Let me pack a bag and I'll be back down in a few minutes."

I turned to leave when he pulled me back, tugging me closer until I was nearly on his side of the car. He pressed a kiss to my lips, his hold both warm and possessive.

"I love you."

"I love you too," I breathed. My head buzzed, my limbs tingled with delicious warmth, as if I'd been given a dose of something strong. The usual attraction between us was now amplified with the full out admission that we were falling hopelessly in love with each other again. My body and brain's reactions were almost more than I could handle.

When he finally released me, I rushed upstairs to pack, a stupid smile on my face. I gave Eli the briefest of updates, which ended in a kind of hopeless shrug that he seemed to understand.

We drove back to Cameron's place. With no sign of Olivia, we settled in. He made us a late lunch and showed me around the building, pointing out all the improvements he and Olivia had made over the past few weeks. It really had come along since the last time I'd been there, and as much as I begrudged Olivia for personal reasons, she'd been a positive force in his world since arriving. In the spirit of moving forward with Cameron with an open heart and a lot more hope than I'd given us before, I harbored a little optimism that Olivia and I could find a way around our differences.

"Everything looks great. This is so much space for the two of you though, isn't it? Won't she get her own place eventually?"

"I'm sure she will. I guess I was thinking about the future. I haven't written off the idea of sharing my home with someone yet."

My cheeks heated a little. "It's a lot even for two people. For New York, this is an enormous living space."

He nodded and bit his lip. "Families can get big, you know."

My breath caught. Oh, fuck. He was talking about us. Maybe his little talk with Ruthie hadn't been senile banter. I shifted my weight nervously from side to side.

"Thinking a little far ahead, aren't we?"

He shrugged, and a little smile turned up his lips. We didn't say anything more about it as we finished the tour and returned to the safe haven of the upstairs apartment.

"So I have to head into the gym tonight, make sure Darren hasn't burned the place down or something."

I cocked an eyebrow. "He's a fire fighter."

"It's a known fact that all fire fighters are pyromaniacs. He can't be trusted. Anyway, come with me."

"You don't want me moping around there. I'll be bad for business."

He laughed. "Nonsense. I won't know what to do with myself if you aren't there bitching about the routine I'm giving you."

"You're going to make me workout?"

He flashed a mischievous grin. "Yup. Get dressed."

I rolled my eyes and groaned. "Fine."

He swatted my ass as I turned.

I shot him a weak glare. "What was that for?"

"I recently realized how much I like spanking your ass, and when you say snarky shit, it kind of gives me the perfect excuse to."

I pursed my lips. "I'm not sure I like the sound of that."

"Oh, I do." He wrapped an arm around my waist, spinning me so we were chest-to-chest. His mouth was close, his soft breath dancing on my lips. All kinds of dark meaning shadowed his eyes. "I like the sound of my palm slapping your ass. And I like the sounds you make when I do it too."

I sucked in a sharp breath, heat rising to my cheeks. "All right, you've effectively coerced me into wanting to go to the gym." I disengaged from his hold and gave him a much-needed push before my sex brain took over and let him start acting on these deviant threats.

CAMERON. The gym was fairly quiet. Raina was gone too, with yoga classes being off the schedule until the new year. I was glad for that. I hadn't had a chance to talk to Raina much about Maya, but I would if it meant quelling her concerns about what kind of relationship we had. The line I'd drawn with Raina to keep things professional would have to be redrawn. I'd let her flirt before, figuring it was harmless. That wouldn't fly anymore.

I was doing crunches on the mat while Maya killed some time on the treadmill. Darren came into view as I rose.

"Hey," I said, sitting up.

"Way to bail on us for Christmas, man. That one will go down in the history books, for sure."

I cringed, regret hitting me in a way it hadn't when Olivia was spewing her threats over the phone at me.

"Things with Maya got, I don't know, intense, I guess. I didn't want to leave her alone and I figured you and Liv could hold things down with Mom and Dad. How bad was it?"

Darren blew out a breath. "Uh, pretty unbearable. More than usual, I suppose, because they were freaking out about you not being there. It basically amplified all the usual awkward shit. So yeah."

I had to see them at some point. I'd been able to avoid them for nearly a year. I'd had a lot on my plate, but beyond that, no time ever felt right. Our time felt awkward and forced, and even without seeing them, I knew it'd be the same. I'd spent three years watching life and death play out in the desert, letting days of my life slip by. I couldn't justify wasting another day pretending to be the son they wanted me to be or apologizing that I wasn't. But for Darren and Olivia's sake, I'd have to step up next time.

"Sorry. I owe you one."

"Awesome, because they're coming back for New Year's. You're taking that shift. I've got a date."

"With who?"

"Not sure, but I'll have one, trust me. And don't fucking give me that look. You owe me one, like you said."

I sighed inwardly, hating that I had to deliver on my promise so soon. "Fine."

"Anyway, what's up with Maya? Everything okay?"

"Yeah, everything's good now. Really good."

"Cool. I'm glad to hear it."

"All right, I'm heading out for a while. I'll catch you tomorrow."

"Sounds good."

He walked off and I finished up, eager to find Maya.

We took a long walk, which ended at a bakery near the park. I'd promised her chocolate if she finished an extra set of crunches. She reluctantly agreed and I'd made a mental note to bribe her with chocolate in the future.

We stepped into the tiny bakery, the smells of fresh dough and chocolate wafting over us.

"God, these all look amazing. What are you getting?" Maya's eyes were wide as she assessed the pastries through the display window.

"I'll stick with coffee. Get whatever you want, though."

She spun and looked at me like I had three heads, her

brows knitted tightly together. "You work me to the brink of death, then lure me to a bakery offering mouth watering desserts and tell me you're just getting coffee?"

"I have to watch my figure," I joked. "Can't have my clients giving me a hard time."

"Whatever, you're holding them accountable. Not the other way around."

"Does that mean I should be holding you accountable too?"

"I'm not your client, but I'm humoring you. You can torture me with your workouts, but don't get between me and my chocolate. It could get ugly."

I laughed. "Warning noted."

"In fact, to make this point, I'm going to get two."

I nodded with raised eyebrows. "Ambitious."

She smiled broadly, and I got a small thrill out of her obvious excitement. We took our desserts and drinks to a small round table in the corner of the bakery. She wasted no time tasting the first dessert. She moaned quietly.

"That good?" I teased.

"You're really missing out." She dangled a spoonful of chocolate mousse in front of me.

"Looks amazing, but I'm good. Stop taunting me."

She airplaned the spoon into her mouth and moaned so loud, my mouth watered, but for all the wrong reasons. She opened an eye to catch my reaction. I was gawking, slack jawed.

"What?"

I slid my chair closer, taking the spoon from her. "Here, let me." I scooped out another helping and held it to her lips.

Slowly she parted for me and took it in her mouth.

She licked the spoon clean, her throat working on a swallow. I suppressed a moan of my own. I wanted to be that spoon. Christ, did I ever. I licked my lips and shoved a vision of her licking chocolate mousse off my cock out of my head. How did we get from dessert to dirty so fucking fast?

I lifted a fresh scoop to her lips. She took it and closed her eyes, a quieter moan punctuating the finish. I wasn't sure if she was trying to drive me crazy on purpose. I was too fixated on feeding her dessert to care. We could do this all night, except I was already getting hard and we had a long walk home.

"It's really good, Cam," she said, breaking me from one of a dozen visions blooming from my now suddenly vivid imagination.

"That good?"

She nodded, slowly licking the frothy substance from her lips. "Delicious."

Delicious. I let the word roll around in my mind, letting it dance over the fantasies that were playing out.

I leaned in slowly until our lips nearly touched. "I'll need to try some of it then."

She sucked in a breath but gave no resistance. I angled slightly and licked the sweet curve of her lower lip. Catching her face in my palm, I held her still and kissed her gently.

The clatter of a couple situating themselves nearby broke the moment. She pulled back quickly. I studied her reaction.

"Delicious."

"See, don't you wish you'd gotten it?" Her voice was breathy, our gazes fixed on one another.

"And miss sampling it off your lips? Not for the world."

She paused and contemplated the as yet untouched tiramisu for a second.

"Give me that fork." I took her fork and scooped off a corner of the dessert. I ate it, noting that it would taste far better when I was licking it off of Maya.

She grinned broadly. "I'm corrupting you."

"That's okay. I'll make you pay for it tomorrow."

She slapped me on the arm. "That's not fair. You cheat and I pay?"

"My rules."

"Why are they always your rules? Maybe next week should be my rules. No exercise and I'll have you on a strict diet of chicken fingers and gummy bears."

I grimaced at the thought. "That shit's terrible for you, Maya."

"I know, and I have the ass to show for it."

I frowned, not liking her implication. "I love your ass," I said with total seriousness.

Her eyes flashed to mine and then back to her dessert, which she was systematically mangling with her fork. "Quit," she mumbled, tucking her hair behind her ear and revealing the sudden blush in her cheeks.

The color emboldened me. I leaned in closer, ensuring only she could hear me. "Don't make me prove it right here."

"Yeah right."

I sat back and grinned. "You have an amazing body, though. You shouldn't feel insecure *at all*."

"I don't believe you, but thank you."

"Believe it, or you'll force me to keep

complimenting your ass. It could get really awkward. Like, a lot more awkward than this." I gestured discreetly to the occupied table and the couple who may or may not have been overhearing our ass banter.

She laughed, and I joined her. I loved her laugh, a natural throaty sound that took me back to another time, when we laughed all the time. I resolved to get her to do this more, for her sake and mine.

Contentment flooded me, in a way I couldn't remember happening since...well, since the last time we'd been together.

CHAPTER NINETEEN

MAYA. "Are you mad?"

"I'm not exactly thrilled with how the other night went down, if that's what you're asking. I thought you'd be more receptive."

Jia dropped her napkin on the table, resting back into her seat casually. Even as I struggled to make sense of this situation she'd dropped me in, I couldn't help but be captivated with her simple grace. How far had it taken her to this point, luring people in with that easy confidence, that air of power and control? I'd succumbed to it so easily.

"You blindsided me, Jia. How the hell was I supposed to know that he, and you, expected me to spend Christmas Eve fucking in his office?"

"You seemed pretty open-minded when we went out to the club. I figured after a drink, you'd loosen up and you'd be fine with it. Is it this thing with Cameron?"

I opened my mouth to speak, but couldn't find the

words. I didn't want to admit how he'd utterly freaked out on me after our rendezvous. "He wasn't impressed."

She frowned. "You should be careful with him."

"What do you mean?"

"He's obviously controlling."

"He cares about me. I don't think he's *controlling*." My tone was sharp, surprising even me with how quickly I defended him. I didn't like the idea of someone thinking anyone controlled my life. I also didn't like her attacking the man I loved.

She rolled her eyes. "Right. They wait until you're hopelessly in love with them, and then they start telling you how to live your life. Trust me, I've been there."

I swallowed hard. I couldn't really argue with the picture she painted. Being with Cameron had changed my life, turned everything upside down. Not that I would have been on board with fucking my boss to get a promotion otherwise, but Cameron's better judgment colored a lot of my decisions lately. Falling in love with him had played no small part in that transformation.

As if reading my mind, her eyes softened. "Maya, what happened? I thought you said you wanted to focus on your career. That you weren't interested in a relationship?"

"I wasn't, but...we were in love once. We fell back into it so easily."

She sighed quietly. "Anyway, we have to figure a way out of this mess with Dermott."

The pit in my stomach grew. My job was very likely on the line. Being jobless wasn't how I wanted to ring in the new year. "How bad is it?"

"He's freaking out that you're going to file some sort

of sexual harassment claim with the company and he'll get heat. I promised him you wouldn't, that you weren't like that. I had to blow him just to get him to calm down."

She gave me a look that said, *Thanks for that.*

I wanted to feel guilty that she'd been put in that position, but I fought a wave of nausea with the thought that it could have been me.

"How can you do that, Jia?" I asked, unable to hide my disgust. Dermott wasn't totally repulsive, but his personality was. The idea of giving him access to any part of my body for sexual gratification seemed unthinkable, even more so than it had the other night.

She frowned as she studied my obvious reaction. "Don't look down your nose at me, Maya. Start with that, and any semblance of friendship that we had is over. I told you I'd show you how to get ahead, and that's what we needed to get ahead."

"You fuck people to get ahead?" I threw my hands up, unable to accept her suggestion as remotely normal. "Doesn't it bother you that people think that about you anyway? What kind of role model are we for other women in this company if that's how we get ahead?"

She softened slightly. "Listen, I don't habitually do that, but I saw an opportunity and I took it. But you couldn't sacrifice a few hours of your life for a promotion that would have put you light years ahead of your colleagues."

"I'd sooner fuck the mailroom guy than Dermott."

She grimaced at the suggestion.

"I'm not spreading my legs to prove I can do my job, when I can do it well enough."

She narrowed her eyes. "So that's how it is."

Defending myself and insulting her behavior were one in the same, and that fact wasn't lost on her. I fought the wave of panic that crept over me. I had no idea how this would play out or what she expected me to do from here. I'd let her take the lead, but I couldn't trust where that took me anymore.

I took a deep breath, trying to recover the tone of the conversation. "All I'm saying is you should have more respect for your body...for yourself, than to let someone like him demean you that way."

She let out a sharp laugh. "Respect? Plenty of people respect me. Who respects you, Maya? You were nothing but a cubicle drone until I put the spotlight on you. You let people pass you over every day, take advantage of your talents and your mind so they can take all the credit. What's that if not demeaning?"

I clenched my teeth, hating the absolute truth that spewed from her lips. "You're right, Jia." I held her in a hard stare, seeing her clearly for the first time. "And that's exactly what you did. Or what you would have done, if I'd been stupid enough to let you."

"What?"

"You spelled it all out for me, remember? You told me yourself that you weren't here to make friends, that you were here to get ahead. That it was all about finding out what people wanted and capitalizing on those desires for your benefit."

"This was for *our* benefit."

"Did you really think I'd let you pimp me so you could get a promotion, Jia? This wasn't about me. This was about *you*. But what shocks me is that someone as smart as you couldn't come up with something more original than blowing our boss to get ahead."

Her eyes grew dark, dangerously so. "You're going to regret this."

"Maybe I will. But I'm sure I won't regret it as much as I would have regretted letting Dermott fuck me."

I stood and grabbed my purse, throwing a fifty on the table. "This one's on me."

"That won't help you keep your job."

"I don't need this job, so do what you want, Jia."

I walked out, trying to keep my legs steady and fighting the tremble that coursed through me.

CAMERON. Darren called to me on my way in. He said something unintelligible to the pretty blonde he was training and followed me down the hall to the office. Shutting the door behind us, he stood silent while I shoved my things in my locker.

I circled the desk. He stood awkwardly in front of it. Something was up. He didn't have a smart-ass grin on his face or anything sarcastic to say. In fact, I'm not sure I'd seen him this serious...ever.

"What's up? Everything okay?"

"Do you want to talk to me about anything?" he asked calmly.

I frowned. "No?" I dropped down into my chair, pulling up the schedule on the computer.

"Not anything at all?"

My eyes went wide. I had no idea what the hell he was getting at. "Spit it out, Darren. I have an appointment in ten minutes."

He walked up to the desk, put his hands on the edge,

and leaned in close.

"A ring, Cam? You bought her a fucking ring?"

My eyes shot to the locker where I'd stashed my bags the other day. *Nosy bastard.*

"Stay out of my locker."

"I knew something was up when you came in. You can't hide that kind of stuff from me."

"It's none of your business."

"Really? I'm your brother and best friend. And you weren't going to run that by me? When I was giving you shit about getting her into bed, I wasn't suggesting you run off and marry her. Have you lost your goddamn mind?"

I reclined back in the chair, gaining some distance from Darren's decidedly aggressive line of questioning.

"I don't understand why you care so much. Relationships aren't exactly your forte."

"They're not, but this is insane. Even I can see that."

"You think calling someone back after you sleep with her is insane. No offense, but you're out of your depth here."

"You really think she's going to marry you now after she's already shot you down once?" His voice was strained and bordered on hysterical.

I suppressed a smile. He was genuinely concerned.

He'd voiced a valid point though. I'd asked myself the same question roughly every twenty minutes since I'd purchased the ring. I was nowhere close to presenting it to her, but it would only be a matter of time. I'd made up my mind.

"I have no idea when I'm going to ask her, but when I do, I'm not taking no for an answer."

He let out a short laugh. "Sounds promising. Great plan."

I blew out a breath. I wasn't sure how to make Darren understand this situation, or if he even could. We didn't have many heart to heart conversations about anything, let alone women, and he wasn't the most intuitive person in that department.

"I know this is probably going to fly right by you and get filed under *touchy feely chick shit*, but I'm in love with her. I've been in love with her since the day I left her. Nothing's changed, except now I love her more. What I did…it was a mistake. We both made mistakes, and we both have regrets. I'm not letting her go again." My heart twisted with the declaration. The familiar pang of regret gripped me as I thought about how I'd let her go. Like an immature jerk, I'd never given her a chance to change her mind.

"You need to get your fucking head together, because last time things went downhill with her, you weren't the only one who suffered."

"Yeah, I get it. Liv never lets me fucking forget it." I stood up, leaning in to meet his glare. "The way you two talk, you'd think you were the ones up all night listening to bomb blasts and watching your friends get sent home in boxes for three years. I've had it with the lectures, all right? It was my choice. No one forced my hand, and I'm on the other side of it. I'm sorry that you all went through what you did, but blaming Maya for it is ridiculous. She's been through enough, in large part thanks to me. So that shit is going to stop right now."

He straightened, crossed his arms over his chest, and stared back. The hint of acceptance in his features was the only thing stopping me from wrestling him to the ground to make my point.

"You're serious about this." The way he said it was less of a question and more of a resigned statement.

"You think I'd torture myself in a jewelry store for three hours if I wasn't serious?"

"I can't possibly imagine." His lips curved into a sarcastic smile.

"No shit," I grumbled.

He smirked. "How the hell did you become the romantic of the family?"

I laughed and rolled my eyes. "Maybe someone will make you understand what this is like someday."

"I'm good. Watching from the sidelines while you get your heart thrown in the blender should fill that void just fine."

"Thanks for the vote of confidence."

He sighed, raking his hands through his hair. He dropped into the seat across from the desk and stared blankly away from me.

"I want you to be happy, Cam. I really do. And I hope Maya's the one who will do that for you."

"She already is."

He nodded. "You have to admit that this is kind of sudden though. Don't you think you're going to give her whiplash?"

"I told you, I don't have any plans to ask her right now. I know it's too soon. I just... I decided, that's all. We're still figuring things out between us and getting to know each other again. She's changed a lot, and frankly so have I. But something happened, and—"

"What happened?"

"It doesn't matter. What matters is that something clicked for me. Maybe it was obvious, but all this time that has kept us apart has been hell for me."

"It was obvious, but I thought you were finally over it. Now here we are again."

"I've never been over her. Not a single day can I say I was safe from caring about her or regretting what happened between us. And as miserable as that's been, I realized she went through it too."

"She told you that?"

I hesitated, not wanting to even hint at the debacle with her mother or how I'd come across the poems. Everything she'd written came across as so raw and vulnerable, I couldn't possibly unleash Darren's novice opinions on them. The words were hers, and while I was guilty of trespassing on them, I was grateful that I had. I might have never known how she really felt otherwise, or it might have taken months or years to strip her down and get the truth out of her. I couldn't wait that long. I wanted her now, to know who she was on the inside now. I wasn't going to settle for anything less.

"In a way," I finally said.

"Well for your sake, I hope you're right, and that when you do ask her, she gives you the answer you deserve."

"I don't deserve her, but I really want to. I hope she gives me the chance to."

He shook his head. "You're such a pussy, man."

I laughed. "Get to work before I fire you."

"Hey, you can't fire me until you start paying me."

"I thought you got paid in dates?"

He shrugged and stood. "Yeah. You're right. All

right, but do me a favor."

"What?"

"Can you not keep me in the dark completely on things like this? I want to be supportive, but I can't do that if you don't talk to me."

I nodded. I hadn't needed anyone's blessing to ask her the first time, and I sure as hell didn't need his approval the second time around.

"Support isn't necessary, but I appreciate it. I'll try not to blindside you with any big news though."

"Fair enough."

CHAPTER TWENTY

MAYA. I walked to the gym, hating how drained I was. One day back at work and I felt as if my life force had been sucked from me. I didn't see Cameron in the weight room. I briefly considered changing and getting on with the workout I'd promised him and myself I'd do tonight. Part of my whole not-drinking-a-bottle-of-wine-a-night initiative, which so far had been working well. Except now I wanted to wash away the weight of the day—Dermott's decidedly cold attitude toward me and Jia's threats—with a stiff drink.

Instead, I knocked quietly on the office door, entering when I heard Cameron's voice. He was sitting at his desk, his brow knitted as he stared at the screen intensely.

"Hey."

He looked up, brightening when he saw me. "Hey,

baby."

"What are you working on?"

"End of the year financial stuff. It's giving me a headache. Come here."

I dropped my bag and came to him, curling up on his lap without reservation. He hugged me close. I nuzzled into his neck. I breathed him in, tension releasing immediately.

"Okay day?"

I shook my head.

"Do I need to hurt someone?" His voice held only the smallest hint of humor.

"No. But I'm not sure if I'm going to have a job much longer."

"What happened?"

"I called Jia out on being a manipulative bitch, and she threatened me." I leaned against his strong chest, resting my head on his shoulder. "I called her bluff. Told her that I didn't need the job, which of course is a complete lie. I've done well and saved, but I need that job. I can't afford to keep Eli and me in that apartment without a decent paycheck."

"Then move."

"Do you have any idea how difficult it is to get an apartment with a bedroom that size? I had to jump around for a few years to find that place."

"Move in with me. I've got three floors to choose from. And fuck the job. You hate it anyway. We'll find you something else. Maybe you could help me around here for awhile."

I laughed. "You are seriously living in a dream world. My place is not in this gym except when you force me or guilt me into coming here."

"I meant on a business level. I'm up to my ears in paperwork. I had the vision for the gym, and I have a vision for more. I got the investors I needed and made it happen. But the rest of this shit is driving me crazy. It's going to catch up to me one day."

I sighed. A little part of me leaped at the portrait he painted of how things could be. Another part of me brushed it off as completely unrealistic. I couldn't ditch Eli, and I couldn't give up on the career that I'd worked so hard for. As much as I wanted to run away, I was trying to do less of that lately.

"I'm happy to help, but I need to make this work. There are lots of banks I can work for if things don't work out."

"What if they make it difficult for you to switch companies? Aren't they all sort of incestuously connected?"

I stared down at my fingers, noting the few nails I'd lost to today's anxiety. I'd briefly considered that Jia or Dermott could blacken my name, blocking attempts to make at least a lateral move, but even that seemed too low for Jia. Had all of our interactions been a farce, or could I count on anything from our friendship?

I closed my eyes. "I don't want to think about it. What's the point in worrying when it's all out of my hands now? She and Dermott will do whatever they decide to do because I won't play their game."

"Sure you don't want me to talk to them? I could give them some powerful insights."

I smiled, looking up at him again. His lips lifted into a grin, but I knew he was serious too. "Thank you for wanting to go to bat for me, but I promise I can handle this one myself."

"Just say the word."

I pressed a chaste kiss to his lips, so grateful for him and his impossible desire to be everything for me. After a moment, he broke the contact.

"How do you do that?" he murmured.

"What?"

"You make everything still. You're all I can see. Everything goes out of focus but you."

A slow smile curved my lips. "Is this a new development?"

"No. When I saw you again for the first time, with all the chaos on the street, I'd actually wondered if I'd recognize you. But I did in an instant. You could have had a spotlight on you. You light up the room, Maya."

My cheeks heated, as I fell under his potent gaze. "Maybe it's who lights me up."

His expression softened. "I hope so."

I held my breath, waiting for him to touch me, wishing he would. He brushed his thumb over my cheek lightly and fingered the teardrop pearls that hung from my ears. Leaning in slowly, he kissed my jaw, pressing his warm lips against my skin and then my lips until I was tingling everywhere.

His hands went to my hips, sliding down to my thighs. His fingertips slipped under the thin fabric of my skirt. I touched his chest, itching to run my fingers over every hard curve of his body.

He slid his hand up and down my legs, caressing the sensitive skin above my knee.

"I like this. You don't usually wear skirts to work, do

you?"

"I was feeling saucy, like I needed to make a statement when I faced them today."

He hummed, smiling under my lips. "Are you still feeling saucy?"

I bit my lip, sifting my fingers through the hair that curled at his neck. A tiny spark lit inside me with his words. "Maybe."

"Long day. I think you deserve a little stress reliever. What do you think?"

I nodded slowly. His gaze turned molten, stoking my spark into a healthy glow. His hand slipped between my thighs, tracing teasing circles all the way up, but evading the place where I needed him the most. I shifted restlessly, hoping he'd take the hint. Instead he lifted me off of him, pushing me back against the desk.

He shoved a few stacks of paperwork aside, making room for me to sit farther back on the desk.

"Lie back."

I obliged, and he divested me of my skirt and panties.

"See if you helped me out with some of this, I'd have a better surface to fuck you on."

I laughed. "I'll take that into consideration."

"Do, because I can already see I'm going to want to work this into your fitness regimen."

He sat down and rolled closer, resting my feet on the arms of the chair so I was wide open to him. He kissed his way up my leg. I jolted at the barest brush of his stubble across my sensitive skin. I was already hypersensitive and on edge, too eager for the rush of his mouth over me. I craved it.

"Can't wait to make you come, Maya."

My breath hitched. Anticipation crept over me with every soft, teasing touch. He brushed his thumb along the seam of my folds, following the path with a broad stroke of his tongue. A quiet whimper escaped me. I threaded my fingers through his hair, moving in time with the expert strokes he lavished upon me. He rotated evasive licks with tiny flicks of his tongue over my clit. I wanted to enjoy every minute of this, being spread over his desk and pleasured, but I burned for him. The need to reach that mindless release took over.

I fisted gently when he increased the pressure, waves of warmth washing over me. My skin prickled.

"Cameron, I love your mouth."

He sucked my clit between his teeth, and I cried out. He hummed, cursing and muttering delicious and obscene admirations against me.

The edge of my orgasm sharpened as he pushed one and then two fingers inside, doing what I sincerely hoped his cock would be doing to me in short order. I responded immediately, my body pushing to the very edge of the cliff. I needed this. I needed him. The pressure of his tongue on me increased, lavishing and tormenting me.

"Fuck. I'm... Oh fuck, I'm going to come." I slammed my hand down on the desk and tightened helplessly, waiting for him to push me over.

"Do it, baby. Come all over my hand." The words shot through me. His breath teased my wet skin, and I was at his mercy.

He pumped inside me, sucking my clit and punishing my G-spot until I cried out. I cursed, coming hard. My body quaked with the lingering shudders.

I was still coming when he stood. He lowered his shorts enough to free his cock. He was hard as stone, thick and so very ready for me. He wasted little time shoving into me. I bowed off the desk. The rush of him filling me sent my tapering orgasm back into overdrive.

"Fuck," he groaned. The strain was evident in his features. "Jesus, you're so fucking tight."

I fluttered around him, tightening beyond control.

He hauled me up into his arms, lifting me off the desk completely only to drop me down onto his hard length. I tightened my legs around him, hoisting myself higher for better leverage.

He bit his lip. "You like that?"

"Love it," I breathed.

He carried us a few steps to the wall, working me over his cock the whole way. I wasn't sure how he managed it, but then again, he was a beast of a man and spent all day in the gym. My back hit the cool surface, giving him enough leverage to find new depths. His hands spread under my ass. He still held me up like I weighed nothing, He pinned my hips to the wall roughly as they met his.

"Oh God." A shudder worked its way through me, my nipples hardening painfully against the laboring muscles of his chest. The brute force only added to my perilous climb. I loved that he could control my body so easily, take me to the edge of pain and still give me unspeakable pleasure.

"I want to hear you. Tell me what I do to you."

My eyelids fluttered open. "I love you so much. I need you, Cam. So much." I leaned in, crushing my lips against his until we were breathless.

His arms tightened around me. We were so close, wrapped up in each other, singularly held in this moment.

His answer was another series of punishing drives into my sensitive tissues. My core clenched, and I went slick allowing him to push deeper still. The bite of his depth was like an electric shock, a snap of mind-frazzling sensation that rendered me speechless and breathless every time he hit the end of me.

My lungs struggled for air. My nails scored down his shoulders. Every muscle froze as we bound ourselves tightly together, only the friction of his brutal entry over and again between us.

He held me with a possessive kiss, claiming my mouth with his, robbing us both of precious air.

"Maya."

The hard rasp of his voice sent a shiver through me. Everything went into the background save the force of the climax as it raged over me. The voice I heard didn't sound like my own as I screamed his name, letting him take us both over the edge.

He went still, a sweep of raw vulnerability softening his face. His lips parted with jagged breaths. The hot liquid of his release filled me as he held himself deep. I clung to him helplessly, wishing that somehow we could stay this way. Forever entwined, creating a new reality that I'd never need to escape from.

CAMERON. A rapidfire rattle echoed in the background of my mind. My muscles tightened, ready to act. Covered in sweat, I shot up, opening my eyes to the dark room.

Maya.

I reached over, finding only emptiness in the mess of sheets where she should have been. The inherent panic carried over, and worry churned inside me. Realization dawned as my eyes adjusted, taking in the familiar shapes of my room. My chest expanded on a long, sobering breath. Fuck.

I threw my legs over the edge of the bed and hung my head, willing my brain back to reality. Panic flitted through my veins. I was on high-alert, the way I'd been for days on end over the course of many years. The state of being was one I'd grown accustomed to. I couldn't talk my brain out of it sometimes.

I rose slowly, making my way to the kitchen. I downed a glass of water. My breath finally slowed. I was far away from that life. I kept reminding myself. Yet a niggling irrational dread lingered that one day I'd wake up there again. The mere thought seized my gut. It was a dark hopeless feeling, a repetitive nightmare that wouldn't quit. No way out. A prison all its own.

I slumped on the couch. Conscious enough to separate dreams from reality, I was now too awake and alert to sleep. I tried to relax. Closing my eyes, my thoughts drifted to Maya. A familiar ache filled me, the one that wanted her with me every minute that she could be. She'd gone back to her apartment after a few days, wanting to check in on Eli and get settled back into her usual work routine. Maybe it was the late nights loving her until we were utterly wasted, but having Maya in my bed kept the specters at bay.

I reached for my phone on the table, flipping

through the photos until I found one of Maya. Her blond hair was pulled up tight, loose tendrils framing her face. Soft brown eyes stared back at me, full of hidden meaning. She was posing, dressed for the holiday party I'd nearly dragged her out of. After, I'd made love to her all night. God, I would again if she were here right now. I'd have my way with her, tell her how I loved her, how I never wanted her to go. Buried deep inside her, I'd make her believe it. She'd never doubt it.

I needed this woman. To possess her, to have the world know she was mine to love and to keep. To cherish.

I closed my eyes, memorizing the image in my mind as I drifted back to sleep.

CHAPTER TWENTY-ONE

MAYA. The day was coming to a close. Again, the day wore on me. Any hope I'd harbored before about my work life improving had effectively been squashed.

Tension between Jia and me was evident. She avoided me when we crossed paths. I barely saw Dermott. That wasn't unusual, except now I had no idea what he was thinking. I hoped eventually enough time would pass that we could call it water under the bridge.

At a quarter to five, my phone rang. In a clipped voice, Dermott asked to see me. My stomach fell. Shit, this was it. The end. I took a deep breath, determined to keep my composure.

I stepped inside his office. When he didn't look up to greet me, I took a seat across from his desk. I wondered if he'd heard me, until he cleared his throat and looked up at me. The moment was brief. He shuffled through his papers, dropping a clipped pile to the edge of the large desk in front of me.

I swallowed hard. "Are you firing me?"

A tight smile pinched his features. "I think it's best if we move on. Your work on the Cauldwell deal was admirable, but clearly there's going to be tension here."

"There doesn't have to be. Obviously it was a gross misunderstanding." Gross might not have been the best word, but in a way, it was. Letting the scene play out from Christmas Eve would have been horrible. My skin crawled just thinking about letting him touch me. Thank God I hadn't let things go that far.

"Regardless, what's done is done. We've never exactly had a great rapport, and frankly, I think you'd probably find yourself more fulfilled elsewhere."

"You're firing me, just like that?"

"You'll get three months' severance in exchange for signing a release indemnifying the company of any allegations. Just in case you have any ideas about discussing our little misunderstanding."

"What about references?"

He sat back in his chair, a discontented grimace on his face. If he hated me before, he despised me now. All because I wouldn't let him screw me on his desk.

"If you need a reference, I'm sure it could be arranged."

How big of him. I reached for the paperwork, reading through it.

"You can bring it back after you've read through it and signed."

"I'll read through it now. I'd like closure on this matter. I'm sure you'd agree."

"Fine," he muttered.

I skimmed through, focusing on the clauses that highlighted the severances and the terms of my silence. It was buttoned up tight. Money would close the chapter on this little mess. Jia and he could go about their business, whatever that now entailed, and I would no longer be a liability. All for a healthy severance that was pennies to the company.

I bristled at the thought. I tossed it back to him.

"You can take this agreement and shove it up your ass, Dermott."

Breath hissed through his teeth, barely containing his rage. "Excuse me?"

"This is unacceptable. I didn't do anything wrong here."

"Really? Jia said you came onto her at a nightclub. That doesn't exactly paint you in a favorable light."

"She came onto me, and besides, that was on my time. There's no fraternizing policy with the company. I've already checked."

"And what about that little incident in Jia's office with your boyfriend?"

Panic hit me. *Oh, fuck.* Then I relaxed, realizing he had no way of knowing what actually went down in there. Jia would have told him she'd given us access to her office while they were gone, but that meant nothing.

"Prove it."

He let out a smug laugh. "I can prove it no more than you can prove anything out of the ordinary happened here last week. If you were smart you'd sign this. I'll only make this offer once." He pushed the stack of paper back toward me. I didn't give it a second look.

"Actually, firing me and trying to shut me up with

313

severance proves something very out of the ordinary happened. Surely that isn't an everyday occurrence." I shook my head, disgust for him renewing my anger. "You couldn't even wait to give me a few poor reviews, get the paperwork in place to let me go clean. I was blatantly propositioned and offered a promotion to have sex with you both. How do you think that will sound? Let's not bullshit. Something is troublesome enough about all of this that you need to be rid of me as soon as possible. Well, trust me, I'm happy to leave, but I'm not getting steamrolled."

His lips tightened. His gray eyes hardened, filled with the mutual dislike that we shared for one another.

"You want to wipe your hands of me, Dermott?"

His silence was answer enough.

"Twelve months severance, and I want recommendations in writing. From both of you and at least one of the officers after you explain to them how I busted my ass on the Cauldwell deal. They'd better be glowing too."

He gave me a hard stare, the vein in his forehead decidedly more pronounced.

"What makes you think you can make demands?"

"Make the changes or I'll be getting a lawyer and every face you see here will know exactly what you two did to me. Not to mention your wife. It's that simple."

A few hours later I was walking hand-in-hand with Cameron toward the Plaza. I'd feigned a smile and assured him my day had been fine. It was New Year's Eve after all, and he'd made plans for us. I'd tell him later about what had gone down today, but for now, I didn't want to spoil our night. He'd be upset and probably would want to beat Dermott to a pulp all over again.

Begrudgingly, Dermott had agreed to my terms and promised to have a revised draft to me in the morning. But until it was signed, nothing was certain. This was my fight, and I was very close to winning it. Even if losing my job wasn't considered a general win, at least I wasn't going to be hung out to dry.

I was relieved I never had to go back to that place. The thought of finding a new job at another bank seemed the natural next step, but I wasn't sure about that. I hadn't had much time to contemplate what my future might look like before I left for the day and met with Cameron.

We found our way to the quiet hum of the lounge. Already on edge, I was a little stressed about facing Cameron's parents. Surely they'd known some details of our breakup, especially if Olivia had been vocal at all about her disapproval of me. He promised she'd be on her best behavior, but I had doubts.

Seated at a round table, the three of them laughed and smiled, drinks in hand. They fell silent as we approached. I clung to Cameron, trying not to look as uncomfortable as I felt. I leaned gently against his large frame, steeling myself for the reintroductions.

"Maya, you remember my mother, Diane?"

"Maya, it's lovely to see you again." Her lips lifted to a smile that didn't meet her gray eyes.

Her gaze traveled the length of me, giving me an obvious visual appraisal. Her expression only betrayed mild interest. Thankfully there was no hint of Olivia's disapproval there. Maybe she was as superficial as Cameron had promised and in all the ways that might have mattered to her, I fit the bill.

I returned her smile and shifted my gaze to his father who sat across the table from where we'd be. He was attractive, but a whisper of a man compared to his strongly built sons. Wearing a suit coat and stiffly starched white collared shirt beneath, he nodded in my direction and smiled.

"Mr. Bridge."

"Call me Frank, please."

I nodded quickly. Bits of memories of meeting with them while Olivia and I were at school together floated back to me. I'd see them fairly often, for parents' weekends, holiday pick-ups, or the few times they'd dropped Cameron off to visit us. They would invite me, Olivia's unfortunate parentless friend, to fancy dinners where they pressed her about her grades and major, plans to travel abroad in the summers. I'd sit, mostly quietly, and pretend I could relate to anything they were discussing. I didn't dislike them because they could give Olivia those opportunities. In fact, I was happy for her. What I hated was being looked at like a pity case. I hated that they spoke a language I'd never been taught, one that I'd only learned over time. By the time I had enough money to do all the things they talked about doing, I'd fallen too far from wanting much of it.

We sat down. Cameron gave me a warm, reassuring smile. I relaxed a little and stared at my menu. Cameron had promised we'd make this short and get dinner together later so I set it back down, regretting that I had nothing to distract me.

Frank piped up after taking a deliberate swig from his brandy. "So, Maya. Tell us about your work."

"Maya works on Wall Street as a financial analyst."

Cameron said before I could speak.

Frank's eyebrows rose. "My old stomping grounds. I'm impressed. Tell me more."

A twinkling of hope filled me. I launched into my practiced summary of what I did, omitting the fact that for all intents and purposes I was unemployed.

Usually people's eyes glazed over after the first twenty seconds, but Frank seemed interested. We went back and forth while Olivia chatted quietly with her mother. Cameron sat back silently, a quiet satisfaction in his eyes, as his father and I discussed financial news. He still held my hand in his, giving it a small squeeze under the table. So far so good.

Frank spoke quickly, more engaged than I ever remembered him being before. "So what are some of your long-term plans? That position has a high burn out rate. I'm surprised you're still at it, actually. Are you staying with the company or...?"

I hesitated, weighing my answer. I was feeling relaxed enough, accepted enough to think that maybe I could tell him the truth. "I'm going to be looking for a change soon. Very soon, actually."

His eyes went wide. "Really? Have you considered private equity?"

I smiled. "Other than helping Cameron with his year-end taxes and settling up with his investors, no. I'm not ruling anything out, though."

Diane interrupted her quiet murmuring with Olivia. "Perhaps Cameron could use you after all. He's in desperate need of an accountant to help get his finances straight with the gym. He refuses Frank's help." Diane waved her hand absently at Cameron.

Frank slapped his leg, the sound making Diane start.

"Maya, you should come work for me. You're exactly the kind of person we hire, and we need more women in our office."

"Frank, be serious," said Diane.

He sat back. "What? I am serious."

"Well," she laughed, a half-hearted sound, as if that alone was hardly worth the effort. "You can't possibly think Cameron wants you to hire his, I don't know, ex-whatever she is to come work for you." She brought her martini to her lips.

"Mom," Olivia admonished quietly.

Diane glanced over at her daughter. "What, darling?"

Olivia shot me a sympathetic look, a rare admission of regret passing behind her eyes.

The moment was uncomfortable, and I wanted to be offended. I wanted to be livid at all of them, but what more could I expect? Everything about Diane's reaction confirmed the reservations I'd had about sharing the details of my embarrassing family life with Cameron or Olivia. Dressed to the hilt with a job only the best education could afford still wasn't enough.

I almost laughed at my foolish hope when Cameron's grip on my hand tightened. He leaned in. "You're being really rude, you know that?"

Diane frowned. "Nonsense. I'm saying what everyone here is thinking. And don't talk to me that way. I'm still your mother."

"No, actually, you should apologize to her, right now."

"I'll do no such thing." Her voice lashed across the table like a whip.

Cameron's jaw clenched tight, his breath nearly audibly as he seethed. "You'll apologize to her, or we're leaving and you'll be lucky if you're welcome in my home ever, let alone in another year."

She held his gaze, unwavering. "Don't be ridiculous. I'm not apologizing to this girl. Why she means anything at all to you is beyond me."

"She's not some girl."

Her lazy gaze slid over to me. "No? She looks like some girl to me. You could have half a dozen just like her. I'm not impressed. I wasn't then, and I'm not now. You aim too low."

I tugged on his hand. "Cameron, let's go." They'd both gone too far, said too much. Much as I wanted to see him berate the bitch that was his mother, nothing good could come of us staying.

He barely acknowledged me except to bring me up with him as he rose. "This isn't your life. You have *no* right to pass judgment on her, or on any of us for that matter."

She straightened, as if the stick up her ass wasn't propping her up enough. "You're my children. It's my job to want the best for you."

"You're doing a great job of driving us all out of your lives, and that's about all you're any good at. I don't expect you to understand, but maybe one day you'll get the picture when she's my wife. You'd be lucky to call her your daughter. Until you can come to grips with that, stay out of my life."

She shook her head, the look of disgust plain. "You'd marry her just to spite us?"

An angry, frustrated growl tore from his throat, and he

walked away, pulling me after him.

CAMERON. We walked across the street into the park in silence. We slowed at the bridge. The old stone walls bowed over the stream, every surface bathed in a moonlit glow. Wind whipped through the air enough to chill me, yet neither of us moved. Blond wisps of her hair flew around her beautiful face.

"Are you okay?"

She nodded. Her jaw was strong, but couldn't hide the defeated look in her eyes. Her gaze lingered everywhere but never found me.

"I'm sorry." I paused, wishing she could know how sorry I really was. "I shouldn't have brought you there. I don't know what the hell I was thinking. I had no idea my mother was already going to be lit and lash out like that. Olivia has been venting to her. I'm sure that didn't help matters. Now you know, anyway, what I'm up against with them. They won't let up—"

"Stop." She held up a hand. "It's fine."

"It's *not* fine. She was terrible to you. I'll never forgive her for the things she said."

She let out a tired laugh. "The sad thing is that she's right. You have tension with them, but I'll never belong in that world."

I frowned. "Neither will I."

"It's different for you. I can dress the part, but under it all, I'm still some poor girl who's climbing her way up. You were born into a successful family with so much going for you. You've lived a different life and struck out on your own. I admire that. I've done it too, you know, in my own way. But you shouldn't alienate them for my sake."

"I was alienating them before you came back into my life. What they think has no bearing on how I feel about you. It never did. Regardless, their unattainable expectations only seem to drive a wedge between us, which is all the more reason to shut them out."

"You may regret that one day."

I wouldn't, but I knew what she meant. She'd never had the luxury of shutting out her family. What lengths would she travel to have her mother back in her life, even with all of her shortcomings?

"No, but they probably will. I'm not changing my life to make them comfortable. I meant what I said in there, about us."

"You shouldn't have said it. They're probably freaking out."

I took a step closer, grasping her hands in mine. She was trembling, maybe from the cold.

"All I care about right now is being with you."

"I want to be with you too. I wish I didn't care what they think of me, honestly, but a part of me hates that I'll never be what they want for you. That they'll be disappointed in you because of me."

I tipped her chin, lifting her gaze to mine. Searching her eyes, I wished for an answer to the question I hadn't had the courage to ask again.

"You're what I want. You're everything to me. The good, the bad, and every moment in between. Everything we've been through has made us who we are, and I wouldn't change a minute of it because I love you so much right now it hurts." I swallowed hard before freeing my next words. "I want everything we had and more. I want this...us, forever."

"Cam." Her lip quivered.

I traced its curve as her mouth fell open. I wanted to pull her closer, to kiss away every insecurity she ever had. But I had to tell her everything. I had to get the words out, even though this wasn't remotely how I'd planned it.

My lips went dry. I fought to breathe. Nerves, the weight of our past, like a bag of stones pressed down on my lungs. I reached into my pocket and retrieved a small black velvet box. I held it loosely between us, my fingers not quite ready to release it yet. I tensed, every instinct held me back and shoved me forward at once.

"I love you, Maya. I've always loved you. Every part of you, no matter what you think or what anyone says. The day I met you, something drew me to you. And I haven't found anything like it since. I'm not in love with who you used to be, or who you strive to be. I'm in love with your soul. That's all I see. Nothing and no one is going to ever change that."

When I looked back to her, tears brimmed her eyes. She shook her head and something like dread seized me.

"Please...don't, Cameron. Not now. I can't do this, not with everything else that's happening right now."

A tear slid down her cheek. I wiped it away. My heart broke for her, for both of us. Why couldn't I fucking get this right? Was I living under some sort of curse? I'd promised myself I wasn't going to take no for an answer. I drew in a steadying breath.

"Marry me, and we'll face it together. That's all I've wanted from the beginning."

"You don't need to be dealing with all my baggage, problems that I still need to work through."

"I'll tell you what I need. You. You're all I need. I can't fucking sleep at night without you next to me. I can't think straight when things aren't right between us. My life has been a goddamn wreck since the day I left you. I want us both to finally be happy again."

"If it doesn't work... I can't live with hurting you again."

I sighed, fighting the wave of emotion that hit me. "Then don't... Say yes. Marry me, and I promise you that we will make it work this time. We'll get through whatever crap life throws at us. Together."

Her eyes glittered with emotion, tears that she could no longer hold back slid down her cheeks.

"Maya. Baby, I'm asking for your heart, and the promise that I'll always have it. After all we've been through, that doesn't seem like too much. You said you loved me, that you wanted to be with me. Prove it. Let's make this real."

She didn't need to say anything, because I could sense the answer. Her gaze lowered to the box that I still held firmly. Would it matter if I opened it, or would that simply deepen the old wound of her refusal? I shoved the box back in my pocket. The motion felt like I was putting my heart back into my body after I'd held it out in the cold for her to take, to keep.

"I'm sorry. Cameron, Dermott fired me today. Between that and your parents, and now this..." She stared down at the ground between us, her shoulders bowed. "I love you and I'm not saying no, but I need time to sort through my life. Everything is off kilter. I'm literally reeling, and I can't tell up from down, let alone make a lifelong commitment. I'm begging you to give me time to make sense of all of this."

My throat tightened. I was in disbelief that we could be in this place again. I tried not to think about the last time we'd been here. Everything played out in slow motion and I analyzed each step, each word, scared to death it would lead us out of each other's lives again.

She sighed heavily. Her dark eyes were a billboard for how emotionally destroyed she must have felt in that moment, and I was right there with her.

Time.

That was it. I could give her that, right? As much as I wanted an answer, yearned for the simple affirmation and to know deep down that she meant it, I convinced myself that I could wait a little longer for it.

She hadn't said no. She hadn't rebuffed the admittedly half-baked proposal. I hadn't even shown her the goddamn ring. Not that it would have mattered, but I wasn't exactly doing this by the book. Again.

"Okay," I finally said.

She looked up, worry written all over her face.

"I'll wait. Take the time you need. I'm not going anywhere, okay?"

Unmistakable relief glimmered in her eyes. I pulled her close, warming us, making myself believe that she'd come back to me if I let her go this time.

"Thank you," she whispered.

CHAPTER TWENTY-TWO

MAYA. I woke early and with purpose. The dawning morning was a dim mixture of pink and gray. Untouched white snow blanketed the trees. I took a snapshot in my mind, knowing the quiet beauty wouldn't last.

I shuffled around the apartment, making coffee and toast for breakfast. My body had become used to rising early, and thanks to some miracle of willpower, I had no hangover to sleep off. Now that my world was effectively turned upside down, I was fiercely determined not to muddle it further.

Finally I sat down at the coffee table. The two notebooks lay open in front of me—Cameron's gift and my own, the one he'd read. I still wondered how much he'd read, but I pushed the thought away. It didn't matter. Today had nothing to do with guilt or arguing with the past or lamenting circumstances that were well beyond my control. I was determined to start the slow and overwhelming process of rebuilding my life. That meant facing my past in a way I never fully had before.

With all the idealism of an optimist writing out his new year's resolutions, I resolved that today would be the beginning of a new me. And I had the good sense to know I wasn't the new me yet, and that I was going to have to work to find that person. I was grateful and utterly relieved that Cameron had accepted my indecision last night. I genuinely needed time, and time was the only thing that would put me in the right place to give him the answer he needed, the answer I so badly wanted to give him. I had no idea when that might be. I only hoped he could wait for me to get there.

Over the course of the morning, I filled the new notebook with final copies of the scribblings that had cluttered my original spiral bound. The thoughts were clean. Instead of shaming the words—whether or not Cameron's eyes had grazed them—I'd given them a place to live, and hopefully, to rest.

The book had represented years of fleeting moments, the deep toil of emotions around Cameron, my mother, work, and the unknown future. Until recently, I'd barreled ahead through so much of that pain with little to no regard for my health or any adult kind of respect for my life and the people in it. I refused to accept that as my reality any more.

I finished, tossed the old notebook in the trash, and placed the new leather bound copy on the shelf next to my favorite books and photos. I'd spent the morning reliving every emotion in every word. Now, I was ready to start living my future.

I spent the next week wasting afternoons in cafes,

writing more, thinking, researching job possibilities. Dreaming. I walked everywhere. Unhurried, cold, and sobering walks that took me to places in the city I'd never bothered going before. Everything was open and possible. I only had to choose my path.

Dermott finally sent the agreement with the glowiest recommendations I'd ever read, which gave me no small amount of satisfaction. I'd signed it, more grateful than ever that I'd never grace that office again. I didn't rule out the possibility of crossing paths with them in the future, but I hoped that enough time would go by first to fade some of the resentment I now harbored.

Eli was out with his new boyfriend most nights. I mostly read and slept in the evenings. Cameron and I talked once a day. I even popped into the gym a few times to help him get his taxes sorted. His lack of organization was staggering, and being handed the task of straightening it all out was unexpectedly fulfilling. I was enjoying the reprieve from work, but I desperately needed an occupation. That much was becoming clear.

Much to Cameron's surprise, I worked out of my own volition. I did my yoga and pretended that Raina wasn't teaching it. In a further attempt to keep things on an even keel, I reassured myself that my recent absence wasn't providing an opening for her to make a renewed try for Cameron's affections.

We were taking time, but nothing had lessened the strength of my feelings for him. I saw the asking in his eyes. He invited me to dinner, but I turned him down as politely as I could. I wanted nothing more than to spend time with him, but he clouded everything with the addictive pull he had over me, the drug that was loving him. At least for now, I clung to the clarity this break was giving me, determined to find and solidify the person I needed to be before rushing back into his arms.

CAMERON. Olivia brought the last of the dishes to the table. Darren dug in without ceremony, piling her homemade pasta onto his plate like a starved man. Olivia smiled.

"Looks great, Liv. Thanks."

"No problem. We haven't had a family dinner in awhile." Her smile faded a second later, her gaze flashing to me. "I mean…"

"It's okay. This is what I consider a family dinner anyway."

The next few moments passed in awkward silence as we ate. I contemplated that night with our parents, warring with who to blame for how it all turned out. At first I'd blamed Olivia for raising concern to begin with, prompting the second of two visits I'd considered entirely unnecessary. I even considered blaming Darren for not being there to run interference, but even his easy charm wouldn't have distracted Diane from saying what she had.

I blamed Maya's boss for ruining her day and possibly her career, pushing her to the emotional edge. Over the past couple days I'd seriously considered paying the asshole a visit and giving him the sound beating I should have given him the night he'd propositioned Maya. If she ever learned of it though, I'm sure it wouldn't earn me points with getting her back.

Her job drama aside, I blamed myself for making the mistake of bringing her to see them, for rushing into the

marriage conversation when she obviously wasn't ready
for it. I'd been selfish, wanting to bind her to me. Now
all I wanted was to simply be with her. I could point the
finger all I wanted, but ultimately the blame fell squarely
on my shoulders. Married or not, I just had to have her
with me. I refused to accept that I could lose her again.
I'd even considered returning the ring, as if that symbolic
step backwards could undo this separation. If only it
could be that easy.

The events of that night had ultimately pushed Maya
back out of my life. Not forever, but enough that I
deeply regretted the distance between us. I ached for her.
I slept like hell, if at all. I'd been withdrawn and growly
at work, which is likely why Olivia arranged this dinner.
A peace offering, maybe. She'd taken the brunt of my
mood. We were a unit, albeit a small one, but we had to
be strong for each other.

"How's work, Darren?" she asked.

"Good. You know, it's fire season. Plenty of people
trying to heat their apartments with toaster ovens. Makes
for interesting days."

"Any new recruits?"

He twisted his lips up. "Nah."

I cocked an eyebrow. "What about the blonde? She
seems like she's all over you. Easy pickings, right? Isn't
that what you always say?"

He ran his teeth across his bottom lip and glanced to
the side. "I don't know. Not my type."

I laughed loudly. "You're joking, right?"

He smirked, finally meeting my gaze. "Fuck you,
man. What's up with Maya anyway? Hate to shine a light
on the elephant in the room, but you've been impossible

to be around lately. Is it over with you two, or what?"

I leveled a glare at him at the mention of her name. I'd made it pretty clear I didn't want to discuss it. Olivia stared at her plate toying with her food, her lips pressed together.

"We're taking some time, that's all."

"She's still coming by the gym though. Are you cool with that?"

"I'm fine. I lived without her for five years. What's another few weeks or months? I should be a pro at this by now." I worked my jaw. Somewhere in the back of my mind, I wished I had somewhere far away to be right now. It was a dark thought, to want to be someplace shadowed in memories that kept me up at night. Anything to be free of this brand of agony.

When she'd come to the gym, I had to keep myself from hauling her into my arms and kissing her breathless. Instead I'd watched myself pull away a little more every time I saw her. The less we interacted, the easier it seemed. Having to see her and not be able to touch her or tell her how I felt was a slow torture. She'd asked for space, and God knew I'd pushed her hard enough already. She hadn't said no, and as much as I hated the idea of giving her time—spending any unnecessary time apart—I didn't get that sinking feeling that we were over.

Impossible as it seemed, I would try like hell to give her the time she needed. I just worried how long I could survive it.

Darren took a swig of his beer. "What about you, Liv? Anyone catching your eye?"

She shrugged. "I don't know. You'd think in a city this big, I'd be dating someone by now."

"Plenty of beefy guys at the gym." Darren gave her a silly smile.

"Right." She rolled her eyes. "Like you two wouldn't be pulling your usual overprotective routine the second one of those guys asked me out."

"Hey, that's what big brothers are for, you know." Darren reached over and mussed her hair.

She swatted him away, unsuccessfully hiding a grin.

We finished eating and she rose to clear the table when Darren stopped her.

"I'll get it, Liv. You cooked. Let me clean up."

She settled back down, fidgeting with her napkin as he disappeared into the kitchen with our plates. The silence was heavy. We'd barely spoken since New Year's and the more time went by, the harder it'd become to breach the tension that had come between us.

"Cameron, I'm sorry. A part of me feels like this is all my fault."

I resisted the urge to tell her she was completely right. I wanted her to feel a fraction of the devastation that I did. The regret in her eyes softened that urge. Instead of the meddling spitfire who'd taken charge of the finer details of my life the past couple months, all I could see was my baby sister. I'd seen her through enough that I knew what genuine regret looked like on her.

"Water under the bridge, okay? Let's get past it. Just promise me you'll never pull that shit on me again, all right?"

Her shoulders relaxed with evident relief. "Thank you. I'm going to talk to Maya sometime too. Maybe when things are more settled between you two. But I owe her an apology. I realize that. I've been a complete bitch. I know it's not an excuse, but I hope you understand that I was only trying to protect you."

"I get it. I'm protective of you too. That'll never change. Hopefully I don't inadvertently end up scaring off your reason for living though."

The regret was back. The corners of her lips turned down a fraction.

I reached for her hand, giving it a small squeeze. "Enough of this heavy stuff though. Want to watch a movie?"

She brightened a little. "Sure."

"Go pick something out. No chick flicks."

She laughed and rose. "Right. Wouldn't want to see you two tough guys getting all weepy on me."

CHAPTER TWENTY-THREE

MAYA. Vanessa rushed into the cafe, stress written all over her face. I didn't miss that look. For a second I thought I could actually see the shackles on her ankles as she joined me at the table. I'd never been so happy to be a free bird.

I rose and she gave me a firm hug.

"How are you doing?" The question was rhetorical. I knew Reilly was definitely still making her daily life pure hell.

She sighed and dropped into the chair. "I miss you like crazy, Maya. I'm so happy you've moved on, but I also kind of hate you, you know?"

I laughed. "Sorry. I'll try to get down here more often for lunch."

"Are you job hunting?"

"I'm seeing what's out there, but I haven't applied anywhere. I've been helping Cameron out with some business stuff at the gym. Otherwise just kind of taking a break. Trying to figure out where to go from here."

"I'm sure Cameron is psyched to be able to spend more time with you."

I stalled, unsure of where to start. I didn't really want to get into where things stood with Cameron right now, but I'd have to eventually. Thankfully the server came and took our orders. I hoped that would distract her, but her focus was fully trained on me, a concerned look in her eye.

Vanessa must have read the hesitation on my face. "Are you two still together? What did I miss?"

"We're kind of taking a break."

"Was that your decision?"

I nodded.

"What did he do? Was he a jerk to you?"

I laughed. "Twenty questions, Vanessa."

She threw her hands up. "I'm out of the loop. Seriously, fill me in. Fast. Who knows when I'll be beckoned again?"

I sighed. "He wasn't a jerk." Far from it. He'd been sweet and poured his heart out to me.

"Well, what happened? For fuck's sake, spill it."

"He kind of proposed."

A deep groove marked her brow. "How does one 'kind of propose'?"

"I guess you get about half way there before the person you're proposing to gets that deer-in-headlights look and stops you before you can get down on one knee."

"What? You stopped him? Why?"

I thought back to that moment. I'd stopped him in his tracks. I hadn't wanted to hurt him, to play out the old memory that had ended terribly for us both. My anxiety that night had reminded me of the certain misery I would face if I said no, yet I was gripped with what it meant to say yes.

"Vanessa, I lost my job, his mom basically told me outright I was trash, and I'm trying this new thing where I don't drown my problems in booze. It was too much. If I'd put one more emotionally intense situation on my plate, I was going to snap."

"So you told him no?"

"I told him I needed time. I didn't say yes or no. I mean, we talk and we've seen each other a few times, but the break has been good for me. I've had a lot of time to reflect and sort of get balanced again. I can't remember the last time I've felt this...I don't know, stable, I guess."

"But you haven't addressed the proposal at all since then?"

"No. In fact we haven't addressed much of anything. He's been kind of distant the past couple times I've been by."

She laughed. "No shit."

"What?"

"I think if I proposed to a guy, which by the way will never happen, and he didn't give me the answer I wanted, I wouldn't be throwing myself at him afterwards."

"Thanks." I rolled my eyes.

"I'm not trying to make you feel bad, but have you thought about what he's going through? You've been dying over this guy for years. Yet you've shot him down twice, and he's still in this. That's nothing short of a miracle."

"I don't want to rush into something that emotionally I can't see through. I'm being responsible for once."

"Maya, listen to me." She leaned forward, her eyes gentler. "You love Cameron. I can see that. I'm pretty sure someone would need to be legally blind not to see what you two have. But I'm not *you*. I don't know what it must be like to live in that hurricane of emotion, and I sure as hell can't tell you when to take that leap. I just want you to be happy, and I don't want to see the person who makes you happy walk because you can't bite the bullet. "

The server brought our food, briefly interrupting Vanessa's rant. I felt sick suddenly. Vanessa's reaction made all my self-assurances these past few weeks seem shallow and absurd. My eyes welled up with thick tears. I blinked them away before they could fall.

"He does make me happy," I whispered. "Like I never knew what being happy truly meant until he found me."

"Stop fighting it then. *Be* happy. You deserve happiness, and Jesus, so does he. He's so crazy in love with you, Maya."

"I just wanted to have a chance to be better for him, for both of us, you know?"

Her lips curved into a sympathetic smile. "Honey, I think all he probably wants is you. Just the way you are."

Vanessa's eyes glistened, and my heart twisted more. I was grateful she cared as much as she did. Her phone lit up a second later. She groaned before answering it with a forced smile. After a few terse words, she hung up.

"Reilly is calling me back. I have to go. Are you okay, hon?"

I nodded quickly. "Yeah, I'll be fine."

"You sure?"

"Go." I waved her off. "The boss needs you. I'll figure this out, I promise."

"Keep me posted. I need updates. We can't go this long without getting together."

I agreed and gave her a hug goodbye. She lingered, hugging me tightly. I was going to start crying if she didn't let go, so I was relieved when she finally left me alone with my untouched lunch. My thoughts all swirled around Cameron now.

I texted him on the way home.

M: Dinner tonight?
C: Sure. What time?
M: Pick me up at 6?
C: It's a date.

I smiled at the reference. We'd gone so far past my juvenile relationship limitations. Making plans to see each other and talk sent a rush of anticipation through me, but Vanessa was right. I'd had some time to sort myself out and I was stalling at this point. Avoiding my deeper relationship with Cameron meant sidestepping the emotional albatross of his proposal. I couldn't lose him, and I only hoped I hadn't pushed him too far away.

Just inside the stairwell leading up to the apartment, my phone began to ring. Not recognizing the number, I answered tentatively.

"Hello?"

A man's deep voice greeted me. "Is this Maya Jacobs?"

"Yes, who is this?"

"I'm sorry to bother you, Ms. Jacobs. My name is Officer Ray Stevens. I'm with the Greene County Police Department."

My heart fell into my stomach. I sat down on a step immediately. "Is it my mom? Lynne Jacobs? Is she okay?"

He cleared his throat, drawing out the silence long enough that I nearly interrupted him before he began again.

"I'm very sorry to tell you, Miss Jacobs, but your mother has passed away."

"What?"

"She was found this morning. It appears she overdosed. We were able to track you down as her next of kin."

"No." Everything around me spun. This couldn't be. *No, no, no. God, no.*

"I'm sorry."

His voice was lower, muted by the thundering sound of my heart and the screaming denial of my mind.

"I understand if you need some time. Maybe I could call back a little later to discuss your plans for arrangements."

I shook my head. She wasn't gone. This couldn't be happening.

"Miss?"

I took a sharp breath. "Yes, later. I can't talk now."

That was all I could manage before lowering the phone. I dropped my head in my hands. My thoughts spun, the beginning of a never-ending search for answers I'd never have. For all my focus these past couple weeks, nothing made sense now. Nothing could, because I'd been in the dark for too long. Our lives hadn't intersected for years. I had no information, and I likely never would. The puzzle pieces would never fit together.

She was gone. Irrevocably lost. All the guilt, worry, and regret I'd tried so valiantly to put away all crushed down on me at once. I was buried in it.

I dragged myself up the stairs to the apartment and headed straight for my room. I wanted to fall onto the bed and cry until my tears ran dry. I wanted to upend my dresser, break everything, scream, and cry some more. But for the life of me, I couldn't find that person. I couldn't find the tears that had come so freely lately.

Maybe this was shock, but I knew none of that would quell this kind of pain.

I turned and headed into the kitchen, past Eli, whose gaze was fixed on the television. I found a glass and contemplated the faucet. Water wouldn't relieve this thirst. The dull craving I'd been getting good at ignoring no longer pulled. It didn't ask or beg. It screamed, like a ravenous hunger that compounded my pain like nothing ever had. It demanded relief.

With trembling hands, I reached for the cupboard and pulled out the whiskey we saved for pregame shots and really bad days. I poured several ounces worth into my glass, not bothering with ice. This wasn't about savoring anything. This was about making the hurt go away as fast as humanly possible. I lifted the glass to my lips. I inhaled on instinct and released an audible sigh with the sheer anticipation of it.

"Maya."

Eli's voice startled me, and I dropped the glass. It shattered in an instant, the contents splashing everywhere.

The sharp smell of whiskey covered me. The liquor was wet on my hands and saturated my shirt. My stomach turned. As desperately as I'd wanted it in me, I suddenly wanted all traces of it off of me.

"Shit. Are you okay?" Eli rushed to me, grabbing a towel.

I shook my head violently as I stepped back from the mess I'd made.

"Maya, talk to me. What's going on?"

"Eli." My voice was barely a whisper, the words lodged in my throat. A slow tremble took over, my shoulders shaking with the effort to hold myself together. "Eli, she's gone."

My eyes filled with unshed tears, confirming the truth we both knew could be a real possibility, even if we'd never downright said it. I dropped to my knees, narrowly missing the shards of glass that had scattered across the linoleum.

Eli knelt down, clearing a path with the towel so he could come closer. He caught my hands. "What happened?"

"Overdose. She…she overdosed, and they found her this morning."

Someone else was saying the words, I thought, because I still couldn't believe this was happening. Hot burning tears streamed down my face.

"Honey, I'm so sorry." Eli came closer and pulled me into a fiercely tight embrace. I hugged him back, letting my tears fall free onto his shoulder.

"I couldn't save her. Eli, why? Why wouldn't she let me help her? She didn't have to go through this alone."

Eli's chest expanded with a sigh. "Maybe she was

trying to protect you. This kind of thing…it can destroy people's lives, not just the people using. She probably wanted to keep you as far away from it as possible. Did you ever think of that?"

I shook my head. Could she have been trying to protect me all this time? Maybe, but I couldn't help but feel like I'd failed her, like she knew I couldn't be the one to help her. Because what kind of person had I become in her absence? How could I have given her what she needed when I was barely living myself? Still, I couldn't let go of the belief that I could have changed her course if she'd given me that chance.

"She never gave me a chance. All those years…waiting to make it right for us, to make the kind of life we'd planned for. Everything I worked for. Now…"

A relentless, searing pain twisted in my gut. I wanted her back, to see her smile or hear her laugh, to feel her touch, to relax into the kind of healing embrace only a mother could give. Just one more day, one last glimmer of her love.

But I'd never have it again. My body quaked with the force of my sobs.

Eli hushed me. "It's going to be okay, Maya. She's not hurting anymore."

"No." My voice was a wail.

Her memory was everywhere then, saturating every cell. My skin hurt, everything hurt. The reality that she was forever lost swallowed up any sense my or Eli's words could make.

Tears crashed over me, wave after wave of a deep drowning sadness. Hard as I grasped for her, to keep her with me in this world of the living, I could feel her slipping away, slow like the tide until I was too weak to cry, too tired to hurt.

CAMERON. Eli buzzed me in, and I bound up the steps to Maya's apartment. My brain was a cloud of what ifs since she'd texted me earlier. Texts could be vague but the tone sounded hopeful. One way or the other, we needed to talk.

When I walked in, Eli met me with a concerned look.

"Hey, Eli. What's up?"

"Did Maya call you?" His voice was quiet, almost a whisper.

"No, we were going to have dinner. Is she here? Is everything okay?"

He shook his head, his arms crossed tightly across his chest. My heart dropped. Visions of her blacked out, in danger somehow, gripped me.

"Where is she?" My muscles tensed, ready to spring me in whatever direction she might need me.

"She's sleeping."

I relaxed slightly, but something was definitely wrong.

"Cameron, her mom died of an overdose. The police called her a few hours ago with the news."

"Jesus Christ. Is she all right?"

"She's upset. I mean, she was ready to drink a fifth of whiskey but she kind of broke down instead. Thank God I was here. I don't think I've ever seen someone cry that hard for that long. She finally passed out about an hour ago."

Eli bit his lip.

"She must be destroyed." My mind was still catching

up to the magnitude of this news.

"Did you know she'd been missing?"

I nodded. "She finally told me, yeah. I can't imagine what she must be going through. Can I see her, I mean... Is it okay?"

He nodded, motioning toward the bedroom.

I crept in quietly. A soft amber glow lit the horizon of the sky through her window and darkness was closing in fast. Maya was curled in a ball on the bed, surrounded by tissues and pillows. I sat on the edge of the bed next to her. I watched her slow breathing, in awe as ever of her beauty and all the strength she carried inside of her. Even in the peace of sleep, her eyebrows pulled together. Her face was pink, the skin around her eyes puffy from all the tears she'd cried. I wanted to touch her, hold her. I fisted my hands in restraint. She needed to rest. I moved to leave and her eyes fluttered open.

"Cam." Her voice was hoarse.

"I'm here, baby. I'm right here." I sat back down, relieved that I could touch her. I ran my hand down her arm. Her skin was cold. I was about to reach for the blanket to cover her when she sat up abruptly.

Fisting her hands into my shirt, she levered herself up to her knees and threw her arms around my neck. She said my name again, a watery sob. Silent tremors rocked her frame, and I knew she was crying again. I held her close, but we couldn't get any closer. She was wrapped around me like a vise, as if either of us let go, we'd fall to our deaths.

She murmured something between shuddery breaths, but I couldn't make it out. I hushed her, stroking down her back and over her shoulders. God, I wanted to take her pain away. All I could do was try to comfort her, be a rock for her while she weathered the storm. Her sobs slowed, and her breathing evened out.

She sat back. Her hands went to my arms, her grip still bordering on frantic. I caught her hands in mine, rubbing the backs gently so she'd know we were still connected. I wasn't letting her go.

She looked up into my eyes, seriousness taking the place of her sadness.

"I have to tell you something."

MAYA. A new wave of sadness hit me when I saw the confusion in his eyes. I had to wash that away. Immediately.

"I'm so sorry."

"Why are you sorry, Maya? My God, your mother died. Why are you apologizing to me?"

"Because I pushed you away, and I shouldn't have. I've been so caught up with everything, but I never thought about how much I was hurting you. And I've hurt you enough. God, I've hurt us both...so much." I bit my lip, nearly piercing the flesh.

"Shh, baby, let's not talk about this right now. You need to rest."

"No. I need to say this. I—" I fought the urge to go to him again. I wanted to disappear in his warmth. I squeezed his hands tightly in my own. I wanted to breakdown, to let the sobs I held back pour out of me. I looked into his eyes like he was the only man on earth, because for me, he was.

"Marry me, Cam."

His lips parted and shut again. His expression was frozen, filling me with an empty fear. Suddenly I worried that this was the worst possible time to say these things. But I needed him now, more than ever. And I couldn't let another day pass without him knowing how I felt.

My stomach was a hard knot as I waited for him to say something, anything. It was as if my heart had left my body. Vulnerable and exposed, I realized then what it'd taken for him to say those words to me before. He could put my broken soul back together right now or wound my heart so badly I'd never be able to give it to another person. He held my fate with a word.

Had he felt this way? Had I done this to him?

"You don't have to do this, Maya. We don't have to."

"I want to," I rushed. "I can make you happy, the way you make me happy. I know I can, if you just give me a chance. If it's not too late."

"Why now?"

"Because…" I swallowed hard, pushing the flood of tears down so I could say what I needed to say. "Because I've spent years waiting, trying to control pieces of my life that were beyond my control. Because I'm so goddamn stubborn I couldn't see what I was giving up when you asked me the first time. I see it now, more clearly than I've ever seen anything. I shouldn't have pushed you away then, the same way I shouldn't have pushed you away this time. I hate myself for it. Because you're the only one I'll ever want, Cam, and we've been through enough. I don't want to fight it anymore. I just want to be with you. I want to be your wife. If you'll have me."

His breath rushed out. He stared at me for a long moment. Before the tears caught up with me again, he caught my mouth, kissing me tenderly.

"Cam?" I looked into his eyes, my question lingering between us. "Will you?"

"Of course. I can't breathe without you. I waited five years, I'd wait a lifetime for you." He cradled me against him, keeping us close. The promise that I would always have his love filled me. My heart pulsed to life, a healing energy radiated across my chest and tingled down to my limbs.

For the first time in my life, I saw love for what it was supposed to be, for what it always should have been. I let it rush in and chase away the pain. I let it soar, nourishing it with every secret hope and dream I'd held for our future.

I laced my fingers with his, holding his hand close to my heart so he might feel it beat for him, for us. If our bodies were two halves once broken, together we were whole again. And I swore then that nothing would break us again.

EPILOGUE

MAYA. My belly was full with hot chocolate and two delightfully fattening croissants from our favorite bakery as we walked through the park. The air was cool, but on the inside I was warm. We settled onto a bench facing the Manhattan skyline. Cameron's legs stretched onto the pathway and I rested against his shoulder, his arm cradling me to him. I smiled.

The past few weeks had been hard, sad in so many ways as I said goodbye to my mother. But having Cameron by my side had reassured me. If I'd had any lingering doubts that he could pull me out of any hell and bring me happiness, they were put to rest. I only hoped I could do the same for him whenever he needed it. I owed him that much. I owed him everything.

In the distance, a small mass of black birds drew a broad path across the sky. A moment later they'd each made landing among the trees around us. Aside from the random shuffling of feathers and the casual chirp, they were mostly silent, almost as if in reverence to the light snow that had begun to fall.

"There are so many of them," I whispered, not wanting to scare them off.

Cameron looked up. "Beautiful. Kind of eerie though."

"I don't think so. You know black birds are actually lucky."

He looked down and gave me a slanted smile. "Really?"

"Yeah. They represent transformation. They're supposed to connect us with life's magic."

"That sounds corny, but promising," he said softly.

I smiled, reveling in Cameron's own magic, the spell only he could put me under. "I think so too. Not corny, but the promising part."

I reached up and kissed him softly. When I broke away, his eyes clouded with emotion. Before I could question the reason why, he dropped on one knee in front of me. From his coat pocket, he pulled out the same black box I'd seen before. My heart thundered in my chest. I'd already given him his answer by nearly begging for his, and for the past few weeks that had been enough. I hadn't given the ring or any of the formality another thought. I was his, and he was mine. We'd make it official eventually. I had absolutely no doubt that's what I wanted.

Opening the tiny box, he revealed a beautiful ring that sparkled radiantly even in the dim light of the day.

"Maya Jacobs." His voice was low, thick with love. "I've waited a long time to do this right. I want you in my life forever. Will you be my wife?"

Before he could get the words out, I was nodding, smiling and tearful. "Yes. I will."

Smiling broadly, he slipped the ring onto my finger. When it was securely in place, I didn't waste a second reaching for him, hugging him with all my might.

"Thank you."

"It's symbolic, Maya. I want to give you so much more."

"You already have. You've given me the best times of my life and we've only just begun, Cam."

He pulled me back enough to kiss me, warm tender kisses full of meaning. "And you've given me mine."

"I love you so much."

"Love you too, baby."

I smiled. Warm tears of happiness brimmed my eyes. I drew in a deep breath, overwhelmed and feeling like the luckiest girl in the world. Nothing would ever keep us apart.

With a wild clatter, the birds above us suddenly took flight in groups, and one by one they were all gone. We watched as they disappeared into the snowy sky.

FOLLOW THE BRIDGE FAMILY JOURNEY WITH

DARREN & VANESSA IN

Into the Fire

MEREDITH WILD

ACKNOWLEDGMENTS

Writing this story was like enduring an especially difficult pregnancy. It was uncomfortable and downright painful at times. I just wanted it to be over, but it simply would not be rushed. In the end, finally, a piece of myself was born.

Of course, I have a few people to thank for helping me bring this story to life. As always, thanks to Jonathan for giving me the support I needed to brainstorm, write, edit, agonize, and publish this book. You're a keeper!

Thank you, Kaveri, for not being a prude, for celebrating with me every step of the way, and for giving me critical New Yorker insights!

Thank you to my betas, for your thoughtful and reassuring feedback. Thank you to my girl Krystin and the entire Team Wild crew! You are truly an amazing and badass group of women. I'll never be able to appropriately express what your support has meant to me, but suffice to say, I love you all!

Thank you, Amy, for proofing with two arms full of needy children.

Many thanks to Helen Hardt for being the best editor ever, and for tolerating my perpetual sense of urgency and my propensity for dangling modifiers. I'd love to tell you all of this will change, but it probably won't.

Lastly, for Michael, Mom, and so many others who've walked in the shadows, thank you for inspiring me with your strength.